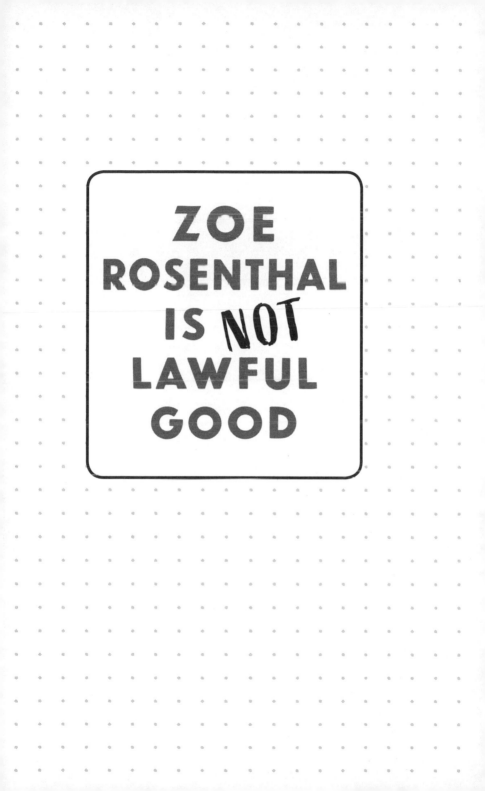

ZOE ROSENTHAL IS NOT LAWFUL GOOD

NANCY WERLIN

CANDLEWICK PRESS

Copyright © 2021 by Nancy Werlin

First edition 2021

Library of Congress Catalog Card Number pending
ISBN 978-1-5362-1473-4

21 22 23 24 25 26 LBM 10 9 8 7 6 5 4 3 2 1

Printed in Melrose Park, IL, USA

This book was typeset in Mate.

Candlewick Press
99 Dover Street
Somerville, Massachusetts 02144

www.candlewick.com

MIX
From responsible
sources
FSC® C103098

For groups of friends,
everywhere

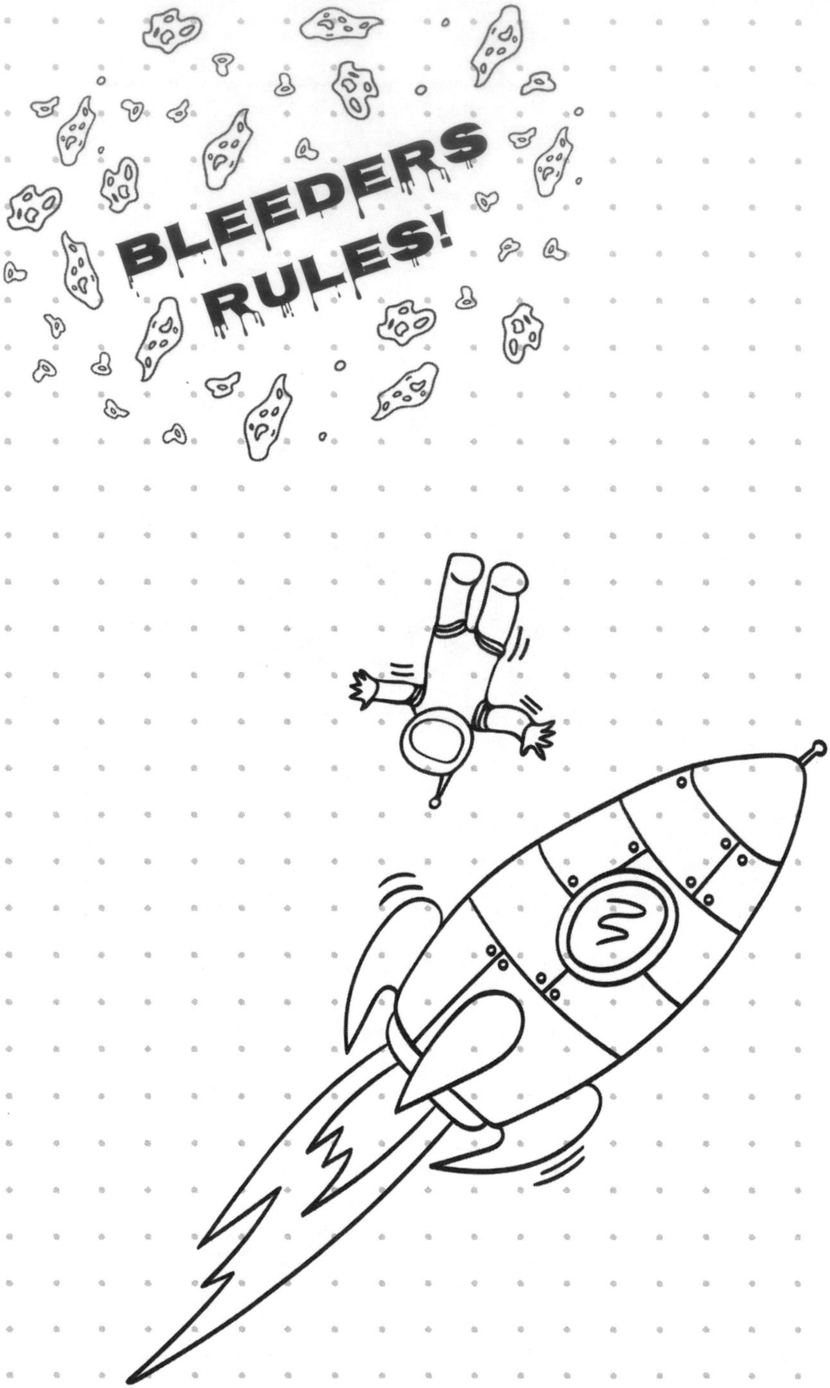
BLEEDERS
RULES!

EPISODE 1

August–September 2018
@Dragon Con

From Zoe's Bullet Journal

TO DO:

☑ Lie

Scene 1

Sneaking

As I waited to board my Friday afternoon flight, I got a text from my boyfriend.

SIMON: Are you feeling better?

SIMON: I'll come over when I get off my shift, OK?

I remained as calm as Captain was when the Bleeder virus—suddenly fully sentient—looked back at her from under the microscope in Episode 2. I knew Simon didn't suspect me. I might have decided spontaneously to do this, but then I had planned every move. (Planning is my superpower.) Also, I was morally in the clear. I was.

ME: Don't come. It's only a headache.

ME: I'm going to nap now anyway.

I boarded my flight. Calmly!

This alternate, obsessed, geeked-out, *Bleeders*-fan version of myself (that I'd only discovered a few weeks ago) was kind of silly. Simon would use a stronger word than *silly*. Nobody could do blistering, intelligent scorn like Simon, although of course he never directed it at me.

I made sure of that. I was the perfect girlfriend. As such, I also knew that he needed his focus on bigger and more important things than my tiny personal ... excursion. My whereabouts for the next twenty-four hours were between me, myself, and (of course) Maggie. And if I regretted that I had to hide from the only *Bleeders* fan I knew personally, well, that was the price. It was too risky to tell Simon's younger sister. At fourteen, Josie had no filter between her brain and her mouth.

I do not take unnecessary risks.

Usually.

I found my window seat and stowed my backpack. I listened to the flight attendant's spiel about seatbelts and exit rows. But I only breathed fully again after Simon sent a funny GIF of some guy getting "back to work."

My parents didn't know what I was up to, either, but I wasn't worried about them. I might even have told them — if I could have figured out how to instruct them never to mention it to Simon. I couldn't, but they were off on a romantic end-of-summer Montreal trip anyway. We'd agreed I'd text them only in case of emergency, which this was emphatically not.

They deserved their time together. They'd been all *croissant au chocolat* and *au revoir* and *je t'adore* before they ran off to the car together. *So cute!* Maggie had mouthed at me. I'd rolled my eyes, but it's true, they're adorable.

Fun fact: my parents got together in high school, just like Simon and me. It was because of their example that my mental bullet list went something like this:

☑ Meet soulmate
☑ Make commitment
☐ Marriage· TO COME! (after college)

The plane took off and my everyday Boston world shrank teeny-tiny and got left behind. I nudged my backpack with the toe of my orange high-top sneaker. I hadn't brought much, since I'd be back tomorrow morning. My con registration. My season premiere ticket. Change of clothes. Of course my bullet journal.

Simon and I had a lot to do our senior year to figure out college together. Once this little fandom indulgence was over, I wouldn't have time to think about *Bleeders*. After seeing the premiere tonight, I might not even watch the rest of Season 2.

And I shouldn't waste this plane time! I pulled out my bullet journal and ultra-fine Sharpie to outline a college application essay. *"Describe a problem you've solved or a problem you'd like to solve. It can be an intellectual challenge, a research query, an ethical dilemma—anything that is of personal importance, no matter the scale. Explain its significance to you and what steps you took or could take to identify a solution."*

I looked out the window at the summer sky. Simon would have a dozen ideas—for himself and for me—but on the plane to Dragon Con, *Bleeders* felt like the only thing of personal importance to me.

The Bleeder virus! When you're infected, the walls of your arteries and veins and capillaries transmute into basically tissue paper. Blood seeps rapidly from every pore, so within seconds, you're a bleeding sack of skin holding in bones and organs. But somehow you stay upright, alive, for a few completely horrifying and totally infectious minutes. (The special effects are riveting.)

Essay. Focus.

I thought of Lorelei in the lab in the first episode. The way she looks into the microscope, down at the virus. Then at Captain.

"We took an oath to save life," Lorelei says neutrally. "All life."

"I'm taking another oath right now," Captain answers. "To stop this." But we see her face as she says it. We see that she doesn't know *how*. And that she's scared. On top of everything else, Captain Paloma is a mother, and the virus is a threat to all humanoid life. She's also levelheaded, deadly, and dedicated to keeping her tiny MOSS (mobile space surgery) crew safe from the robotic Interplanetary Sanitation Force, doing their forbidden scientific research . . . while running and evading and hiding. And when they must, fighting.

But only when they must. Originally, they chose to *flee*. I don't blame them for it. Because: What are you supposed to do against a Really Big Bad? When deep in your heart, you don't believe you can have any effect on it? When, even deeper in your heart, you truly think the worst will surely come? When you can't help but despair, no matter how hard you *pretend* to have hope, especially when you're with the people who really *do* have hope?

You run. It's logical!

And yet I know that if I keep watching, the crew *will* figure out a way to fight and win. Somehow. Because fiction, not reality. Captain, Lorelei, Celie, Tennah/Bellah, Monica, and Torrance will win in the end.

And I want, I *need*, to see that happen.

Yes, yes, yes. It's an imaginary universe with imaginary problems. (Simon's words to his sister about *Bleeders*.) I shouldn't care so much about *entertainment*. But I do, and honestly? I'm truly worried about this season!

Essay! Focus. An idea stirred in me—but no. "No matter the scale" was an obvious trap. I shouldn't write about the personal miracle of a properly organized to-do list. It's not important enough.

Also I have learned that nobody wants to hear it.

There's a real-world virus, Marburg, which is the conceptual progenitor of the Bleeder virus. Also obviously Ebola is a source. But if I wrote about viruses, that might imply I was interested in a scientific career. And I'm definitely not. I haven't settled on anything else yet. Which is extremely frustrating for Simon and me, because it makes our college applications even more challenging.

I decided to spend just a few minutes looking at cat videos. It's research for my job. That's what I tell Simon.

I was shocked by the announcement that our plane was preparing to land. I had wasted the whole flight daydreaming about *Bleeders*, rejecting stupid essay ideas, and watching cats. Great.

Still, I'd gotten to Atlanta. Now all I had to do was get to the right place at midnight. I'd see the *Bleeders* Season 2 premiere (a week early!), get back to the airport, and get home tomorrow morning with nobody but Maggie the wiser. Zoe Rosenthal for the win!

I texted Maggie that I'd arrived. Then I gave myself a quiet little fist bump.

Scene 2

Atlanta

As soon as I got off the subway in downtown Atlanta, I saw it—no, her—no, *them*! Someone was cosplaying Tennah/Bellah! Another *Bleeders* fan was rapidly disappearing on the upward escalator! The crowd was so thick, I couldn't even pursue them.

Tennah/Bellah is two separate people—not personalities, *people*—who happen to share a single humanoid body. Probably we'll learn more in Season 2 about how the Quatos species shape-shifts between their two selves. It hadn't occurred to me that there would be *Bleeders* cosplayers here for Dragon Con. I swiveled in place and craned my neck, but I didn't see any other Bloodygits. Unless they were camouflaged in Muggle clothes like me.

There was certainly no lack of other cosplayers. As the

crowd and I shuffled slowly along toward the escalator and exit, I gawked. I stared. I ogled.

Thranduil, the elf king from *Lord of the Rings*. A Wonder Woman mother and her matching small daughter. Three chatty stormtroopers. Walking Dead. Castiel from *Supernatural*, in his trench coat. Jon Snow and Daenerys (with a stuffed dragon on her shoulder). Oooo—Mr. Rogers in his cardigan! I couldn't help it—I called his name and waved. He shouted back, "Hello, neighbor!" I got a little sniffly. It actually almost felt like Mr. Rogers himself had greeted me.

There were also lots of people simply wearing geeky T-shirts. Moving upward on the long, steep escalator, I glanced self-consciously at my clothing: a billowing, light, sleeveless white top and capri leggings, orange sneakers. I could have borrowed Maggie's WAKANDA FOREVER T-shirt if I had only thought of it. Or maybe done a simple lightning-bolt temporary tattoo on my forehead.

Only no. I wasn't actually *like* these other fans. I'd *never* do cosplay. I was just here for a few hours, for my show. I wouldn't embarrass myself in public. I mean, you could see that some of the Muggles were sneering or rolling their eyes at the cosplayers. Who needs that? I was a low-profile kind of person.

I made it out onto the people-packed street, where the difference in temperature between Boston and Atlanta made itself known. I was going to sweat. That didn't matter. Orienting myself mattered. I started to pull out my map and phone, but someone near me, wearing a bright blue ball gown and a blond Elsa wig, was talking about going to registration with her friend, who wore a brown bodysuit and a reindeer headdress. So I just skulked along behind them.

I kept on staring as I walked.

A medieval Japanese female knight. A leather-clad black cat in a neon-green furry gas mask, with other green fur-ball things stuck all over his body. A steampunk Santa. Ruth Bader Ginsburg arm in arm with Sonia Sotomayor. A man who was naked except for tight silver shorts and silver body paint. A phalanx of Star Trek ensigns in red shirts who spontaneously fell onto the sidewalk together while everyone around them yelled, "They're dead, Jim!"

My mom loves anything Star Trek, including the original series, so I got that one.

The cosplayers didn't seem to mind being stared at. There was a lot of posing and preening.

"Awesome, huh?" said a motherly-looking winged angel. I discreetly checked to make sure this wasn't directed at someone else. It wasn't.

I smiled back. "Who's that?" I pointed to the nearly naked guy in the silver paint.

"The Silver Surfer. He's a Marvel Comics character." She rolled her eyes. "One of millions."

I didn't know much about comics. "Okay, what about the neon cat?"

"That one I don't know. Maybe he's from a game."

I'd lost sight of the Elsa cosplayer I'd been following before. I asked, "Are you going to the Sheraton to register? Can I just follow you?"

"Sure." The angel gestured at some of the people

streaming past us in the opposite direction. "You can tell they're coming from registration because they're all wearing their badges. Stick with me."

I said, "I love your costume, by the way. Should I recognize you?"

The angel wore a long white lace dress that I guessed to be a repurposed wedding gown and wings formed from wire and feathers.

"No, I'm just my own angel. So this is your first Dragon Con?"

"Yes," I said. "You?"

"Oh, I've been coming for fifteen years. You're going to have a fantastic time." A wave to indicate an elderly Princess Moana. "Everybody wearing their inside on their outside! Which is how life should always be."

I suppressed a smile at her naivete. "But it's not how life *is*."

"Maybe not for everyone," said the angel. "But you can make a free individual choice."

"I take it you've forgotten high school," I said dryly.

"Nope. Never." The angel laughed. "What year are you?"

"Senior."

"Planning for college?"

"Yes." I thought of the long list of schools that Simon and I had finalized together over the summer. We had no idea yet where we'd end up; we only knew we'd do it together. That was so comforting.

"Well, unlike high school, Dragon Con is a place where

you can be yourself," the angel said with assurance. "It's why you've come!"

I have come to see my show, I thought, but said, "Any other tips?"

"Get to your programs early. There can be huge lines and then you don't get in."

"Thanks."

We filed into the basement of the Sheraton, where two friends joined the angel, and then I got flowed into a different registration line. I waved goodbye, but I'd already been forgotten.

There continued to be wonderful cosplays everywhere to look at. But I also noticed how everybody else had somebody to talk to.

I really could not have brought Josie. She certainly couldn't have afforded her plane fare and registration, and I couldn't have paid for her. Aunt Kath's birthday money went only so far, and I was totally committed to saving all my earnings from my job. I reminded myself, too, of all the complications of Josie being Simon's sister. The logistics would have required a spreadsheet! That said, if I'd put on my thinking cap, perhaps it wouldn't have been completely impossible—no. I made the right choice. Plus, there just wasn't time.

For company, I texted Maggie.

> **ME:** Are you there?
>
> **MAGGIE:** Yes but no, sorry, cousins galore, chat later.
>
> **ME:** No worries. Have fun!

My line moved forward.

Then, ahead of me at registration, I spied my Tennah/ Bellah cosplayer again. They had figured out a really cool way to indicate Tennah and Bellah, with a vertical body division. A wig had Bellah's braid on the right and Tennah's scraped-back bun on the left, and makeup delineated each face differently. The costume was literally two costumes sewn together: Bellah's loose navy jumpsuit with military decorations on one side and Tennah's form-fitting slinky dress in camouflage green on the other. The chest, however, was even on both sides and preposterously, wincingly, and worst of all, erroneously large for Tennah/ Bellah. But it did make a good base for the stethoscope-garrote riding majestically on top. The only thing that wasn't *Bleeders*-inspired was the cosplayer's round pink glasses.

What if I just shouted out "Tennah! Bellah!" like I'd shouted at Mr. Rogers?

If only I'd had some indicator of my own *Bleeders* fandom on me! Then I might have had the courage. Josie had a Bloodygit T-shirt she'd bought off Etsy, with the stethoscope-garrote printed on the front like a necklace . . . I wished I'd thought to get something like that.

Beep.

SIMON: How are you feeling now?

SIMON: Don't answer if you're sleeping!

Best not to answer. I looked up from my phone, only

to see Tennah/Bellah disappearing under the EXIT sign. Again! I felt bereft. Compulsively, I answered Simon.

> **ME:** Are you at Tropical Foods?
>
> **SIMON:** Yes. We've registered two people so far.
>
> **ME:** That's great!
>
> **SIMON:** Most people are ignoring us but that's OK.
>
> **SIMON:** I wish you were here too.
>
> **ME:** I'm sorry I'm not, but rest is doing me good. I'm going to sleep.
>
> **SIMON:** See you tomorrow!
>
> **ME:** Yes! I know I'll feel all better by then. xo
>
> **SIMON:** xo

I was glad Simon could be upbeat about voter registration, which to be honest I found depressing. But it was sweet to think that we were both feeling lonely for each other at this exact same moment.

This summer, Simon had volunteered a lot at Alisha Johnson Pratt's state senatorial campaign, along with working full-time at his day-care job (children love Simon). I helped with the Pratt campaign too, when I wasn't working for my neighbor Mrs. Albee. But voter registration versus seeing the *Bleeders* season premiere a week early? I mean! The steps I needed to take to be at Dragon Con instead practically wrote themselves in my bullet journal . . . because, listen, to-do lists really and truly can work miracles in your life, and if you also deploy a spreadsheet . . .

The registration line was making efficient progress. Of course I was still excited about the *Bleeders* midnight season premiere. Of course I was still really glad I was here and not at Tropical Foods feeling secretly futile. Only now I wondered, What was I going to do with myself, all alone in this crowd, between now and midnight?

Scene 3

Bloodygits!

I hung my official con membership badge around my neck. Outside the registration hall, I picked up a paper schedule. It was thick and packed with descriptions of thousands of programs organized by date, time, and track. Yes, thousands. There were also floor maps for the hotels. Lists of exhibitors and special guests. And. And. *And.* You'd have to study it for a week to figure everything out.

But all I wanted was something halfway interesting to do between now and midnight. And then something to do after the premiere . . . in the wee hours . . . by myself . . . because I really didn't want to go hang out at the airport then. Aaargh!

"You're better off downloading the app," the guy behind the schedule table advised me. He was massive, elderly, and bald, sporting an *Ultraviolet: Code 044* T-shirt and a handlebar mustache of which he was clearly proud.

"The app keeps you on top of the programming, which you need because room assignments can change. And it's just easier to find things in the app. But—you're a first-timer, right? Thought so. You'll want to rip the hotel maps out of your printed schedule." He demonstrated enthusiastically. "Now, the Hyatt, Hilton, and Marriott are all connected. You never have to go outside!" He said this like it was a good thing. It probably was, given the heat.

"Thanks." I paused as he looked at me encouragingly. "Where can I get something to eat? That's not too expensive and is, you know, somewhat healthy?"

I came away armed with directions to two food courts and also to a place called the Con Suite inside one of the hotels where food was apparently available to everybody 24/7, completely free although not guaranteed to be healthy. I had also been encouraged to attend an orientation session for newbies, and my maps were now annotated with circles and arrows for food, the location of the *Bleeders* premiere, some gathering places for other "military science fiction and horror" sessions (the volunteer assumed this must be what I was into and I didn't bother to explain that I wasn't into anything except *Bleeders*), and several good spots to stand for a parade that was to happen tomorrow morning. (I also didn't explain that I'd be on my way home by then.) He was great, and I felt a little bereft when he said dismissively, "Have fun now!"

Still uncertain, I threaded through the milling, talking, excited crowd until I found a wall to lean on. I downloaded the app and tried to understand it while watching more cosplayers swan past. Lots of Star Wars and elves and fairies and Spiderman and Fred and George Weasley and minions and dragons and Mary Poppins. Also, a surprisingly creepy group dressed in yellow with rubber duckie masks who yelled "Make way! Make way!" Then Abraham Lincoln and medieval and steampunk—and Lisa Simpson! I love Lisa!

And so very many costumes and references that I didn't have a clue about.

Most people seemed willing to pose for pictures when ever you asked, so I texted a few photos to Maggie.

MAGGIE: *Speechless*

ME: Me too.

MAGGIE: Send more. I'm begging.

ME: OK, but promise me you won't show them to anybody.

ME: Because it can't leak out where I am and what I'm doing!

MAGGIE: I promise. Just send more.

ME: Right now? Aren't you busy?

MAGGIE: Yes and no. Sitting in the back.

MAGGIE: My grandparents just renewed their vows.

MAGGIE: Everybody is cooing.

MAGGIE: I'm in danger of crystallizing into a pillar of sugar.

MAGGIE: You're my only hope.

I sent her a giant guy dressed as a rooster.

MAGGIE: Haha. May I request another hot elf?

ME: Mission accepted.

I prowled the area and got more photos, feeling like I was on the sidelines of an enormous party that had been going on for years. People shrieked and hugged as they found one another. They picked up conversations that referenced last year, or five years ago. They were mostly adults—twenties, thirties, forties, fifties. There were smaller kids, with their parents, but I didn't notice many teens who were on their own, like me.

Maggie had gone silent. Of course she had grand-daughterly duties at the anniversary party. I thought about getting a nerdy T-shirt to change into. Even just a Dragon Con shirt. Only I'd never wear it again so it was a waste of money, and while Aunt Kath was probably good for another gift card at Chrismukkah, right now I'd have to dig into my college savings from my job with Mrs. Albee, and to this I say a firm no.

Well, at least I had my Dragon Con membership badge to show I belonged.

I ventured out onto the cosplayer-crammed streets of Atlanta in search of I didn't know what. I tried to walk confidently, though, as if I knew where I was going and that I would meet many close personal friends there.

But then I saw my Tennah/Bellah cosplayer again, waiting in a line that wound at least halfway around the Hyatt hotel, between a steampunk Alice in Wonderland and a couple wearing Sailor Moon T-shirts. Tennah/Bellah was talking to someone who—my heart skipped a beat—was cosplaying Torrance!

Torrance is the only male on the crew of the ship *Mae*

Jemison, and he is quiet. But toward the end of Season 1, he began displaying some interesting depths.

The fan cosplaying Torrance was a girl, a few inches taller than Tennah/Bellah, and she looked about my age, with dark hair cut close that was clearly real rather than a wig. The Torrance cosplay was basic, just a white lab coat with the *Bleeders* medical insignia (a gold snake wrapped around a surgeon's laser) embroidered on the pocket. And the stethoscope-garrote, of course.

The best part: in one hand, she had a small cast-iron frying pan! And her white lab coat was stained on the front . . .

In Season 1, Episode 7, Torrance got cornered in the ship's galley by a Sanitation Soldier and conked his attacker on the head with the pan. Then he vomited on the soldier whose head he'd just smashed in—and later, spent hours in surgery trying to save it. Which was futile because Sanitation Soldiers are half circuitry, and Torrance is a doctor but not an engineer, and Bellah, who's both, flatly refused to help. *Coghead can't be dead enough for me. And don't even mention rehab. You can't handle the programming.* So the soldier ended up in a closet until Celie quietly wired its head into the kitchen appliances two episodes later, but all it can do so far is insult Torrance, call Celie "most exalted and extreme genius," and make toast. (By the way, fans ship Torrance and Celie all the time. There is something kind of innocent and sweet about that ship.)

Anyway, Torrance is a pacifist and this incident was the first time in his life he'd hurt anyone. Or any*thing*, as

Bellah kept insisting. Bellah and Torrance had a vicious quarrel about what it means to be alive, which ended with Torrance exploding that this was going to be the last time he'd touch any weapon whatsoever for any purpose whatsoever, whereupon Captain intervened by saying something about the frying pan.

So when I saw that frying pan, I felt my face break out into an enormous smile, and the girl who was cosplaying Torrance caught it and grinned back at me. It was a tractor beam drawing me in.

I went up to the two of them.

"Hi! Oh my God, hi! Torrance! Hi, Tennah! Hi, Bellah!" I couldn't stop smiling.

Tennah/Bellah bowed, a little awkwardly. He had very thick eyebrows that almost met above his pink glasses. "Bloodygit?" he asked me.

"Bloodygit!" I confirmed excitedly. "Zoe Rosenthal."

Torrance smiled and said, "I'm Liv Decker." A brief pause, as if she was hesitating, and then she held up her badge. There was a little ribbon on the badge that said THEY/THEM.

Because of Simon, at least I didn't hesitate to respond. "Oh, I should have said. I'm she/her." I smiled at her— them.

Simon had a whole speech about including pronouns in introductions, especially when meeting new people, pointing out that the onus otherwise was always and unfairly on the nonbinary or trans person. Here he was being proven right yet again.

Liv smiled back and added, "Just so you know, I don't

take *offense* at she/her. It's just that I identify personally as nonbinary."

I nodded. "But just so you know, I try but I mess up on pronouns sometimes."

"No worries. I happen also to be imperfect."

Tennah/Bellah said, "I'm Cameron Decker. Cam. He/him. I am perfect."

Liv snorted.

Cam said, "We're from here. Atlanta."

"You're siblings?" I asked.

"Twins," said Cam. "But not identical. Just in case that's not totally obvious."

Liv snorted again.

"Wow, I have to tell you, I'm regretting this," Liv said, raising the pan. "I totally should've gone with aluminum."

I said, "But it makes the costume. You know, authenticity." I gestured at their lab coat's vomit stain. "Also, nice touch."

"I had to try at least somewhat, given the competition," Liv said, with a glance at Cam's Tennah/Bellah costume.

"You look spectacular," I said to him.

"I don't see the point of doing things halfway," said Cam airily, and then paused before adding, "when it comes to cosplay."

I said to him, "I love your split face."

"Thanks! Originally, I was going to paint as Bellah in front and use a mask for Tennah in the back, but then I decided to go this way instead. I didn't like the idea of, you know, *silencing* Tennah by reducing her to a mask. It would be like she's permanently dormant."

I nodded. "I see what you mean."

"I don't," said Liv.

I truly did, though. Tennah/Bellah shape-shifts from one person to the other, and even though this is body-sharing, sort of, Tennah doesn't have any access whatsoever to what Bellah knows and vice versa. When one is up, the other is—sort of—dead. Or asleep. They leave each other meticulous voice logs. Also, and this is extremely important, Tennah and Bellah are *not* friends. They cooperate only because they have to and they do not particularly like it, or each other. Oh, and they have quite different tastes in sexual partners, which led to an interesting scene in Episode 5 and, as you may imagine, many more interesting scenes in fanfic. Not that I read *Bleeders* fanfic. Not much at all.

The line that the Deckers were standing in started to move. I walked alongside. "What are you going to?"

"Frank Oz," said Liv. "You know, you could maybe come with us. One person won't make any difference, right?" This was directed to the Sailor Moon couple behind them. "We've been waiting," the man said uncertainly.

"It's not like you wouldn't get in," Liv wheedled.

"Oh, no, no," I said quickly. "I could never cut in line."

Even though I wasn't sure who Frank Oz was, I would have gone with them if I could have. Only I really didn't want to cause any unpleasantness. I said, "Actually, I'm on my way to get something to eat." Then I was brave. "Are you two going to the premiere at midnight?"

"Of course!" said Cam. "You?"

"Yes!"

"Meet you there?" said Cam. "We can all sit together."

"Absolutely," I said. "That would be great."

"Pro tip? Come an hour early. At least. We want good seats."

We.

"Yes," I said. "I will."

Their line was moving, so Cam said, "See you at eleven, Zoe!"

"Eleven," I agreed happily.

Scene 4

Sweet

"Doors don't open until eleven thirty," said the volunteer at the Piedmont Room door, sternly, as he blocked my way. I had arrived on the Conference Center level at the Hyatt even earlier than eleven o'clock.

"Can I just, you know, go in and sit? Save a couple seats?"

He eyed me. "You have a ticket for the *Bleeders* premiere?" When I nodded, he added, "Then you just wait out here with everyone else."

I retreated with my metaphorical tail between my legs. Only a few hours before I'd claimed that I would never cut in line! Apparently I'd just never been really tempted.

I was far from the only one who'd come early. People sat on the floor or leaned against the walls, including a T. rex wearing a Handmaid's white bonnet and red robe. I gave them a thumbs-up, got permission to take a photo (for Maggie), and then looked around for Cam and Liv Decker. Who must have thought eleven meant eleven.

I went up to a skeletally thin, tall kid in cargo shorts and a Doctor Who T-shirt. His Dragon Con membership badge dangled from a purple-and-yellow lanyard around his neck as, sitting, he leaned forward over a book.

"You're the end of the line?"

This guy looked about my age, maybe a little older, with a scruffy chin that he had tried to shave. He closed his book when I spoke. The book had a picture of an elk on the cover and was titled *Modern Java Recipes*.

"Yes, I think so." His voice was loud and subtly atonal.

I said, "Okay if I sit here too? I won't bother you."

"You won't, I mean, I'm not bothered, I mean, yes. Sit down. Fine. That's fine. You can sit. Sit." He scrambled to make more room, although there was already plenty. I had that sinking feeling about him, not the bad one, just the "he likes girls and I'm a girl and I'm here so he's going to try" one. But this was where I had to be, so I sat. I pulled out my phone and ducked my head so my hair sort of curtained my face. "I have to text my boyfriend," I said pointedly, even though in actual fact the only person I needed to text was my employer, Mrs. Albee. Which I should have done earlier, only I'd forgotten. "He's expecting it."

The boy looked interested. "Is he coming too? We can save him a place."

"Uh. No. He—he's not. Two other friends of mine are coming, though."

"We'll save spots for them, then."

I lowered my phone. "That's allowed? Or would it be as if they were cutting other people in line?"

The guy shook his head solemnly. "We just need to tell whoever gets in line after you that we're saving the spots. Someone told me that today when I got in line for Frank Oz. Also, Bloodygits won't mind. We're all fans together! You said two?"

I nodded. "Yes, two. But I'm going to text my boyfriend now, okay?"

"Fine," he said, but just kept on talking. "My name is Sebastian Sweet. He/him."

There was something cheerful about him. It didn't feel like he was hitting on me, after all. And he was a Bloodygit. I smiled. "Hi, Sebastian. I'm Zoe Rosenthal. She/her."

"Hello." Sebastian pressed his hands together and bowed his head. "Namaste, Zoe." He added solemnly, "The light in me salutes the light in you."

I had never namaste'd anyone outside of a yoga class. "Namaste, Sebastian." He kept looking at me expectantly, so even though I felt ridiculous, I added, "The light in me salutes the light in you." It was worth it because then he looked so happy. He was weird, he was definitely weird, I thought. But . . . well, sweet. I added hastily, "So, I'm texting my boyfriend now, all right?"

"Yes, you said you would. Good. Don't you wish he were here? He'll miss the season premiere! Did you have to promise him you wouldn't spoil it for him? Won't it be hard? You won't be able to talk about it with him until next week!"

I bit my lip. "Actually . . . uh, see, Simon's not a fan."

Sebastian Sweet's eyes widened. "He's *not* a Bloodygit?"

"He's never watched it."

"Well, you have to make him!"

"That won't work. Trust me. He's not even slightly interested. We don't talk about it."

Sebastian Sweet looked absolutely horrified. "Zoe, that must be *awful!* I don't think I could be with someone who didn't at least have patience for my stuff!"

"We manage," I said dryly. "It's called compromise." As soon as the word was out of my mouth, I realized that compromise wasn't precisely what was happening in this particular case . . . but I stood by the principle.

Sebastian didn't, apparently. "I really don't know how you do that," he said, looking worried. I smiled at him awkwardly and thought, *Autism spectrum?* If so, I was superglad I hadn't shut him down before. Still, I leaned over my phone decisively; I didn't want to pursue the compromise discussion. Sebastian Sweet took the hint and went back to his book.

He was okay, I thought.

I texted my boss.

> **ME:** Yes, I can confirm that I'm coming over tomorrow at 3 to take more video footage of Wentworth. No need to answer if that's still OK! I'm sorry it's so late. See you then!

My phone rang immediately. Mrs. Albee reads texts but says she can't stand to talk that way. I picked up. "Hi, Mrs. Albee."

"Zoe, I'm so glad you called—"

"Texted," I said compulsively.

"Yes? So, tomorrow isn't going to work? Wentworth needs more rest and relaxation between shoots? And maybe some special treats?"

I pressed my lips together. Wentworth's entire life consisted of rest and relaxation and special treats. They did not help.

"I'm also not sure about your script?" Mrs. Albee went on. "I'm working on an idea that will be less stressful for him?"

"Send script edits my way," I said. "We're canceling tomorrow's shoot, then?"

"Yes? We can reschedule once Wentworth is ready?"

"Fine," I said.

I hung up, banged my own head against my own phone, and looked into the interested, questioning eyes of Sebastian Sweet.

"I am the media marketing manager for my next-door neighbor's business," I explained. "Mrs. Albee's Handmade Organic Kitty Soaps."

"Really? What are your qualifications?"

I blinked. Nobody had ever asked me that before. Even Simon had assumed the answer was just that I lived next door and liked cats. I said, "So I used to make videos of our cat, Riley, and upload them. Just for fun. But then Riley had to go live with my Aunt Kath because my dad got too allergic. I missed him and I just thought . . . well, anyway, I asked Mrs. Albee if I could do a video of Wentworth."

I shuddered, remembering that shoot. That horrible shoot. Only I said:

"Mrs. Albee liked it. And she asked me to do more. And I said yes, and now I manage her Twitter and Instagram and the Etsy store and most everything online."

But it was making the videos I loved. And I had thought, surely, *surely*, with some more experience, and when he was more used to me, Wentworth would be cooperative. Would pick up some basic comfort level with the camera. Some professionalism!

"And so," I concluded. "Here I am!"

"That's great!"

"Not always," I said frankly. "I mean, yes. In many ways, I love my job. It's creative, and Mrs. Albee listens to me and lets me make decisions. But our spokescat, Wentworth . . ."

Sebastian was listening so intently. Suddenly it all burst out of me.

"Wentworth is maybe the most neurotic cat I have ever met, and believe me, I have met a lot of cats! He is simply not emotionally qualified to be a spokescat! And, you know what else? I know *exactly* why Wentworth is the way he is. Ask me my opinion about nature versus nurture. Go on. Ask me!"

I might have snarled the last bit.

"Uh. Nature or nurture?"

"Nurture," I told Sebastian darkly. "The kitty does not fall far from the tree!"

Sebastian Sweet might have shifted ever so slightly away from me. "Um, Zoe? Didn't you need to text your boyfriend?"

"Correct," I said. "I did say that, didn't I?"

Sebastian nodded and retreated rapidly behind *Modern Java Recipes*.

I leaned over my phone, pretending to text, and thought bitterly about my many, many hours of useless Wentworth footage. I wanted to give up on him. I longed to give up! I *wanted* to hire Ellen From Finance! (Her actual name. And a sweeter, more cooperative cat you will never find, plus she lived conveniently just down the street with the Costellos!)

But I didn't know how to get Mrs. Albee to agree.

May I say how maddening it is when an intelligent person won't recognize reality? Wentworth is not suited for stardom. He just plain doesn't want it enough! #fact

I spent some soothing minutes with our college spreadsheet. We had thirty-two colleges, color-coded. I had spreadsheet indicators for the schools that had excellent scholarship and financial aid reputations, like Boston University has this cool Presidential Scholarship, and some (not many) schools promise to meet all your financial need so you don't have to get loans at all. I had included other important factors as well, like location and cost and majors and urban versus suburban versus rural. If you clicked on various cells, you drilled down to helpful auxiliary information.

My parents thought thirty-two was too many. My mother added up the application costs and left the information for me on the kitchen table with a note: "We'll pay application costs for ten. The rest is on you, honeybee. Quick question: Isn't this a lot of money for Simon to throw away, too? He's got to pay for all of his applications, right? His mom can't help."

I knew that! We'd discussed that! Simon said the application fees were an investment in our future together. We needed to try for some choice at the end, because both of us were not going to get in everywhere. And it was complicated! Simon needed more financial aid than me, *and* we wanted schools that had strong political science and economics departments for him. And, since I don't know what I'll major in, we needed schools with lots of options.

How could my parents think I'd forget for a moment that Simon's mom couldn't help him as much as my parents could help me? I'd actually offered to pay some of his fees from my savings, to even things out. (Thanks to kitty soap, I have nearly three thousand dollars!) But Simon insisted he would manage; he had savings from his daycare job, although less than me.

I put away my phone and turned back to Sebastian Sweet.

"Did you say you went to Frank Oz this afternoon?"

Apparently I had not scared him too much; Sebastian eyed me cautiously but willingly. "Yes. Did you?"

"No, but my friends—the ones who are coming here—did. Only, I'm not sure who Frank Oz is? I mean, I think I've heard the name."

At this, Sebastian's native enthusiasm returned full force. "Of course you know Frank Oz! He's Miss Piggy! He's Yoda! He's Bert, and he's Cookie Monster. He was half the Muppets. And he's a movie director!"

I felt my eyes get big. "Seriously? Miss Piggy? Oh, you're right, of course I know him!"

Sebastian closed his book. He rummaged in his backpack and tenderly pulled out a manila envelope. He shook out a photo. I examined the face of the older bald man. He looked so ordinary, but . . . awe filled me.

"He signed it to me," Sebastian said.

"I loved the Muppets," I said. "Miss Piggy—she's just so unabashedly selfish! I adore that, don't you? And it's hysterical."

"I know, right?" said Sebastian.

"She just goes after what she wants!"

"It's inspiring!"

"It's piggy!" I punned badly, but Sebastian laughed. I grinned and stared more at Frank Oz, wondering what it would feel like to be doing good in the world—doing good by creating joy—by making and playing puppets. Puppets . . . but no, I shouldn't dwell on my personal pathetic puppet-related memories. They didn't matter. Frank Oz mattered. I couldn't look away. Here was this old guy who I might pass on the street and probably not even notice, but he'd been incredibly important to me. And to how many others? No wonder there'd been a line all around the hotel waiting for him . . . wow. Wow!

I should have begged the Sailor Moon couple and tried harder to get into that line. Only I just hadn't known I cared.

"So what did Frank Oz talk about? I mean, did he actually have Miss Piggy with him? Or what?"

"It was question and answer. He did voices, though.

Like, when there was a question about Bert and Ernie, he answered as Bert, and when it was Yoda, he answered as Yoda."

I leaned forward. "What did people ask?"

By the time Cam and Liv Decker arrived, Sebastian and I had moved on from the Muppets to the even more important questions about the end of *Bleeders* Season 1. The cliff-hanger: Captain had come up behind Lorelei sitting in the lab and said quietly, "Use that scalpel to cut both your wrists. Set it to SLICE. Do it now, Lorelei. Now, or I'll kill you my way."

The camera had moved from Captain's unwavering gloved hand on the garrote at Lorelei's throat to focus on Lorelei's ice-pale, still eyes . . . then down to the pulsing laser knife with its settings SLICE and KNIT. Lorelei reached for it . . . SLICE—

Fade to black.

What in all bloodiness was AMT—that's the showrunner, Anna Maria Turner—up to? And what would happen next?

Season 2, Episode 1

We sat together in the twelfth row: my new pal Sebastian Sweet, my only-slightly-less-new pals Liv Decker and Cam Decker, and me. Around us sat other fans, everybody buzzing with theories. Most people thought Lorelei was up to no good—was maybe an agent of the government and/or the Sanitation Force—and that Captain had caught her.

I was preoccupied, though. There were many empty seats—and it wasn't as if the room was an enormous auditorium. Maybe it wasn't so amazing after all that I'd gotten a ticket in the lottery?

I said uneasily, "I sort of expected more people."

Liv met my eyes, their forehead wrinkled. "I guess it's because SlamDunk is a newish streaming service?"

Cam spoke up from Liv's other side. "SlamDunk

doesn't advertise much. But I thought there'd be word of mouth. It's worrying."

"No, no, don't worry!" said Sebastian.

"Well," I said. "We should worry. Because here's this fantastic show offering a sneak peek of its season premiere, right smack in the heart of the—" I hoped this wasn't insulting "—of the kingdom of the geeks. Shouldn't this room be standing room only? Even at midnight?"

"Midnight might or might not be prime time at Dragon Con," said Cam. "Hard to say. There's less to do, so maybe they hoped to attract new fans to try it? I don't know."

Liv said, "I see Zoe's point. Something like *Deep Space Nine* offers just a Q and A with actors and that show ended *years* ago. But there's thousands of fans lined up to revisit the past with them."

"Nostalgia is powerful, that's all," said Sebastian. "And Star Trek's always relevant, especially when there's a new Star Trek show on. We can wait to build the *Bleeders* audience. It'll happen. Every show has to start somewhere."

"Shows do take time to build their audience," Cam said. "Even good ones. Maybe especially good ones."

"Yes," I said. I wanted to believe it.

"We're like pioneers," said Sebastian comfortably. "More people will catch up and get on board this season. It's a no-brainer."

"I hope so," I told him. "I can't help wondering if *Bleeders* is having trouble because it's majority female."

"Don't be paranoid," said Cam. "Lots of guys here who like the show." He gestured around.

"I mean behind the scenes at *Bleeders*. Women actors, woman showrunner. Does that mean less advertising revenue?" I asked. "Or other, I don't know, problems with raising money?"

"Unfortunately, that's plausible," said Liv.

Cam shook his head. "Let's not go down that road until there's evidence."

"History is evidence," Liv said. "Why should *Bleeders* be magically exempt from the kind of prejudice women-led businesses have faced since, oh, the dawn of humanity? We should assume that prejudice is a factor unless we see evidence otherwise!"

"Liv, we're just free-associating about some empty chairs—"

"Sure, yes, I'd love some. Thanks!" Sebastian was distracted by someone ahead of us who was passing out Swedish Fish. Probably he was right. I too wanted to be distracted from this particular discussion because it was making me twitchy.

I got some fish.

Then a volunteer up at the front told us to silence our cell phones and not to record.

"Oh my God," said Liv. "It's starting! I can't stand it!"

I clutched my own arms in excitement, and as the lights dimmed, I looked around one last time. So maybe there weren't so many of us, not yet anyway, but everybody who *was* here was grinning like crazy, leaning forward, eyes alight. And this was my *show*, our show! I was here, meanwhile there were other passionate fans out in the world who weren't able to be here (like Josie). I was so lucky!

We Bloodygits were part of an elite group; we were in the know. This was where I belonged. *Bleeders* needed its fans!

I reached up to touch Cam's stethoscope-garrote, which he'd generously loaned me. The screen lit up. Bloodygits went crazy applauding.

On the screen before us, the camera was on the laser scalpel in Lorelei's strong bare right hand.

Lorelei flicked the scalpel to SLICE. It pulsed. She slanted a look up at Captain, seemingly unmindful—as she turned her head—of how the garrote in Captain's gloved hands was already cutting into her neck so that a thin line of blood trickled down.

"Do you have a preference, Captain? Left or right wrist?"

"Lorelei's ambidextrous, remember," a voice whispered loudly from behind us.

"Shhhhhh!" dozens of others hissed.

"How about both," said Captain calmly. "One after the other. On high."

You couldn't be a fan of *Bleeders* and go queasy at the sight of blood. Still, the wrist! I had to force myself to not shield my eyes—

The skin of Lorelei's right wrist came apart in a long, clean vertical cut. Tiny blue and red crystals sparkled beneath the surface. Only crystals. No blood.

"Happy now, Captain?" asked Lorelei.

"Do the other."

Lorelei cut her left wrist, just as deftly, just as deeply. This time, blood welled up, pulsed, pushed. It was red.

I heard Sebastian moan slightly.

Captain and Lorelei watched it gush.

"All right," said Captain at last. She had not relaxed her hold on the garrote; blood still trickled from Lorelei's neck. "You can close those up now."

Lorelei reversed the setting on the scalpel. The skin of her bloody wrist zipped closed. Healed without even a scar. Then, without assistance, the skin over the crystal wrist knit itself back together as well.

Captain released the garrote, holding it easily in one red-gloved hand. Without another word, she sank down into a chair next to Lorelei.

"I'm so sorry," said Lorelei courteously. "I imagine it's a shock. May I make you a cup of tea?"

"With honey," Captain said.

"We only have the Eglantine variety. Not your favorite."

"I'll manage."

"Of course, I do apologize for not being entirely honest with you."

Captain's gloved fist lashed out and hit Lorelei squarely in the jaw, toppling her over in her chair. From the floor, unhurt, Lorelei looked back at Captain.

"Unless you find you don't want tea after all?"

"I'll get it myself." Captain paused, her teeth worrying her lower lip. "Tell me. How long before you turn entirely?"

"Uncertain," said Lorelei. She stayed on the floor, looking surprisingly comfortable there. "The rate has been rather slow so far."

"On the bright side," said Captain, "once the transformation is complete, you'll have no flesh for the Bleeder virus to eat. What about your mind?"

"I have reason to believe," Lorelei said, "that I will still be me. For . . . some years."

"Huh."

Lorelei shrugged. "I don't recommend you make the Lucifer bargain, too. It's not an avenue for everyone. And one of us will do, I believe."

"Is it safe to look now?" Sebastian whispered.

"You didn't watch?!" I was aghast.

"I'm afraid of blood. What'd I miss?"

My voice rose involuntarily. "How can you be a fan and afraid—"

"Shut up!" The woman in front of us whirled and hissed.

"Sorry," I whispered.

Bellah entered the ship's bridge, where Captain sat at the navigation console, sideways in the chair, with her short legs dangling. Captain was listening to someone whose static avatar—a purple amoeba—was visible on the communications console but whose voice wasn't audible because Captain was using an earphone. She nodded acknowledgment at Bellah, rolled her eyes toward the console, and then spoke crisply.

"If you double our fee, I'll consider it. We'd need half up front also. Yes, I hear you. Yes, we believe in humanitarian aid. But we also believe in making a good living." She paused. "All right. We're in business, Mayor. I'll send our team down with supplies. Captain out."

Captain detached her earphone and placed it on the console. "We've got a new job," she told Bellah and Monica. "A town in the jungle. Vaccinations—pretty straightforward, I think, once we do the bloodwork. I'm sending you, Bellah, and Celie and me."

"Not me?" said Monica.

"You have the con."

Monica nodded. "What are they paying?"

"Hm. One thousand universals."

"That's all? Captain—"

"Plus fifteen minutes on a secured, untraceable communications channel."

"Oh," said Bellah. She added slowly, "And you don't think it's a trap?"

Captain straightened her shoulders. Then somehow, subtly, she transformed.

How does the actress—Jocelyn Upchurch—do that? There's a shift of expression on her face, just for a second or two, and for a moment you sort of see into Captain's soul—or think you do, which amounts to the same thing. Captain's a burdened woman of forty with children she hasn't seen in years, a husband who betrayed her, a doctor's oath, 24/7 responsibility for her ship and the lives and well-being of its crew, twenty extra pounds that she claims a little too often to have made peace with, and— incidentally—a self-imposed mission to chase across the universe after a deadly rampaging virus that threatens to destroy humanity. You're reminded of all that just by looking into her face. But that's not all she is, and this too is suddenly plain. She's a canny, charismatic leader you'd follow into hell . . . even when you're not sure what will happen once you get there.

You see all of that.

Then you see her smile.

"Bellah, Bellah, Bellah," Captain said. "My naive one. It's definitely a trap."

Bellah raised an eyebrow. "But you want me, not Tennah?"

"Yes. You and all your poisons."

The Ex-Cheerleader

The Bloodygits (we call ourselves that in homage to the *Bleeders* showrunner, AMT, who is desi and British with the most adorable accent ever) came pouring out of the season premiere in a gossipy geyser, and our little knot of four was in the thick of it.

"What *was* that in Lorelei's arm?"

"Lucifer? What's that? A second virus?"

"Captain didn't seem afraid of catching it, though."

"It's got to do with selling your soul to the devil, don't you think?"

"No, really? Huh! . . . Listen, I loved that mayor creature, didn't you?"

"It was hilarious! I hope we haven't seen the last of it."

"Did AMT write this episode?"

"Yes, but there was also a cowriter on the credits. I'll look it up."

"Did you notice they didn't do that super-close-up on the bugs in the blood this time? It's because AMT doesn't want to cross the line when it's not dramatically necessary. She thought maybe the virus got too gross at the end of last season. She said so in that season promo interview, did you see it?"

"No! The grosser, the better."

"Sebastian! Sebastian Sweet, is it really you? *Sebastian!*"

The voice came from behind us. Sebastian didn't seem to hear. I touched his arm. "Hey. Someone's calling you?"

I pointed backward in the crowd that was rapidly thinning around us to where a young woman was waving madly as she worked her way forward.

Cam laughed. "Hey! It's Captain!"

"Amazing cosplay!" said Liv enthusiastically.

The young woman coming toward us wore Captain's battle headgear. She had realistic-looking laser hilts and futuristic syringes fitted into her black leather belt, and she wore Captain's vest with its embroidered white-and-red medical insignia and the signature gloves, in red latex. (Captain never shows her bare hands.) Her figure was almost as curvy as Captain's. The cosplay didn't match only in that she was white, her hair wasn't in cornrows, and she was way, way, *way* too smiley for Captain. Also, she had a guy by the hand who was wearing a blue-shirt Star Trek uniform, whereas Captain doesn't touch anyone unless she's doing surgery, or fighting, or killing. Obviously, too, Star Trek is another universe entirely, so

Captain holding hands with a blue-shirt is just visually weird. Although I'd realized by now that this particular weirdness was one of the points of Dragon Con.

Sebastian said, "Oh no."

"Sebastian, it's really you!" the Captain cosplayer said, beaming, in a super-strong Texas accent. "Wow, that's fantastic. I never thought I'd see you again, but here you are! Awesome."

Sebastian took a step back, away from her.

The Captain cosplayer's face sobered. "Sebastian, I—I have to tell you that I think about you a lot." She paused, waiting, but when he didn't answer, she added, even more tentatively, "Do you remember me? Melanie Delacroix? From high school?"

"I remember," Sebastian said.

Melanie Delacroix, who was extremely pretty, smiled again. She gestured to the young man with her. "This is my boyfriend, Todd. He's not a Bloodygit—or a Trekker, really—but he likes to do whatever I want, so here we are."

To this, Todd nodded genially and said simply, "Why not?"

I tried and failed to imagine Simon accompanying me to Dragon Con in cosplay because *why not*.

Sebastian was not interested in the boyfriend. He said, "You can't be a Bloodygit! You're a cheerleader."

"What?!" said Todd the boyfriend, arrested. "You are?"

"That's in the past," said Melanie, with a toss of her head. "In high school. I'm on my college dance team now," she added earnestly to Sebastian. "It's much more me. I'm learning to choreograph."

Sebastian clearly did not care about this. A combative, angry expression had taken over his face. He said, in too loud a voice, "So somehow they let *you* into college?"

I exchanged a concerned look with Cam and Liv.

Melanie's smile slipped slightly. "Yes . . ."

"Meldel's an English major," the Trekker boyfriend told us, as if that had anything to do with anything. "I'm studying music tech." He turned to Melanie. "What's this about your being a cheerleader in high school?"

She shot back at him, "What's wrong with that?"

"No, it's cool." He leered. "But you never told me . . . you said you were a nerd . . ."

"I was a nerd. Secretly in my heart!"

"If so, it was like a state secret," Sebastian spat. He turned to Todd. "Nerd or cheerleader, the *problem* was that she was a truly terrible *person*. And she hung out with other truly terrible people, and they were truly terrible together. In *uniform*." He glared at Melanie. "I was totally happy to never think of you or high school again. And I was having a really good time here tonight with my friends." He gestured a little wildly at me and Cam and Liv. "I'm not talking to you anymore." He pressed his lips firmly together.

I blinked. Sebastian was here by himself—like me. And Cam and Liv, they had just met us. We were all strangers. But Sebastian clearly wanted—or needed—this Melanie person to think we were his good friends.

Melanie Delacroix looked self-conscious and awkward, but she stood her ground.

I met Liv's eyes—and then Cam's.

So this is a thing that happens to me sometimes with

Maggie, when we look at each other and we know we're thinking the same thing. Here, it was simply that we would all support Sebastian. On faith. At least for now.

So Liv said to Melanie Delacroix, "We hope you're not going to upset our friend Sebastian. I don't know what happened between you two in the past, but we were having a good time together here and we'd like to go on doing that."

"That's right," I said. "Let's just all walk away, okay?"

"No hard feelings," said Cam. "No drama."

I heard Sebastian exhale in relief.

But Melanie didn't move. She held out her hands. "But, see, I don't want to upset him either! Or interfere with anybody's good time. I just, I saw Sebastian, and I only wanted to say hello. And maybe, maybe . . ." She glanced over at her boyfriend and then back at Sebastian. "We're older now. We're in college. Where are you, Sebastian? Texas Tech?"

"I am at NYU." Sebastian's mouth tightened. "Not that it's any of your business, but I wanted to get as far away from Lubbock as I could."

"I wanted to get away too! I'm at UT Austin," said Melanie. "That's in Texas," she added, as if Cam and Liv and I might not have heard of the capital of Texas.

"What are you trying to say to Sebastian, Melanie?" asked Cam.

By this point, the six of us were alone; the other Bloodygits had gone off, presumably to sleep or to do one of the seventeen dozen things you can do at Dragon Con at two in the morning. I suddenly realized that I'd seen my show, and therefore I could excuse myself. I could head to the airport and wait there for my morning flight.

Only I didn't want to leave the Bloodygits.

Melanie said, "I meant—that is, I'd like to—oh, this is hard to say . . . but I have recently taken a fearless moral inventory of myself and I owe you an apology, Sebastian. I was—not nice. I want you to know how sorry I am and how much I regret it and that I am not that person anymore."

"What exactly did you *do* to him, Meldel?" asked Todd the boyfriend.

"It wasn't just her," said Sebastian softly.

"I don't want to say. I'm ashamed. Do I have to say?" Melanie looked pleadingly at Sebastian.

He shoved his hands in his pockets. "I don't know. No." A pause. "You're really sorry?"

"Yes. Yes, I truly am. I've prayed about it."

"Oh?"

"I believe I was led here," Melanie added earnestly. "Not just because my creativity demanded it, but also to see you and apologize."

Sebastian had been looking softer, but at this, he grimaced. "And I believe that kind of thinking is delusional."

Melanie smiled gently, forgivingly—infuriatingly, I thought. But at least she really was apologizing for whatever bullying—I assumed—she had done to Sebastian.

Cam and Liv were whispering. Then Cam said, "So, Liv and I have a hotel room, thanks to our parents. We were going to invite Zoe and Sebastian up to hang out and talk about the premiere and have snacks. So Sebastian, what do you think about my inviting these dudes, too? You and Melanie can maybe talk privately, and then we can all talk about *Bleeders*. But not if you don't want to."

Melanie smiled gratefully at Cam and then looked hopefully at Sebastian. "I'd like that. If you're willing. And I'm really dying to talk about *Bleeders* with you all, too. I don't know any other fans."

Sebastian hesitated, then said to Cam, "Did you say something about snacks?"

"Yes."

Sebastian smiled then. "Okay."

"Oh good," said Melanie.

"Cool," said Todd the boyfriend amiably.

Then suddenly we were all doing introductions. I made sure to say my pronouns, which led to everybody else doing it too. It went smoothly except that instead of just saying "he/him," Todd bellowed, "I identify as a man!" and actually beat his Trek-uniformed chest.

"Todd also identifies as immature," observed Melanie without embarrassment.

I wanted to giggle but managed to suppress it. I hoped that Liv wasn't offended. I stole a glance but couldn't tell. Liv was looking at Cam. Then we were all walking.

I could have said goodbye then.

But my plane didn't leave until seven o'clock. And I'd certainly rather be with Bloodygits than alone at the airport or alone somewhere else at the con.

So I went with them.

A Nice Cold Facecloth

I awoke on the rug in Liv and Cam's parentally subsidized, air-conditioned hotel room. I was curled up, fully dressed except for my sneakers, with a pillow under one cheek and a blanket over me. Sunlight streamed onto the floor over my outflung arm. A stethoscope-garrote, Torrance's iron frying pan, and my orange sneakers were inches away.

I was clutching my phone, which was off. Because—I now recalled—I had powered it off to save battery.

My last memory was of everybody talking. Including me.

The others were still talking.

"So the way I see it, Lorelei is basically amoral, and Torrance is too moral. But he also just doesn't have any balls! That's really what I object to." This was . . . I squinted. It was Todd the boyfriend. He was lounging half on, half off one of the beds.

"Don't say 'balls,'" a now-familiar Texas drawl objected. Meldel. At some point before I fell asleep, Melanie Delacroix had insisted that she was to be called Meldel. She sprawled on the other bed, with Liv.

"What am I supposed to call it? I'm not being sexist. Torrance is a guy. Cis-het, even. He literally has balls. Except he doesn't have *metaphorical* balls, is my point."

"Torrance takes his do-no-harm oath seriously!" snapped Liv.

"So you're insulting the rest of the crew? All of whom are women who *do* have metaphorical balls?"

"Is it really only about women?" Cam asked. "Tennah/Bellah is very obviously a they. That metaphor—if we're going to talk about metaphors—could not possibly be more clear. Plus, you seem to be defining 'balls' as being willing to kill."

"To kill *enemies!*" Todd insisted.

Fear clutched my throat as I watched my phone go through its maddening cutesy start-up routine.

"The problem is with the meaning of 'balls,'" Liv said with obvious patience. "It has a history of exclusion. We can do better."

"Disagree-e-e!" Todd said. "The word is bigger than its literal meaning. It is beyond gender." He raised a half-eaten Twizzler in a toast to Meldel. "For example. Balls of steel has Meldel."

Twizzlers. That was what I could still taste.

My phone informed me that it was 8:38 a.m.

I almost threw up the Twizzlers.

Instead, I looked around at the room full of strangers.

They hadn't felt like strangers a few hours ago, when we'd been talking and arguing. But now . . .

How had I allowed this to happen? To *me*?

"If you're going to take 'balls' away, then I need a replacement term," Todd was insisting.

"Something female," said Meldel. "Yet sharp. Single syllable."

"Something that applies to everyone," said Liv. "Nongendered."

One blessing: Simon didn't know I was here in this room with these strangers.

"It absolutely has to be vulgar," Todd said.

"Granted," said Cam, as Meldel nodded and Liv said, "Sure."

And Simon must *never* know.

"We'll have to invent something," said Liv.

"Femball?" said Todd.

"That's idiotic!" said Meldel. "And you're not listening. Neutral!"

"I may be idiotic and a bad listener, but I'm charming. You're charmed by me."

Meldel sighed—and then giggled.

"Actually, all of you here are charmed by me, even against your wills. I can tell. I'm the Celie of this little group. Meldel? Will you love me when I'm a girl? Will you love me *more*? Or at all?" He waggled his eyebrows up and down.

Liv and Cam side-eyed each other. I agreed with what they were obviously thinking about Todd, ugh, but most of my attention was fixed despairingly on my phone as it presented me with a backlog of automated texts from the airline. These told the story of my folly: directing me to a gate, informing me that the flight was boarding, that the flight was closing its doors, what number I should call to reschedule, and that, in the event of rescheduling, there was a fee on top of the charge for a new flight, click link for details.

I was about to click the link when another bunch of texts arrived.

> **SIMON:** Good morning sleepyhead!
>
> **SIMON:** Should I come by with bagels soon?
>
> **SIMON:** No rush but today's voter registration shift is at noon.
>
> **SIMON:** You're all better now, right? We need you today!

I levered myself to a sitting position. Sebastian, on the desk chair, waved at me. "Zoe!"

For a terrifying moment, I actually thought Simon could hear and see him. Me. Us. Here in this Atlanta hotel room.

It was time to panic. Even Maggie couldn't save me. She was offline all day today, doing—something. Something else family. I knew exactly what it was, but I couldn't remember because my brain was frozen. Oh God. Oh God.

"Good morning, Zoe," Liv was saying, and the others said hello, and then Liv leaned forward. "Zoe? Are you okay?"

"No," I said. "I am not." Thank you for noticing.

"What's wrong?" asked Sebastian.

I looked down at Simon's texts. Luckily, he'd sent them

only a few minutes ago. Unluckily, I had no idea what I could or should text back.

"Zoe?" said Cam.

I said, "My life is over."

"Can it be over *after* the parade? We have to leave in ten minutes," Cam said. "Our mom is saving us a spot near the Sheraton. She has muffins and coffee. You'll feel better once you eat."

"I will never feel better," I said.

"Your mom is inviting all of us?" asked Sebastian. "Really?"

Liv nodded. "Sure. You'll like her. And our dad is marching. You have to see him. The parents are total geeks, by the way, in case that wasn't easily inferred. Zoe, you want the bathroom before we leave?"

"I'm not going to any parade," I said. "You don't understand. My life is over. Parades will not help."

"Coffee and muffins will, though," repeated Cam. "And really, you don't want to miss the parade."

"I don't drink coffee." I put down my phone. My hands were shaking. I buried them in my hair. "And I will never eat again. Also, I hate parades."

"Not this one," Cam insisted.

"I hate parades, too," said Todd. "Especially if there are clowns. Will there be clowns?"

I scrambled to my feet and gave them all the hairy eyeball. "Listen! This is not a joke! I was supposed to be on a plane home already. Only my best friend knows I'm here, but what's most important is my boyfriend doesn't. I was a total freaking liar about coming here, but I just had to see the *Bleeders* premiere, and I didn't intend for anybody to ever know! But now I've missed my plane and my boyfriend just texted and he wants to come to my house with bagels and I'm supposed to go do voter registration with him today. Because hashtag resist." I waved my arms. "Only now he'll probably text my parents and get them all upset, because he's like super-responsible and he'll be worried if he goes to my house and I'm not there, and so it's all going to come out that I'm not home. And that I lied! I lied! Over a TV show! So, like I said, my life is over! Over!"

I realized too late that I had screamed the last word.

"Ah," said Meldel.

Ashamed, I cleared my throat. "Uh. Sorry."

"You're a total sneakasaurus girl," said Todd admiringly. "Awesome. Have a Twizzler." He tossed the container to me. Automatically, I caught it and fished out a Twizzler and viciously bit its head off and only then remembered that I never wanted to eat a Twizzler again. I ate it anyway because sugar.

"But your boyfriend isn't even a Bloodygit," Sebastian said.

I glared at him. Then I looked pleadingly at Liv and Cam. "Can I just stay here in your room while you go to this parade? I need to figure out what I'm going to do. There's got to be something—wait, I know, I'll just go straight to the airport and find the next plane—I don't know how I'll pay for it, I'll have to use my parents' credit card—they'll be pissed off—but I guess it's an emergency—only it's my fault it's an emergency. Okay, I'm getting ahead of myself—first I have to text Simon! What do I say to him? Oh God."

"What's he look like?" asked Cam.

Grimly, I called up a picture of Simon on my phone and handed it over.

"My ears and whiskers!" said Cam admiringly. "I quite see why you want to stay in with *him*." Meldel tried to take the phone from him, but Cam held it out of reach, staring, until Liv held out an imperious hand.

"Down, boy. He's not for you."

"I'm just window-shopping," Cam said, but he handed it over, and the phone then went from Bloodygit hand to Bloodygit hand.

"And that's just Simon's outside," I said smugly.

Liv handed me back my phone. They had modified their Torrance costume by winding three different scarves around their neck. Liv said firmly, "First. Breathe."

I almost stamped my foot. "You aren't listening! I—"

"Don't you worry your pretty little head about your flight *or* your yummy-yummy boyfriend," said Meldel. "Auntie Meldel will get you home with nobody the wiser. Trust me, Zoe. I've been in trouble on a few occasions in my life. What I have learned is that there's always a way out. With the Lord," she appended piously.

"But Simon just texted me," I said. "And—"

"Bless his heart. Give me your phone." She took it from my flaccid fingers. "Perfect, you told him you had a headache yesterday!" Meldel ran her thumbs rapidly over the phone face. "There. You've had a terrible relapse!" Her smile nearly blinded me. "You can thank me later."

I tried to take my phone back to see what she'd texted.

"No, no, I'll keep your phone for now. Until hottie

Simon and I finish talking!" said Meldel. "Because he and I are going to have a nice little chat. Whoops, I mean, you and Simon. Don't worry. You're off the hook with him. Or you will be." She started texting again. "He'll never know I'm not you! Promise! I'm an excellent writer and a quick study. I'm imitating your texting style very closely. I see you're a stickler for punctuation and spelling, and so is the hottie. I approve. Todd, take a lesson."

I stood there.

Liv unwound one of the three scarfs from around their neck and draped it gently around mine. It was covered with My Little Ponies and rainbows. "Better?"

The rainbow ponies were ridiculous, but the scarf felt soft and silky.

"Yes?" I asked tremulously.

"A scarf always helps. People don't coddle their necks enough. You can keep this one as long as you need it, Zoe. Wear it to the parade."

"We really have to go now," said Cam. "Parents."

"No problem," said Meldel. "I can walk and text Simon at the same time. Now, take that worried face off, Zoe. I'll talk with the airline next. Everything will be *fine*."

"That's my girl," said Todd proudly. "The Melster has got awesome powers."

I sighed. I wrapped the soft rainbow pony scarf more securely around my neck and decided to hope for the best. What choice did I have?

Scene 8

Before the Parade
Passes By

On Peachtree Street, the dragons marched by first. They had papier-mâché heads and colorful hides and giant feet, but that was about all they had in common because different people had made them. One enormous black dragon had outstretched wings and snapping jaws and a guy on his back wearing a horned helmet.

"He's on stilts that operate the legs," Liv said analytically. "And he's using puppetry to work the head and jaws."

Puppets again. "You're sure there aren't two people in there?" I asked, craning my neck.

"Yes."

I stood on tiptoe to follow the black dragon with my eyes. "It's so good—do you think that guy's a master puppeteer? Like Frank Oz?"

Liv and Cam's mother answered, "Maybe, but I doubt it. Chances are, he read up and tried things and figured out how to make what he wanted. That's how cosplay tends to work. Hey, here comes the steampunk group! Check out that woman with the top hat and monocle! I love steampunk!"

The next hour was full of charm and delight, albeit not enough to make me forget about Simon and that my life was now over, and also that I had no idea how and when I was going to get home and how frustrating it was that I couldn't even text Maggie. (Well, I could text, but I wouldn't get an answer anytime soon because—my memory had unfrozen enough to inform me—Young People's phones were always confiscated during the annual Kwan family picnic.)

I had to trust that Meldel was going to figure it out for me.

There were no better options.

Ghostbusters went by, with cars and vans and blaring music. Then medieval lords and ladies with high head-dresses and knights on horseback. Somebody clomped along behind this group wearing a suit of armor in which they just had to be sweating buckets. Next came storm-troopers, including one in head-to-toe pink.

There were fandom groups I recognized and some I had to ask about: *Agents of S.H.I.E.L.D.*, *Firefly*, *League of Legends*, Walking Dead, Tolkien, Hunger Games, Star Trek—all different kinds—and *Handmaid's Tale*.

The Handmaids included the giant T. rex I'd spotted yesterday. In a white bonnet and red robe, this dinosaur galumphed along at the back of the group with hands clasped and eyes meekly downcast. Enchanted, I pointed it out to Liv. "If I weren't committed, I'd sort of want to resolve right now to date him. Or her. Or them. I mean, if they were available and interested."

"I just do not get that," Liv said. "Even as a joke. You don't know that person! But then—" They paused, looked at me, and then nodded as if they'd thought about it and made a deliberate decision to go on. "I can barely understand it when people are romantically attracted to someone they actually do know."

"You don't want someone?" I asked slowly, carefully, not wanting to offend my new friend but needing to know. "Even someday?"

Then I relaxed, because Liv snickered. "I really don't *think* so! I never have even really fantasized about it to this point. Whereas you do, right?"

I groaned and fanned myself with one hand.

"Exactly," said Liv triumphantly. "And I just bop along in my own skin. You know, sex aside, sometimes I wonder if having a twin ruined me even for the idea of partnership. I mean, I never even got to be independent in the womb!"

Oh, I like you, I thought.

"Nobody's independent in the womb," I pointed out. "You're tethered to your mother."

"Don't be so literal. You know what I mean. I've been sharing and compromising since conception. I love my brother, but it's enough already! Space, please."

I laughed. "I get it." I paused before confessing the way Liv had: "But I have to tell you, I'm entirely the opposite. I've wanted a boyfriend since I can remember. And, oh

God, now that I say that aloud, I feel embarrassed. I sound so . . . needy. Or boy-crazy." I winced.

"Yeah, well, you're not alone at least. Look at my brother. He's been having massive crushes since forever. But he's way too shy to make a move on anyone. He suffers in silence. At least you don't have that problem."

"I always had an idea that it was easier for gay men. Cam is gay, right?"

"Oh, yes he is, and no, it's not easier. Not for Cam, anyway," said Liv. "Of the two of us, he got all of the sexual longing and none of the confidence to go with it."

"But wouldn't other guys chase him? So all he'd have to do is respond?"

"He says the ones he likes are always out of his league."

"Now that starts to sound like my friend Maggie," I said. "And with her, what it really means is that she's terrified. Whenever it gets too real, she bolts."

"I've wondered about that with Cam, actually."

"But that's not you?"

"I don't think so, no. But that's just me. Lots of enby people are really into sex and romance."

I nodded, remembering Jordan O'Halloran, an enby person at my high school, older than me, a music geek who'd had a reputation as definitely being into sex.

At that point, I realized that I hadn't had such an easy time talking to someone new since, well, Maggie.

Then Liv's mom yelled, "Here he comes! There's Dad's group! Gerry! Over here! *Gerry!*"

She pointed as the Disney princesses were replaced by the Borg from Star Trek. Cam and Liv's dad was covered in black rubber and coiling hoses, with only his right eye exposed. "Gerry!" yelled Ms. Decker again, and Mr. Decker waved at us stiffly, robotically, with both arms. I took a picture for Maggie—one of a very long series.

Next came elves and hobbits, and then more super-heroes than I could shake my frying pan at. (About the frying pan: feeling like a misfit in my regular clothes, even though I had the scarf, I'd again borrowed Cam's stethoscope-garrote and grabbed Liv's discarded cast-iron frying pan, too. To my regret, because it really was too heavy.)

Star Wars, with many incarnations of Princess Leia. Someone who'd done a mash-up of Han Solo with Elsa from *Frozen*. The writer Jane Yolen in a tiara waving from a convertible. Pennywise the clown, dancing alongside Beetlejuice, which made Todd hide his head and scream, "Clowns! Minions of evil!"

The parade grand marshal was greeted with loud cheering. This was a comics guy I'd never heard of, but the crowd certainly had. "He's got the beauty queen wave," Cam observed with delight. "Elbow, elbow, wrist, wrist."

"What?"

He demonstrated. "Southern girls learn it. Elbow, elbow, wrist, wrist. Touch your pearls, blow a kiss." I did it too, with the stethoscope-garrote.

I found out how the parade works: Any con attendee is welcome to march. You register yourself and your intended costume in advance. When the organizers put the parade together, they assign you to a group. So, let's say you cosplay Scooby-Doo. When you line up for the parade, you learn that you've been put with two Velmas and seven Shaggys and a Fred and a Daphne and two other Scooby-Doos. You all march together. If you're lucky, their cosplay doesn't make you feel ashamed of yours. But it might.

Cam said, "People look down on costumes that you buy. You're supposed to make your own. It can get a little snobby."

"What do you mean, snobby?"

"If you don't care enough to put in the time and effort to make your own cosplay, then people might not respect you."

These were new definitions of *snobby* and *respect* for me.

"But everybody should at least *try*," Cam said, and quirked an eyebrow at me. "Even Liv put in a sort of quarter effort. Like, it can help build the fandom, if people see you're out there."

"Fine. I get it. I'll work on my Lorelei," I said rashly. A moment later I remembered it was impossible.

Sebastian was listening. "I could just be a random bleeder," he said. "I was thinking about a mechanism for the blood."

I turned to him. "Didn't you say you're afraid of blood?"

"I want to get over that. I can't believe I missed the key scene last night."

"You could just keep your eyes open next time. See what happens."

"I'd faint. I know it. But if I cosplayed a bleeder, then I'd know the blood was fake because I faked it myself. That's different. I think that would give my brain the right message and I wouldn't faint."

"What do you have in mind for the mechanism?" asked Todd.

"I could freeze thin layers of ketchup in plastic bags and then poke pinholes . . ."

I eased myself over to the other side of our group, where Meldel was using Captain's headgear to play peekaboo with a toddler in Princess Leia earmuffs. Before I could say a word, Meldel gave me a thumbs-up. "I haven't forgotten your flight. Don't worry!"

I decided to believe her, at least for now.

Meanwhile, Ms. Decker was talking to the toddler's mom and dad. "Trends come and go, right? A few years ago, *Battlestar Galactica* was huge, but I'm not seeing them lately. *Game of Thrones* is fading a bit now."

"Star Wars is always so huge."

"Uh-huh. And the Leias are now not really just Leia anymore but a tribute to Carrie Fisher." Ms. Decker blinked mistily. "You know, Carrie—Princess Leia—she was the very first woman hero I ever saw in science fiction. In Episode IV, when she just grabs the gun and blasts a hole in the wall—oh, dear. Sorry." She sniffed. "I was only a kid when I first saw that, but it had *such* an impact."

Liv hugged their mother. The toddler's mom and dad nodded agreement.

Meldel's attention was elsewhere. "Oh, Bloodygits! Don't miss it!" she sang out as bare-chested Spartans complete with oiled six-packs approached.

"Hm," said Cam appreciatively. "*300.*"

"Not bad," said Meldel analytically. "Now, if only there *were* three hundred of them."

"Ugh," said Todd and Sebastian and Liv together.

I laughed. And that was when I realized that I was actually glad—oh, except for an anxiety level that was worthy of Wentworth in front of a camera—that I'd missed my plane. Glad to be here at the parade. Really! I had expected it to be totally nerdy and dorky and I had also expected—to be honest—that it would embarrass me even to be here, watching it. But I didn't feel like that at all.

I thought it was *awesome*.

And I loved being with my Bloodygits.

I clapped and shouted until my hands ached and my throat was sore.

Scene 9

Fettered

Liv said, "You know what I've been thinking? It's that Bloodygits have a big problem, and if we don't do something about it—and I mean *us*, specifically—we'll regret it for the rest of our lives."

"Dramatic much?" asked Cam.

"I'm serious!"

It was Saturday afternoon. The six of us sat against a wall in the long corridor connecting the Hyatt with the Marriott. I was back to feeling like I'd known them all for years. After the parade, we'd wandered the hotel lobbies, talking and looking and talking more. We had just visited the Con Suite for a free lunch, which for me consisted of a golden not-so-delicious apple and a chocolate very-delicious donut. Balanced!

Liv's face had a look of concentration and intensity. "We need to do something. The time is now."

Now? Like, right now? I eyed her warily. Under no circumstances was I going to miss my new flight at 8:40 a.m. tomorrow. (With only a fifty-dollar change fee! Meldel had blessed the heart of the agent who'd been under the impression that I should pay for a new ticket, escalated her call to a manager, and fed that manager a breathlessly long and involved story about how it was all *her* fault that I'd missed the flight because of my being such a good friend in Meldel's hour of totally desperate need. This desperate need somehow involved lost glasses and a bichon frise named Geranium. Meldel did not once pause for breath. My suspicion was that the manager would have done anything to get her to stop. Maybe I should ask Meldel for advice on how to persuade Mrs. Albee to replace Wentworth with Ellen From Finance.)

Everything was good with me now, however. I'd made a new checklist and ticked everything off. Texting with my parents, who were having a great time in Montreal. More pictures for Maggie. And an actual phone call with Simon, who had gone safely off to voter registration alone. Simon totally believed in my continued headache and my need for a Me Day involving a bubble bath and sleeping and "female restoration" (this was all Meldel). But also, he was preoccupied with something that he was dying to tell me, only he didn't have time right then, and actually, on second thought, he was going to save his news for when he saw me in person. (It was good news, though. That much I had learned.)

In short, I was getting away with it, just as if this longer and friend-filled version of Dragon Con was, after all, the actual treat that a benign universe meant for me to enjoy.

"What are you thinking? What's the problem?" I said to Liv, but Todd cut me off.

"You may have a problem, but I don't. I am footloose and fancy-free."

"You don't even know what that means," said Meldel. "You have a girlfriend, me. By definition, you're *not* footloose and fancy-free."

"So I'm, uh . . .?"

"Tied down," I suggested. "Attached. Committed. Fettered."

"Okay!" said Todd. "I'm fettered. Yay. Fine. That's good too."

Liv said, "Well, I guess it isn't Todd's problem if he doesn't want it to be. It's a problem for Bloodygits. What I mean is—"

Todd cut in again. "I'm totally on board with being a Bloodygit. No conflict. I mean, what Meldel likes, I like. I'm fettered."

"That's great, darling, and let's hear Liv out, shall we?" said Meldel.

I mentally (and smugly) compared Todd to Simon. Simon was the winner, and not only because he wouldn't have interrupted Liv. If Simon were to reveal his bare, oiled abs in Spartan cosplay, he would not disgrace himself. (Not that Simon ever would do such a thing, if he even knew there *was* such a thing. Never *ever*.)

"As you know, we did not have a good turnout at the

season premiere," Liv said. "It should have been packed, right? But there we were in a not-so-big room and there were actual empty seats. And in the parade, did you notice? Not a single Bloodygit. What *Bleeders* has here"—they contemplated a raisin—"is a visibility problem. Which frightens me."

"We should have marched in the parade, Liv," said Cam. "Even if it was just you and me. We could have carried a *Bleeders* banner."

"We hadn't even figured out our cosplay by the time we would've had to register for the parade. What I'm saying really is, what can we do *now*? We need to help our show."

"If we accept that it's our responsibility to do something," I put in. "I mean, shouldn't SlamDunk be advertising more widely? Maybe they have a whole marketing campaign planned for this season. Maybe the premiere at Dragon Con was just the start."

Liv looked skeptical. "Corporations don't care. Even a little one like SlamDunk. If one thing isn't a hit, another thing will be. They close the books; they move on. I think we have a responsibility as fans to help *Bleeders* survive."

Sebastian said, "You mean, literally the six of us?"

"Literally the six of us."

"Correct use of *literal*," Meldel put in. "Excellent."

"Only how do we do that?" asked Sebastian.

"We discuss it. Fans have power. We just need to deploy it."

"I could write fanfic," said Meldel. "What do you think? Captain/Monica?"

Cam scrunched up his face. "Ew. No. I don't care that

it's a common ship! It does nothing for me. Also, Captain still loves her husband. Or at least, she's obsessed with him."

"But he's a bastard. She should move on. Or she could love him still but have a slow-burn thing happening with Monica."

"Please not Monica," I said. Monica is so desperately in love with Captain, it positively hurts to watch her silent suffering. I'm not a fan of hopeless love in real life and I don't even like it as a story line.

"Wait. You write fanfiction?" Sebastian said incredulously to Meldel.

Meldel shrugged. "Mostly Harry Potter. I specialize in Draco/Luna. But I could change to *Bleeders*. I should, actually. Stretch my skills."

Cam cackled.

"What?" demanded Meldel. "Why not fanfic? We need *Bleeders* fandom visibility. This is something I can do. I happen to be good at writing!"

"No, no, I don't mean—" said Cam.

"Cam writes Harry Potter, too," Liv cut in. "Neville Longbottom stories."

Cam said apologetically, "They're not very popular. I don't put any sex in them. I'm more into humor. Meldel, I was laughing because I read Draco/Luna. It's my favorite. What's your pen name?"

"Melisande Du Lac."

I was shocked to see Cam go starry-eyed. "What? Really? That long one last year, where Luna was in blood debt to the Malfoys? Fantastic! I checked for updates like every night. I always thought Luna didn't get enough screen time in canon, and you just totally exploded that. I love you! You should be, like, published for real."

Meldel looked shy. "Thanks. So, uh, who are you?"

"Orphan Shortbottom. I don't have many readers, like I said. I'm not in your league," he added humbly.

"I'll look up your work right away. So, we should write *Bleeders* fic! Collaborate?"

"Do you mean it?"

"Why not?"

"Because you're—you're Melisande Du Lac! You haven't even read my stuff yet. Really, I'm, like, not worthy."

"I'll read your stuff today," promised Meldel. "Mine could do with some humor. We'll want a totally different tone for *Bleeders* anyway. We'll invent a style. And with two of us, we can have twice the output. Good for visibility."

Sebastian was looking stunned. He demanded, "Did anyone in high school know you wrote fanfiction?"

"Of course not," said Meldel. "Why? Do you write also?"

"No. I'm not really into Harry Potter."

"I mean, do you write anything? It doesn't have to be Harry Potter."

"No. No writing. I'm not creative that way." Sebastian blinked at Meldel. "I actually don't read fanfiction. It's just—I'm surprised you write it."

"I don't read, either," Todd put in. "Not anything. I prefer watching shows. With emotionally manipulative music so I can see how it's done! Not that I'm thinking about my future career or anything." He guffawed. "Who has time to read?" There were some glances exchanged among the rest of us, but this was left tactfully alone.

I thought about Josie, because Simon had confided in me that he suspected his sister of secretly writing *Bleeders* fanfic. He was worried about it. My other thought was that Josie would have been at the premiere if she could have been, filling another seat. Showing SlamDunk there were more fans.

"The fanfic is a good start," Liv was saying. "What else can we do?"

I opened my mouth to say that I was getting pretty good at marketing videos, especially with cats, and maybe I could put Ellen From Finance in Captain cosplay. But no, no, I wasn't going to have time, between school and Simon and college applications and kitty soap, not to mention my secret plan to unseat Wentworth and give Ellen From Finance the legitimate, paid spokescat job she deserved.

I said instead, "Let's not panic. There are probably lots of other *Bleeders* fans, but they just couldn't show up for Dragon Con."

Liv shook their head. "That's kind of beside the point. We need to get the attention of the kind of people who *do* show up for Dragon Con. We need the big fans, the loud fans, the committed fans. Those people aren't watching. And what that means is . . ." Liv reached for the stethoscope-garrote I was wearing. I handed it over. Liv did a fake-strangle thing with it. "They could cancel the show."

"No." Sebastian shook his head. "*Bleeders* will catch on. It's only Season 2. What happens is, people binge-watch the previous season and there's word of mouth and it all just takes time. It will build. Zoe's right."

Liv shrugged. "Maybe. But think about *Firefly*. It got canceled because the fandom formed too slowly."

"Wait, what?" I said. "*Firefly* has lines around the block! They have legions of fans."

"But their big fandom happened in kind of an underground way," Sebastian said. "Liv's right. *Firefly* only got one season. Then TV execs pulled it because they didn't think there was a big enough fan base. Which was wrong, but the fans weren't noisy enough, the build was too slow, and the TV execs didn't give it time." He paused. "Of course, that was the olden days. Before you could stream an entire season."

"So that won't happen to *Bleeders*," I said.

"It still could." Liv leaned forward. "It could already be happening. The people in power at SlamDunk know now that *Bleeders* fans didn't exactly swarm the season premiere. And remember what you said before, Zoe? About maybe the show not getting support behind the scenes because AMT is a woman? That could be true. I bet the clock is ticking, and if *Bleeders* doesn't build a big, vocal, visible audience, and soon, there won't be a Season 3."

Silence.

"I'll write a new fic every week," Meldel vowed. "I mean, Cam and I will."

Cam looked alarmed. "I have to apply to college this year."

"You'll fit it into your schedule," said Meldel firmly.

"Just do what she says," advised Todd. "It saves time."

"We all will fit in what we can," said Liv. "I repeat: What else can we do? We need something big."

"We are humble folk, Liv," said Cam. "We are ordinary fans. We are powerless."

Liv raised their fist. "No! Fans matter! And anyway, if you think you're powerless and therefore you don't do something, then nothing changes. It's a self-perpetuating prophecy. In life, you have to stand up to be counted."

This was what Simon always said, too. Only he'd never say it about wanting a TV show renewed. *Are you kidding me? You're wasting your time on this frivolous, inconsequential thing when there are real-world problems demanding our attention?*

"I have an idea," said Sebastian. "I'm not sure, I mean . . ." He went pink in the face. "What if we all went to New York Comic Con next month? In the best *Bleeders* cosplay ever? And, like, we photobomb everything we can? As a group?"

We stared at him.

"I *know* I can make a costume that actually bleeds," he said. "That would be very high visibility. There's no parade, but if we go around as a group, everyone would want to take our picture. And we could have a *Bleeders* banner, like Cam said before."

"Huh," said Liv.

"Can I be Celie?" asked Todd. "She's the cutest one, like me."

Liv said, "Sebastian, that is not entirely crazy. Cam and I wanted to look at New York colleges anyway. Let me just look up the con dates . . ."

"First weekend in October," said Cam, who was already on his phone. "That could work."

Sebastian's face was alight. "You can all stay with me at NYU!" He waved both arms expansively. "Cheap! And we'll just take the subway to the con! In full cosplay! Visibility!"

NYU was on my list with Simon.

"I'm always up for New York City," said Meldel eagerly.

"Excuse me? Have you ever even been there before?" asked Sebastian. It sounded like he hadn't entirely forgiven her, not yet anyway.

She raised her chin. "Not yet, no, but one day, I will be published by a big New York publisher."

"We'll go to New York Comic Con," said Todd grandly to Meldel. "I'll take you. What else is my mom's credit card for?" Meldel smiled at him.

"Excellent," said Sebastian, looking a little abashed. "Stay with me. Everybody's welcome."

The Bloodygits exploded into animated talk and planning. But not me.

Of course I couldn't go. It wasn't realistic. Boston to New York isn't far, and yes, we were applying to NYU, but it wasn't all that high on our list, and I had other priorities, like preparing applications and keeping up my grades, and Mrs. Albee counted on me, and my money from Aunt Kath was mostly spent, and Simon would want me volunteering with him at Alisha Johnson Pratt's state senate campaign as much as possible until the November election. Also, lying and sneaking around behind Simon's back was exhausting. This had been a one-time thing, and I'd gotten away with it (so far), and it had been wonderful.

But.

I was going back to watching *Bleeders* on my laptop, in my bed, late at night with my headphones on. Alone. I would not discuss it with anyone. That was just how it had to be.

It was pure delusion anyway, to think we six could affect whether *Bleeders* got a third season. I wasn't going to sneak off to another con next month in order to cram into Sebastian's dorm with my new friends and dress up like—like—well, Lorelei.

Lorelei. Because Lorelei was obviously who I would be. Captain and Torrance and Tennah/Bellah were taken, and Sebastian was going to be a bleeder, and Todd wanted Celie. That left Lorelei and Monica. Lorelei with the crystal arm. Lorelei who had apparently made some deal with the devil. For what? I guess we'd find out soon.

If I were going to New York Comic Con, I would go as Lorelei. Only I wasn't going. Definitely not.

EPISODE 2

October 2018 @NY Comic Con

From Zoe's Bullet Journal

TO DO:

- ☑ Secretly take more video of Ellen From Finance
- ☑ Plausible cover story for con weekend
- ☑ Cosplay items ordered
- ☑ Con membership
- ☑ Bus ticket

The Most Terrifying

My suitcase got loaded into the belly of the Megabus.

"Don't be nervous about traveling by yourself," said my mom. "You can handle it, and it's excellent experience." She began running through her solo New York City travel advice again.

I wasn't nervous. I wasn't going to be alone. Looking at my earnest mother, though, I reviewed my decision not to tell my parents my complete weekend plans. But I came to the same conclusion. I couldn't ask them not to mention the con part in front of Simon. Impossible!

Secret of effective lying: keep the lie simple and close to the truth. Only I wasn't really lying. I was omitting. And Maggie knew everything.

Maggie thought it was hilarious.

"You can call or text us anytime," my mom said

anxiously. "And of course the program for visiting prospects at NYU will take good care of you."

"Sure," I said.

Not a lie there, either. The program consisted of our leader, Sebastian Sweet, and visiting prospects Liv, Cam, and me.

"I mean, I didn't have parents schlepping *me* to schools when I was your age. My best friend and I flew to California together to see Berkeley and UCLA. And you're so responsible and trustworthy!" My mom's voice was happier on this last sentence. Luckily I had pulled out my bullet journal to check my list and had an excuse to hide my guilty face.

Boarding was called. We had already hugged goodbye when my mom took a deep breath and blurted, "Zoe? I'm glad you're going without Simon. You need to put your own needs first."

I froze. "What exactly does that mean?"

"Just . . . oh, honeybee, just that your father and I think it's good to see you striking out on your own with this trip."

"You're trying to say something, Mom. What is it?"

"We'll talk later. You'd better board now."

There was no time to probe further. And she'd known there wouldn't be! Now my mom shouted reminders to text and that my dad would pick me up when I got back on Sunday night. Fuming, I got on the bus.

I'd had a strange feeling lately when I talked to my parents about my college plans with Simon. And now this! Had my mom just been insinuating that something was wrong with Simon? With me? With us?

I found a window seat and pretended not to see my mom waving goodbye. I stewed until my phone beeped, just after the bus got on the highway. It was the Bloodygit group text.

> **TODD:** Mel and I just landed at the airport. Sweet, what's your address?
>
> **SEBASTIAN:** I told you yesterday. Scroll up.
>
> **MELDEL:** Got it. See you soon.

Everybody else was already in New York—Liv and Cam had arrived a few days ago to visit Sarah Lawrence and Columbia first.

My bus couldn't get there fast enough. I wanted to be in my *other* life, my fandom life, my escape life.

For the last month we'd texted *constantly*, planning our PR assault on the world of fandom. I wasn't even sure when or how my certainty that I couldn't-shouldn't-wouldn't go morphed into longing, then into decision. But after careful work on a to-do list, I figured out exactly how to manage.

It was easy.

Simon was *grateful* to me for checking out NYU for us in person. He even apologized that he couldn't come too. He was busier than ever, not only with school and college applications but—and this was his amazing news!—also with his duties in his *paid* position at Alisha Johnson Pratt's campaign!

He'd temporarily given up the day-care job and was earning eighteen dollars an hour at the campaign, the same amount that I earned with Mrs. Albee. I was so proud of him. His job would end after the election next month, unless Alisha actually won, because she'd told Simon there might be a permanent job for him then.

The polls said it was possible.

Simon had told me it was his dream. "In that case, I'd definitely want to stay in Boston for college," he had said. "And keep the job. It would be an irreplaceable opportunity for me."

"Of course we'd stay here!" I'd answered.

As my bus turned off the Massachusetts Turnpike, I saw the first New York City sign. My heart leapt. I turned to keep the sign in view for a couple of seconds longer. Then I thought of my mom implying that I shouldn't go to college with Simon, and scowled. Defiantly, I texted him.

ME: ♥

A second later, my phone beeped, but it wasn't Simon. It was the Bloodygits again.

SEBASTIAN: Guess what, Zoe? Cam and I just tested part of my costume.

SEBASTIAN: All systems go! I'm feeling almost cured of my fear of blood.

CAM: Fingers crossed.

SEBASTIAN: No worries bro. I'm going to bleed slow and gruesome.

MELDEL: Can't wait to see everyone!

TODD: We're in the Lyft now!

LIV: Zoe, we're on track to meet you. Look for us when you get off the bus.

LIV: Then we can go straight to the Javits Center and get our badges and stuff.

ME: Sebastian, did you get my cosplay?

SEBASTIAN: Yesterday.

ME: Thanks again for letting me send it to you. It needed to be secret.

SEBASTIAN: Because of that Simon?

ME: Yes.

SEBASTIAN: Dump him.

LIV: She's not dumping Simon.

ME: What Liv said.

SEBASTIAN: Then you have to convert him.

ME: Again. He's never going to be interested in *Bleeders*.

SEBASTIAN: Then it's never going to work.

ME: Oh, Sebastian, Sebastian.

I wasn't offended, even though I had been offended by my mom. Sebastian had confirmed to us that he was indeed on the autism spectrum, and also that he tended to over-perseverate (his term). He was always texting us. He truly seemed to think nothing was important besides *Bleeders*. I hoped he was keeping up with his college courses. He never mentioned studying. But I had seen him reading that book on coding at Dragon Con. He was wicked smart, too.

I would focus on studying more myself after the con. My bullet journal for next week's overdue tasks extended onto a second page. I was just a tiny bit behind because of texting the Bloodygits and figuring out my cosplay and doing my part for our online PR campaign, which included being a beta reader for the fic that Cam and Meldel (a.k.a. Orphan Shortbottom and Melisande Du Lac) were writing as fast as they could.

I'd recommended Simon's sister, Josie, as a beta reader, too. She was thrilled.

That impulsive kindness had nearly gone off the rails, though. Josie believed that Melisande Du Lac and Orphan Shortbottom had found her on their own in the *Bleeders* online forum, and she was so excited, and of course she told her mother and brother. I hadn't realized in advance that would happen. Predictably, Simon tried to stop it, and Josie fought back, and ultimately their mother decided it was okay for Josie to be a beta reader if she showed her mom what she was doing. Which left Simon absolutely steaming and hating *Bleeders* even more than before. He paced back and forth waving his arms about how trash TV infected the mind, and people were watching Hulu and Netflix and so on instead of paying attention to the world, and then he used air quotes to say that TV was the "opiate of the masses."

In short, involving Josie had been a mistake, even though my part was never even close to being revealed.

I made sympathetic (okay, hypocritical) noises at Simon. I didn't correct him about the Karl Marx quote that he got wrong in let-me-count-the-ways. I understood Simon's attitude. He was overworked, and the upcoming election was important, and he considers himself responsible for helping his mom with Josie's upbringing. And I really can't imagine what that feels like, in my privileged situation with married, working parents and no siblings who also must be educated.

My bus was passing New Haven, Connecticut, when Simon finally texted me back.

> **SIMON:** The polls now say Alisha has pulled within the margin of error!
>
> **SIMON:** We are going to win this thing!
>
> **ME:** Yay! But don't stay at headquarters all weekend. Get some sleep.
>
> **SIMON:** I can sleep when I'm dead.
>
> **SIMON:** Guess what? Alisha stopped by my desk and thanked me! She knows my name! She says I'm valuable to the campaign.
>
> **ME:** That's so great! Of course you are!

I thought of what my mom had said. She just didn't get it about Simon and me. I was *better* when I was with Simon. He always got me believing and hoping good things about the world. I *wanted* to feel like Simon did—hopeful, active, optimistic, full of fire about making a better future. Saving the environment, decimating racism and poverty and sexism and hunger. He was just so good. He was good for me.

How I Got Hooked

Flashback!

It was the start of my junior year. Simon and I had been together only a few months and everything was feeling sooo right. I was still incredulous to have a boyfriend, let alone such a hot, smart, kind, and emotionally mature boyfriend. I was basically radioactive with happiness. Maggie would elbow me and say, "Zoe? Take that look off your face. Now, I said *now*. You're with me. Be here."

I'd try.

Bleeders was newly out in the world, but I hadn't heard of it until one evening when Simon's younger sister, Josie, she/her, then thirteen, slid into her chair late for the Murawski family dinner. She got a frown from Ms. Murawski, but Josie acted oblivious. Anyway, a frown is as far as Simon's mom ever takes it—which Josie knew. Simon had told me how his sister shamelessly manipulated their mother, though he also said Josie was basically a good kid, if a little headstrong.

"I was watching my new show again." Josie waved her fork. "I am hooked! I can't wait for the second episode tonight!"

Ms. Murawski shuddered. "I'm not watching anymore."

"The blood's not that bad," Josie said earnestly. "Really, Mom. It's not like it's *gushing*, there's only a few seconds when Captain goes to examine that guy. They give you plenty of warning, so you can look away before the virus makes their skin completely dissolve. Also—"

Simon said, "Josie, we're having *dinner* here. And we have a guest."

"Oh, Zoe doesn't count as a guest!" Josie turned to me excitedly. "You have to watch! *Bleeders!* It's streaming on SlamDunk, and it's free if you watch the commercials. Have you heard about it? It's about women doctors! In space! There's this terrible virus."

Simon made a little sound.

I shook my head. "I don't have time for a lot of TV."

"Zoe's bookish," Simon said. We smiled at each other. We'd spent an hour yesterday talking about a serious book called *Infinite Jest* that he loved, and a science fiction series by N. K. Jemison that I had successfully talked him into reading the first book of, once he understood that it was at its core about institutionalized racism. We talked about how some books were hard going and complicated but repaid your attention.

"You'd love the show," Josie insisted to me. "It's intellectual and feminist and science-y."

"It's fantasy science, space opera, not realistic science." Simon turned his face so his sister wouldn't see him roll his eyes at me. But she must have sensed it anyway.

"The virus," said Josie dangerously, "is totally scientifically plausible."

"I'm guessing you read that in some PR release?"

"So what? How can you even have an opinion? You haven't watched *Bleeders*."

"You haven't shut up about it for the last week, that's how. I draw my own conclusions."

"Which are totally wrong. I can prove it. I'll send you links about real viruses!"

"I know about real viruses, Josie. I happen to think that's where we should focus our attention. On reality. Not fantasy."

Josie's eyes flashed.

Ms. Murawski intervened. "Don't you find it disturbing, Josie? You had nightmares for days after watching the Red Wedding."

"Oh, *Game of Thrones*," Josie said. "At the time, it was upsetting, I suppose, but I was younger. That kind of thing doesn't bother me at all now."

"Now you're a year older and so wise." Ms. Murawski mimed banging her head against the table, but she was grinning.

Simon told me, "Josie wasn't actually *allowed* to watch *Game of Thrones*. She was sneaking it on her laptop, under the covers, by dead of night. I caught her."

"But then Mom let me watch it," Josie said coolly. "With her."

"There was," Simon explained to me, "a carefully negotiated truce."

Josie went on excitedly—unstoppably—about her new show. By the time dinner ended, I had heard all about Season 1, Episode 1, of *Bleeders*. Her mom smiled at her and participated. Under the table, Simon held my hand, his face carefully neutral except for a compressed mouth.

So until Simon walked me home afterward, I didn't realize how truly worried he was about his sister.

Simon knows he can't take his father's place as an authority for Josie, and he doesn't want to, and he also understands he's a kid too. But still, he tries to do whatever he can to lift some of the burden of being a single parent from his mother.

"If she was just going to watch this new show once a week until the season is over, I guess I wouldn't worry. But with her, that's just the tip of the iceberg. She likes, you know, *fandoms*. I've seen this before. She'll rewatch. She'll analyze. She'll spend hours and hours online with the freaks, obsessing. It's not good for her! And she's wasting time that should be spent on better things."

"What does she do online? Talk about the show?"

"Yes. But also, there's fanfiction, which as far as I can tell is written by people who have nothing better to do with their lives. Josie can spend hours and hours reading fanfiction. Which isn't good, serious literature like what *you* read, Zoe."

I smiled and said nothing. Simon didn't know that my reading tastes were ... eclectic. That *good* and *serious* wasn't always what I was in the mood for.

My dad jokes that most people don't date each other directly; their *ambassadors* date each other. I suddenly understood what he meant. It was helpful to know that this was normal and what everybody did.

We had arrived at my house. It was a beautiful late-summer evening with school due to start in three days. Junior year was going to be wonderful, together. I had no intention of doing or saying anything to put that at risk.

And yet ...

"You think fanfic is always badly written?" I asked.

"By definition, it's got to be crap, right? No originality. Derivative. But that's not really what bothers me. Or, not only that." Simon moved his shoulders uncomfortably. "A lot of it is *porn*. I was suspicious, so I checked and I actually found some Harry Potter fanfiction on her laptop. Hermione and Bellatrix—" He blushed. "Never mind. You can probably imagine. I'm sorry."

I *could* imagine. Hermione and Bellatrix Lestrange. Hm. Interesting ...

Simon was looking everywhere but directly at me.

And then I realized: He checked his sister's computer. Behind her back. And read her private stuff ...

"Listen, you'd worry, too, if you had read what I did," Simon continued gruffly, eyes on the sidewalk.

I tried to think of what to say.

Simon's and my relationship was progressing at an appropriate pace, for us both being sixteen and being each other's first boyfriend and girlfriend. He was very considerate, and we'd decided together to go slow sexually, with lots of talking. This was unlike, for example, Maggie's ex-boyfriend from last year, who'd been both inarticulate and seriously pushy for the two weeks he lasted. Simon felt and said that I should set the pace. So we were in complete agreement. We could talk about *us* and how we felt and what we wanted.

It was comfortable. In contrast, this conversation felt uneasy. Maybe because it was his sister we were talking about.

I finally said, "Could you say more about it? I'm listening."

"Just that I don't think Mom really gets it about what Josie sees online. Even though I showed her! She says she'll intervene if she needs to. But I don't think she's all that worried about the—the porn. I don't get it! I actually showed it to her—well, I told you that—but she said she'd take it from there and it wasn't my business, it was hers and Josie's."

Whew. That sounded exactly right to me.

"Good," I said. "Your mom's on it. It's not your—our—business."

"Yes, only Josie's still reading that . . . stuff. I know it, Zoe. I looked again. And this . . . stuff . . . I can't even tell you . . ." He actually blushed. "You would be shocked. I was. Josie is only thirteen! I want to protect her!"

I didn't think I would be as shocked as he thought.

Also, I wondered, at Josie's age, would I have appreciated having an older brother who looked out for me? Made decisions for me? Advised me?

Checked my laptop?

No.

I might not want to, but I absolutely had to say something. "Simon. You shouldn't look at Josie's computer ever again. Never. Or at anything of hers that you know is private."

"I know. My mother said that too. And she's right. You're right. I won't."

"Good."

I was relieved! So relieved! I said, "So can we stop worrying about Josie and focus on us instead?"

Simon grinned. "Gladly."

We kissed good night for a long time. Our practice was definitely paying off.

I wasn't intending to watch *Bleeders* that night, or ever. But I was thinking about Josie, and what she said about the show and how enthusiastic she'd been, and I found myself searching for it. And then, well, I watched.

Episode 1 begins with the crew finding out that Celie has programmed the ship's computer to supply constant encouragement, like *You feel energetic and alive!* and *You love challenges!* Meanwhile, Captain is contacted in secret by someone who wants to sell her information about her husband and kids, and she arranges to meet them on the planet they're orbiting on a medical mission. Except Lorelei says they can't go down now—out of nowhere, the

Bleeder virus has infected the planet and it's on a rampage. Captain goes down anyway—and that's where we first see the virus in action.

The next thing I knew, Episode 1 was over and Episode 2 was going to be available in fifteen minutes.

Scene 3

Lorelei

My bus was inching south in traffic in New York. I texted the Bloodygits:

> **ME:** I'm in Manhattan! We're close!
>
> **LIV:** We're waiting for you!

I bounced out of my seat when the bus arrived. The Bloodygits were right there, and I fell into them, all of us hugging and screaming (Todd screamed in a fake falsetto, ugh). It was the best arrival I'd ever had in my life!

Meldel, Cam, and Liv were cosplaying the same as at Dragon Con: Captain, Tennah/Bellah, and Torrance. (Liv had a lightweight frying pan this time, and four scarves— I understood by now that Liv didn't consider themselves dressed without at least two scarves.) Todd was looking good as Celie, with his hair teased high and sprayed and wearing thick smoky oversized glasses, a frilly dress over olive green leggings, combat boots, Celie's white medical backpack, and a stethoscope-garrote.

Cam had made stethoscope-garrotes for all of us. I put mine on right away.

Sebastian, like me, wasn't in costume yet. He didn't want to risk wasting the "blood." He also had a bag with all the Lorelei stuff that I'd ordered online and had sent to him.

"To the Javits!" Sebastian pumped a fist and pointed.

The Javits Center is an enormous convention hall on the west side of Manhattan. Walking there wasn't like being in Atlanta for Dragon Con; the streets were filled with regular people, not other cosplayers. Some people stared at us and smiled, but even more people didn't pay any attention to us, because—Sebastian explained—New York is where you go to be invisible.

Still, I felt self-conscious walking in public with cosplayers. I didn't start feeling at ease until we were waiting in line at registration. Then, among all the fans (costumed and not), I remembered being at Dragon Con all by myself. And suddenly all I wanted was to get into my cosplay and fit in with my new people.

I pulled out the white wig I'd ordered and looked it over. "I was hoping to make a bun out of this. It's shorter than I thought it would be."

Meldel eyed it. "I can make it work, once you put it on. I have Todd's hair spray."

"You think? I just couldn't find the exact right thing online, not cheap enough anyway," I apologized. "I hope I'm not letting you Bloodygits down. Your cosplays are so amazing."

"No problem! You'll clearly be Lorelei just because you're with us," Liv said encouragingly. "Even if you don't look exactly like her. And cosplay is about playing with the character representation just as much as it's about being the character." They considered. "Maybe more."

"Nobody's tall enough to really be Lorelei perfectly anyway," Meldel said. "Except Todd, who really wanted to be Celie."

"I don't have the complexion to carry off white hair," said Todd. He twirled clunkily. "I feel pretty!"

(I don't quite know what to make of Todd. In fact, when I explained all the Bloodygits to Maggie, I said that Todd didn't seem like a real person to me. "A poser?" Maggie asked. And I said, "I don't know, maybe?" I was supposed to report any further conclusions to Maggie after the weekend.)

We got our badges, and then Liv and Meldel came with me into the ladies' room and I turned myself into Lorelei.

Lorelei is the chief surgeon on the *Mae Jemison*. She's the oldest person in the crew, in her sixties at least. She is very tall and very thin and very silent. While she refuses to carry any weapon except for the regulation stethoscope-garrote, she is not a pacifist like Torrance. We have seen her fight only once—in the Season 1 finale—but in another sense, we've *never* "seen her fight." What we saw was a close-up of Lorelei's eyes, which went entirely opaque and silver, and then we saw the aftermath, with three dead that she had somehow killed, no mess, no fuss, and then the season was over without any explanation of how she did it—until we saw the crystals in her arm in the Season 2 opener. Which explained nothing either, really.

There is a growing fandom taboo against shipping Lorelei with *anyone*. I think it's ageism, but Liv says no, it's aro/ace representation.

I put on tight black leggings and a black turtleneck and flat black boots with very pointed toes, and the white lab coat with the red insignia on the pocket, totally simple, and a heavy silver pendant. I had a laser pointer that was supposed to represent Lorelei's surgeon's laser scalpel. I had my white wig, which Meldel styled somehow into a tight bun. We rubbed makeup onto my face to turn my skin tone blueish. Finally, on one arm, I pulled a beaded crystal elbow-length glove that I got on Etsy for twenty-five dollars.

I had obviously had to spend some of my Mrs. Albee's kitty soap earnings to pull all of this together, but it was worth it.

Captain, Torrance, and Lorelei stood in a line and looked at ourselves in the mirror. I snapped a photo for Maggie. Behind us, an Elastigirl said, "I don't know who you are, but you all look fantastic!"

"We're from *Bleeders!*" Meldel said. "Streaming on SlamDunk!"

Elastigirl gave us a thumbs-up on her way out.

Meldel remarked thoughtfully, "I could choreograph a dance for us."

Liv slid their eyes to me for a second. "Like, an interpretive dance?"

"Yes!"

"No," I said, alarmed.

"Why not?" said Liv impishly.

"Because I said no," I said. "Also, and more to the point, nobody on *Bleeders* dances. Why would they dance? They're on the run! They're doctors!"

"But art," Liv said, and giggled.

"You're goading me, Liv," I said. "I get it now, and I refuse to react."

"It would be like a pantomime," Meldel said dreamily. "Like a medieval masque, and we would sort of mime out our roles—"

"No," I said.

"Coward!" Meldel said.

"Finally, you understand my character," I said.

Skittish

The six of us positioned ourselves just outside one of the doors to the con's show floor. Things didn't start well. Our giant sign said BING WATCH BLEEDERS ON SLAMDUNK! When I pointed out Todd's spelling error, he shrugged. I had to squeeze in the missing *e* with my black ultra-fine Sharpie. We had two giveaways: an informational flyer about the show, which Meldel had written (her spelling is perfect, what can she possibly see in Todd?), and Meldel and Cam's newest story, located under another sign that said FREE! NEW BLEEDERS FANFIC BY MELISANDE DU LAC AND ORPHAN SHORTBOTTOM!

However, the passersby expressed no interest in the giveaways.

We'd pinned our hope on the skit, an abbreviated version of Season 1, Episode 1, written by Meldel and starring

Meldel, which was fair enough because even though the show opener introduced the entire crew of the *Mae Jemison*, it centered emotionally on Captain. Besides, Meldel could act.

So she had claimed.

"My husband betrayed me!" she cried, and smote (there is no other word) her breast with one fist. "He stole our daughters from me! And now, our universe is threatened by a virus for which there is no cure! The entire universe quakes in fear! The government has unleashed deadly robots to hunt down carriers. They are out of control! We are doctors! We are female! Except him [points to Torrance]! We seek a cure, and personally, I seek the return of my daughters! Here, see their pictures in this hologram!"

She thrust a snow globe into the path of a surprised Rey from Star Wars.

"My daughters!" insisted Meldel as she shook the snow globe in Rey's face. Inside the globe, fake snow fell around the Golden Arches and a hamburger.

"Uh, delicious," said Rey.

Meldel went nose to nose with Rey. "See the clever look in my daughters' eyes?"

Rey exchanged a look with a little person in a Darth Vader mask, who was accompanying her.

Meldel shook the snow globe anew. She pointed at me, yelling, "Lorelei!"

I used an outdoor voice. "Our small crew of doctors has stolen this broken-down spaceship!"

"We have banded together in rebellion!" yelled Celie/Todd.

"Sounds like a *Firefly* rip-off," observed the little Darth Vader.

"Now we are fighters, we are lovers, we are healers, and we are mothers and sisters," Tennah/Bellah/Cam said tonelessly.

"Are you also cousins and aunts?" asked Rey with a snicker. Whereupon Darth Vader suddenly sang, using a carrying baritone, "I am the monarch of the sea, the ruler of the Queen's Naveee!"

Meldel opened her mouth, but a dozen strangers in the area cut her off, singing, "And we are his sisters and his cousins and his aunts!"

Our skit collapsed like a punctured balloon as Vader took center stage, bellowing an entire song from what I later learned was an operetta. Random people around us joined in on the chorus about the sisters and the cousins and the aunts, as well as another line about "what never, no never, well, hardly ever!"

When Darth finally finished, there was laughter and wild applause from the gathered crowd. Darth took a deep bow.

Meldel got in his face. She yelled, "You ruined our skit! Do you not realize how rude that was? Do you not?"

Todd interrupted, with a hand on Meldel to draw her away. "She's just passionate," he explained to a flustered Darth. "And this was her very own thing, you know. Sorry!"

Meldel wrenched her arm away from Todd. She said, "I was speaking for myself!"

Darth and Rey looked appalled. Darth said, "Sorry. It was just, uh—the mothers and sisters thing, I couldn't resist—and it wasn't just me—everybody was singing. And—"

That was when Sebastian ran up to us.

Screaming.

"It burns! Help! Get it off me! Help!" He skidded to a stop, looked down at the ketchup oozing out from the tight fabric of his sleeves. He paled, tottered, and abruptly thudded onto the floor in a dead faint.

Umpteen people whipped out their phones and called 911.

Character Alignment

It was night. Tails between our legs, we'd retreated to Sebastian's residence hall for pizza and reassessment. I chewed a leaf of the salad I'd insisted we also get, reflecting that in-person publicity was a whole different animal from using social media. Marketing kitten-shaped soap for Mrs. Albee had clearly not taught me enough.

Everybody else was obviously depressed, too. Except, possibly . . .

Todd tucked into his fifth slice. "Hey, Sweet! Where'd you get all those ketchup packs anyway? Steal 'em?"

"I *collected* them." Sebastian shivered visibly. "Over time. But I didn't realize how they were going to feel on my skin. It was basically a couple hundred tiny ice packs! I'm going to need a whole different approach. Nothing yet, but don't worry, I'm thinking."

Sebastian was down but not out.

Liv said, "I'm wondering, would they have worked without freezing them first?"

"No, they would have leaked too soon," said Cam.

Sebastian nodded. "I need a slow ooze. Look, I knew it would be *uncomfortable*. I just wasn't aware of what exactly it would feel like. And . . ." He lowered his head to between his knees. "I knew it wasn't real blood, but that didn't matter. I'm so embarrassed," he added miserably. "I ruined our skit."

"No, no, it was that mini Darth Vader who ruined everything," Meldel said. "Not you. We could have ad-libbed your screaming and fainting right into the skit."

Sebastian's brow crinkled in puzzlement. "Really?"

Liv and I exchanged a glance.

"May I ask exactly how you suggest we would have ad-libbed in the arrival of the first-aid team?" I asked Meldel.

She waved a hand. "Oh, Zoe. *Bleeders* is a medical show! We would have been creative. Surely you can think of a dozen different ideas. Don't make me do all the work."

"That's my Mel," said Todd.

Meldel narrowed her eyes. "Which reminds me. Todd? Don't ever apologize or make excuses for me again! Or intervene when I am talking to someone!"

"What are you talking about?"

"I was telling mini Darth off and you intervened!"

"Oh, that. You were overreacting. I just wanted to help."

"Darth was totally rude and I had every right to say so."

"A little diplomacy was a better idea. We don't want to alienate our potential nerdy allies, now do we?"

"Don't *now-do-we* me!"

I was trying to remember exactly what had happened as Meldel added, "You were one microsecond away from calling me an emotional little girl-creature who was out of control. And *then* you apologized on my behalf! You're my boyfriend, not my keeper!"

"That wasn't what I meant."

"It *was* what you meant." Meldel took a deep breath. "But we'll talk about it later. I care about you and your emotional growth and I would like to cure you of your ingrained male condescension. Or at least make you conscious of it."

"And can I try to cure you of your superiority complex?" Todd snapped. "Or is this a one-way thing?"

They were leaning forward, their faces close, glaring at each other. I was thinking that they were both right, and that my Simon would never, ever have apologized for me — but the next second, Todd and Meldel were kissing. And it wasn't just a quick peck, either.

"Ahem!" said Cam loudly. "Ahem! Other people! Other people are here!"

Sebastian muttered, "Faint again. Please. Let me faint."

Meldel pushed her fingers into Todd's hair. Todd made a noise that I wished never to hear again.

Liv took up an unopened can of Fanta orange, shook it briskly, and exploded it on Todd and Meldel.

They broke apart, dripping.

"That was rude," said Liv sternly.

Meldel said, "Sorry!" but Todd did not apologize. He wiped soda off his face with his fingers and then licked them. The rest of us winced. Sebastian threw Todd a wad of paper napkins. "Faces. Floors. Look under the sink for cleaning products. Also, no more of that . . . that. Not in my dorm room. No arguments, no kissing! No *nothing*! And here I thought *I* was the one with socialization issues!"

"Learn something every day," Cam said.

"I know, right?" said Sebastian indignantly.

"Todd will clean up," said Meldel.

"Yes, Todd clean up," said Todd, still grinning. "Todd happy. Todd looking forward to makeup sex."

"Shut up shut up shut up," I said.

"I'll help clean," said Liv primly, getting up and heading for the sink. "I apologize, Sebastian. But something had to be done."

Todd said, "Don't fret, little children. One day, you will understand."

"No," said Liv bluntly. "If anything, you have added cement to my lack of interest."

Once the soda spill was cleared to Sebastian's satisfaction, Todd and Meldel were sent to sit in separate corners. Then Cam cleared his throat and hammered the wooden floor with the bell of the stethoscope-garrote.

"Back to business, Bloodygits! We need to try something else tomorrow. Something that doesn't involve skits or blood."

As we pondered in silence, my phone buzzed.

MAGGIE: What's going on now? Sebastian recovered from his faint?

ME: Yes but more drama ensued. I'll tell you later. Everything OK there?

MAGGIE: Great! Guess what?

MAGGIE: I'm about to learn how to snake electrical wire up into the ceiling!

ME: And why would you do that?

MAGGIE: To install a ceiling fan, silly. Or a light fixture.

ME: Won't everything be wireless soon?

MAGGIE: Do not speak of mysteries that you do not understand.

ME: You're getting weirder and weirder.

MAGGIE: Says you, Lorelei?

I was still smiling when my phone buzzed with another text, this time from Simon.

SIMON: Josie came with me tonight to address voter postcards.

ME: How's that going?

SIMON: Well, she's eating the cookies.

ME: I take it her presence is not entirely voluntary?

SIMON: It's for her own good.

SIMON: She'll appreciate it later.

ME: ♥

ME: Are you maybe a little bit bored too?

SIMON: Maybe . . .

ME: Missing me?

SIMON: Yes. I wish you were here.

SIMON: Maybe you won't have needed to check out NYU.

SIMON: I'm really hoping now we'll want to stay in Boston.

SIMON: Alisha is going to win. I know it!

ME: I hope so.

SIMON: Back to work! xo

ME: xo

When I looked up, Meldel was making one last pitch for us to try the skit again. "We attracted a crowd. Well, a small one. It was good PR, even when we got mocked. And you know, maybe we should be thankful for mini Darth."

She got to her feet. She marched back and forth, hands behind her back, looking at us like she was Captain and we were sorry recruits. "Let us reframe. We were trying to get attention. We got it! Bad attention is as good as good attention! Bad is good!"

"There's this book, Meldel," said Liv. "A little dystopian classic called *Nineteen Eighty-Four*. You might have heard of it. 'War is peace. Love is hate.' Or something like that."

"'Ignorance is strength,'" I added.

Meldel beamed at all of us. "You're getting it now! Use your minds to conquer and change reality!"

I said, "So you're saying—by implication—that there's no such thing as actual truth."

Meldel shook her head. "No. There is truth, but there is also sometimes *reframing*."

"That's dangerous," I pointed out sharply. "In the political realm, for example." Simon would be proud of me.

"No politics, Zoe," said Cam. "Please, I'm on vacation from politics."

I squelched a sympathetic impulse and said sternly, "You have to be aware of what's going on in the world. Meldel, what you're talking about is, um, well, evil."

We sat there. Somehow, I had killed the discussion.

Then Todd broke the spell. "Zoe, let me explain Meldel to you. She's not evil. But she is on the chaos axis."

Meldel smiled, Cam laughed out loud, and Liv and Sebastian nodded thoughtfully.

"What?" I said.

"He's talking about where Meldel is on the character alignment chart," Liv said.

"What?" I repeated.

It turns out that in role-playing games, an "alignment chart" is used to quickly pinpoint the essence of a character's moral code. There are nine potential types, which Sebastian called up on his laptop and showed me, with various Muppets as examples.

Kermit was Lawful Good and Miss Piggy was Neutral Evil and Animal was Chaotic Neutral, which is what Todd said he was too, while (he claimed) Meldel was Chaotic Good.

Cam said, "It's deliberately crude. Think of the sorting hat! It provides a rough insight into character. I think I'm Neutral Good, depending on the situation."

"The character alignment has applications to people," said Meldel. "But what I really love is analyzing shows with it."

That took everyone off into *Bleeders*. True Neutral for

Captain, Chaotic Good for Celie, Lawful Good for Torrance.
They were arguing about Lorelei when I finally spoke.

"Simon is Lawful Good," I said.

"Oh, for sure he is," said Liv. "From what you've said."

And so am I Lawful Good, I thought.

	EVIL TO GOOD →		
	LAWFUL GOOD: Combines a commitment to oppose evil with the discipline to fight relentlessly.	**NEUTRAL GOOD:** Does the best that a good person can do.	**CHAOTIC GOOD:** Acts as their own conscience directs with little regard for what others expect.
	LAWFUL NEUTRAL: Acts as law, tradition, or some personal code directs.	**TRUE NEUTRAL:** Doesn't have strong overriding beliefs; morality is real but situational.	**CHAOTIC NEUTRAL:** Avoids authority, resents restrictions, and challenges traditions. Personal freedom comes first; the good of others is secondary.
	LAWFUL EVIL: Plays by the rules but without mercy or compassion.	**NEUTRAL EVIL:** Does whatever they can get away with. No law or morality, but will not go out of their way to hurt others unless there's something in it for them.	**CHAOTIC EVIL:** Arbitrary and unpredictable. Sees no reason to consider law or others. What they want is all that matters, and they don't care how they get it.

LAWFUL TO CHAOTIC →

Scene 6

The NYU Tour

Sebastian led Liv, Cam, and me out into the early-morning autumn air for our personal tour of NYU. Our plan was to get the tour done before hitting the con with Meldel and Todd later.

"Coffee," said Liv, staggering toward a Starbucks.

I got an orange juice. Sebastian got hot chocolate. Liv and Cam got coffee. Cam was wearing shorts that flirted with being a skirt, and a T-shirt with a dinosaur and the words ALL MY FRIENDS ARE DEAD. It was the first time, I realized, that I had seen him wearing anything but Tennah/Bellah cosplay. And it occurred to me to wonder...

"Hey, Cam and Liv," I said. "When I think about it, I'm surprised that Liv is Torrance and Cam is Tennah/Bellah. Why not the other way around?"

"Uh," said Liv. "You think it's more natural that the person assigned male at birth ought to play the male role and vice versa?"

"Oh," I said. "Yeah. Sorry."

"Also." Cam pointed to Liv. "It needs to be said that we picked the cosplays we picked because someone is lazy."

"I just wanted a simpler costume. I'm busy."

"While I lead a life of pure indolence and pleasure," said Cam.

"No, but some of us play a varsity sport."

"Some of us have no time for team sports because we pursue a full interior life."

"Too interior, some think."

"What sport, Liv?" Sebastian interrupted.

"Basketball," said Liv.

"Cool," I said, impressed. "That'll help with college, right?"

"Maybe. We'll see. I'm good but not, you know, Division One recruiting material." Liv paused and added, "I've decided that I'm looking for a Division Three school with a decent basketball program where I can major in gender studies and hopefully get some scholarship money if I play. As part of that, I'm also considering a couple of women's colleges with good teams. Which I admit feels somewhat weird." Liv shot a glance at Cam.

"No kidding weird," Cam muttered. "Since you don't identify as female."

"So how can you apply there?" asked Sebastian.

Liv said, "Well, there's stuff on the Smith College website—that's one place I'm looking at—about their support for gender diversity." They rolled their eyes. "Their language is a tiny bit contradictory. They say they're open to nonbinary and trans and nonconforming students, but at the same time, they want you to self-identify as a woman."

"Which, hello, you don't," said Cam to the air.

"But I don't identify as male, either, and I never will," Liv countered. "And when I search my soul, I feel female loyalty. Esprit de corps or whatever."

"Wouldn't an all-female atmosphere be worse for you than a college that admits all genders, though?" I asked.

"I'm not sure that's true. I like being around women — like, I'm totally comfortable with my team. My summer basketball camps were all-women, and those have been some of the friendliest experiences I've ever had. It was actually the first place I ever met another enby person." Liv shrugged. "In the end, the atmosphere probably depends on the specific school, right? Anyway, this is just one idea I'm exploring, and I'm going to be careful, so stop looking at me disapprovingly, all of you. Okay? I know what I'm doing."

"Sorry," said Sebastian.

I nodded, a little disappointed. If Liv chose a women's college, there was no possibility we'd end up at the same place. But their situation was obviously just as complex as figuring out the right college was for Simon and me.

Liv added, "Basketball is one reason why I also use she/her. It's just made things easier when I'm on a girls' team."

"You think they'd throw you out over your pronouns?" asked Sebastian incredulously.

Liv shrugged. "I don't know and I haven't wanted to find out."

"That's why the scarves?" I asked. "Camouflage?"

"No! My scarves are not femme window dressing. I love them! This one is so warm, I don't even need a coat. Thirteenth Doctor." Liv fingered a fringed end lovingly. "My mom made it. Scarves forever! But the thing is, beginning with college, I want to just be me, without having to worry about what other people think about how I dress or how I act and how it fits their ideas."

"Good luck with that," said Sebastian gloomily. "My experience? The worry never ends completely. But at least I'm myself around Bloodygits."

"Me too," I said. Impulsively, I flung one arm around Sebastian as we walked and the other around Liv, and Cam reached out on Sebastian's other side, so the four of us were walking together, arms around one another, smiling.

We had walked a few blocks south during this conversation. Sebastian stopped, disentangled, and waved a hand. "Here! These buildings all belong to NYU."

NYU didn't have a dedicated campus; it was merged with the city in lower Manhattan. I wondered if Simon would like that, before remembering that now Simon hoped to stay in Boston, supposing Alisha Johnson Pratt was elected and gave him a job.

"It must feel like being really grown up, going to school here," Cam said. "You're living in the city. You're surrounded by real people all the time, not just students."

I nodded, thinking of the apartment Sebastian shared with his roommate in the residence hall. I wondered whether Simon and I could be in an apartment-dorm together. Would that be allowed? Would I want that? It would be sort of like being married already. Probably my parents wouldn't like this idea. Especially given what my mom had said yesterday.

"There are flags and signs to identify the NYU buildings," said Sebastian, and we looked at the purple flag and the lettering on the building before us: the Andre & Bella Meyer Hall of Physics. I took a picture for evidence I'd been there.

I said, "I don't think I'd ever take a college-level physics class."

"They have psychology in this building, too," Sebastian said. "And I had Nat Sci here last year. You want to see inside?"

"Definitely," said Cam.

Sebastian opened the door using his badge. We looked at an empty lecture hall, which had concrete walls and seats cascading down theater-style to a stage with a speaker's podium, electronic monitors, and sliding blackboards. Sebastian demonstrated how you could sit in a chair and set up the folding desk that came out of the chair's arm. I took a picture of him, a close-up shot that wouldn't show all the empty seats around him, and that might imply I had attended a weekend lecture. Then I had Liv and Cam sit down so that I could take a picture of all of them and claim that they were part of my tour group.

Which they *were.*

Neutral Evil: Does whatever they can get away with.

I winced.

Liv was examining the writing on the blackboards. Cam stood with his hands in his pockets. Suddenly he spun in a circle and burst into a song about New York being a wonderful town. When he stopped, he was grinning. "I'm so sold on NYU."

Sebastian beamed. Liv, who had wandered back up the stairs to us, snorted. "You said the same thing about Sarah Lawrence a few days ago."

"I hadn't seen NYU yet."

I asked, "What about money? Do you have to think about that? You mentioned a basketball scholarship for Liv."

Cam said, "Yes, it's definitely a factor. We're both hoping for aid. What about you, Zoe?"

I nodded. "Money's an issue, for sure. That said, there's only me, and my parents started saving when I was born. But Simon needs as close to a full scholarship as possible, and that affects my situation. He can't be a burden on his mother."

Cam asked, "So what happens if Simon doesn't get enough scholarship money? Or any? What will you do if his needs are different from yours?"

"We'll cross that bridge when we come to it," I said primly.

"I didn't mean to make you uncomfortable."

"I'm not."

"My plan is community college for a couple of years, if I don't get enough scholarship money," Cam said. "I can live at home, then transfer later."

"No!" Sebastian exclaimed. "You can't do that. I mean, I couldn't have stood it, to stay at home. I had to get out of there!"

"You could have done it if you had to," said Cam. "And community college is a great option. I like having a plan B."

Sebastian shook his head. "If I'd stayed home, it would have been bad. I'm afraid that I'd have flunked out and stayed in my room and played video games."

"And, like, never showered?" Liv asked. "And eaten Fritos?"

"Cheez-Its. But yes."

Cam said, "No. Give yourself some credit. You'd have made it work if you had to be at home for a few years. Because you'd have known it's a slippery slope. If you're living at home, you can't just hang around and pretend to be fourteen, pretend your life isn't happening already. That way lies, you know, total self-destruction. So, you put limits on yourself. Or else." Cam made a motion with his hands like he was setting off an explosive. "Not that I've thought about it for myself at all," he added. "Not that I'm preparing myself just in case. I don't want that to happen; I want to be in New York!" He rotated again, flinging out his arms. "But I'm not going to think my life is over, either. No matter what. You have to be flexible."

"Have alternate plans," I said.

"Exactly."

We all smiled, but a serious feeling remained, hovering like a rain cloud.

I said compulsively, "Simon will get a lot of aid. He's really, really smart. He has all As and good SATs, and he's taking two AP classes this year. And he might be able to get a recommendation from—well, someone impressive." I was taking four AP classes myself, but that wasn't what we were talking about, and Mrs. Albee was certainly not going to write the kind of impressive recommendation that a maybe-state-senator would. In fact—now that I thought about it—Mrs. Albee was capable of writing me a recommendation in the persona of Wentworth. *Meow, Zoe is a very smart human person, meow!*

I winced and pulled out my bullet journal.

☐ Do not ask Mrs. Albee for college
recommendation. Unless I can draft it for
her? Or at least see it before she sends
it? (But you're not supposed to do that.)

I like Mrs. Albee. I really, truly do.

It's Wentworth I can't stand.

I was tucking my bullet journal away when Cam asked me, "If it doesn't work out, would Simon do community college to start? Hello? Zoe? Hello?"

"Sorry," I said. "I was thinking about a cat." After a moment, I said slowly, "Simon is very practical. So yes, he'd make the best of it. I'm sure he would." It would hurt his pride, though. Especially if I got in somewhere he wanted to go. Only I couldn't, wouldn't. I would certainly *never* go somewhere that he had to turn down because of money, or that he didn't get into. I wouldn't even *tell* him if I got in somewhere he didn't.

We were going to be together. There would be at least one school in the middle of the Venn diagram, overlapping with the circles of where he got in, where I got in, and what was financially feasible.

"Would you stay home with him?" asked Cam. "Go to community college also? In that case?"

I exhaled. "Yes." And then: "I don't know! All right? I don't know! I'll think about it if the situation comes up. Which it probably won't! Is that all right with you?"

"Of course it's all right," said Liv, with a reproving glance at Cam. "Sorry. It's just that Cam and I have talked about what happens if one of us leaves home for some fabulous college and the other one doesn't. Our parents said we needed to think about it in advance."

Cam said, "I didn't mean to make you feel bad."

I took a deep breath. "I know. I'm sorry. I didn't . . . it's just that I'd never really thought about that possibility before." I wondered if maybe Simon was thinking about it, silently, and hadn't wanted to bring it up. I would have to talk to him.

"Really and truly?" said Cam curiously. "There's no page in your bullet journal about it?"

Liv elbowed him. "It probably won't happen," Liv said.

I looked at them. My new friends. My friends.

I said, "Bloodygits, you would really like Simon."

"I know I would," said Cam, instantly and sincerely.

"Since you like him," said Liv, more temperately, "and we like you, I know we would like him."

Cam said, "He really is awfully cute. I completely get what you see in him."

"He's more than just a pretty face!" I forced a smile. "Sebastian? Onward?"

"Sure. Follow me."

Scene 7

Love and Robots

The rest of the weekend flew by. We roamed the convention center in our cosplay. We ate bad food. We posed for pictures whenever asked, which—surprise!—was often.

Maybe it wasn't so surprising. We looked good as a group, and we now had an awesome *Bleeders* sign. Meldel and Todd had made it while the rest of us were touring NYU. Using Sebastian's white bedsheet, they'd written BLEEDERS in ketchup, with artistic splashes of red dripping below the title, no misspellings, and spot-art accents like hypodermics and knives and a spaceship, added with my Sharpie.

Sebastian explained to photographers: "I'm supposed to be bleeding slowly from every pore, but I haven't figured out how to make that work." This turned out to be an effective conversation starter. Some people hung out for quite a while to discuss potential solutions. They usually also said they were going to check out the show, and wanted Sebastian to let them know what he decided to do about bleeding. He collected a lot of contact information.

We attended sessions for *Firefly* and Stargate and Star Wars and Star Trek—any show that had something in common with *Bleeders* and that had a session that wasn't impossible to get into.

And of course we handed out flyers. Meldel said it didn't matter if they got tossed, so long as people saw the *Bleeders* name. We did pick them up off the floor and reused and recycled whenever possible.

The whole time, we talked and talked and talked about our show.

"So there's been *nothing* so far this season about how Lorelei killed the five Sanitation Soldiers in the Season 1 finale." This was me.

"Well, Lorelei does practice that tai chi–looking thing," said Meldel.

"But then why wouldn't they show her using it to kill them?" asked Liv. "It's got to be that the crystals make her deadly."

Sebastian said, "I think she's turning into a robot. I think she grabbed them by the neck maybe with her mind somehow and . . ." He made a twisting motion with both hands.

Cam nodded thoughtfully. "More and more, it looks like she's AI."

I said, "Is she on the way to becoming one of the Sanitation Force robots?"

"We can't rule that out," said Meldel. "We have no idea how the robots are made, but we know they're part-humanoid."

"That's what Josie thinks," I said. I don't talk to Josie about *Bleeders*—obviously I can't do that—but I interact with her online using my Bloodygit alias, LoreleiWillBiteYou.

"TBD," said Todd. "We'll see what happens."

"But don't you want to figure it out now?"

"They'll let us know in good time."

When we weren't talking about *Bleeders*, we talked about whatever came up, from Todd arguing that music sampling should always be considered artistic freedom and not theft to my explaining Simon's passionate political convictions to Cam's love life—or rather, lack thereof.

"I'm like Saint Augustine," said Cam as he eyed a muscled Spiderman walking ahead of us. "I want to fall in love, but not yet."

"He said that about chastity, not love," I said. "'Grant me chastity and continence, but not yet.'"

"How do you know that?" Cam asked.

"I'm the daughter of history teachers. My mom does history of religion. Also, that's a pretty famous quote. Everybody just loves it because, you know, it's so relatable."

"I knew it was about chastity," said Cam. "I was just being delicate when I said 'love.' But what's that about continence?"

"Did Augustine have trouble toileting?" asked Todd. He snickered. "Of course he did! Because there were no toilets!"

"There were too," I said indignantly. "Ancient Rome

had excellent plumbing. Running water and covered sewers and everything. But continence actually meant mostly the same thing as chastity or abstinence then. Nothing to do with, you know, control over peeing."

Meldel said, "I wonder when it started meaning pee. It might be a translation thing."

"Google knows," said Todd.

Liv looked on their phone. "No, actually, Google doesn't."

"You're probably just not using a good search term," I said pompously—even I knew it was pompous as it came out of my mouth—but then I couldn't find the information, either.

Sebastian offered, "I'm ready to fall in love anytime. But I don't expect it to happen very easily for me, because even if girls like me sometimes, it's only ever as a friend." He sounded both pragmatic and sad. It made me wonder if I could maybe fix him up with Maggie. Maggie claims she's looking. But then of course I reminded myself that I had to keep my worlds separate. Even though Maggie knew everything.

"You just need someone to stick around for long enough to get to know you," said Meldel to Sebastian. "It'll happen."

"It really *can* just happen," I added earnestly. "The right person simply comes along, and that's when you get it that the person from before who you thought was right really wasn't, after all. You made yourself miserable for nothing when instead, you should have been patient and trusted and been happy."

Sebastian said, "What?"

I reviewed what I had said. "Oh, sorry. I mean that if you had, you know, like, a near miss? Somebody you thought you wanted to be with? Who you obsessed about afterward because you weren't with them?" I paused. "Do you do that ever? Obsess over somebody you liked, but it didn't work out for whatever reason, but still you can't forget it?"

"Oh yeah," said Sebastian gloomily.

"All the time," said Cam.

"I once lost a really good friend and did a lot of obsessing over what went wrong between us," said Liv.

"Sure," said Todd, although Meldel said nothing.

I explained, "Well, there's no need to obsess. Because when the right one comes along, then you let the old dream go. And it follows logically: if you knew in the past about your happier future, then you wouldn't be sad in the past."

"What?" said Todd.

"But you can't know in the past what's going to happen in the future," Sebastian pointed out.

"Yes, but you'll find out in the future. When you fall in love for real, you'll realize you didn't need to be miserable before, so you shouldn't be miserable now, in anticipation of how much better you'll feel later. Does that make sense?"

"I lost you long ago," said Sebastian.

"It makes sense, but it's wrong," said Cam.

"Interestingly wrong, though," said Meldel.

"Yes. Love you anyway, Zoe," said Cam, and blew me a kiss.

"Being single is a great, rich choice, too," Liv said. "And that's another good reason not to obsess, if I may take

Zoe's side in the true love argument for a different reason. You don't need that wrong person in your life. Being unpartnered doesn't mean being alone and sad! Freedom! Lots of friends!"

"But that's a totally different conversation, Liv," said Todd.

"No, it's an *expansion* of the conversation. There's all kinds of love in life. Many kinds of important relationships. Not just romantic partnerships. You have to look at the full picture of life. Life and love."

"That's not being *in love*. I'm *in* love with Meldel," Todd said. "Even though she's not in love with me. But my eyes are open. And I think she loves me."

A rare moment of vulnerability from Todd. Meldel elbowed him and smiled but didn't dispute this.

We were quiet for a while.

"I know she's out there," said Sebastian finally. "My true love. Somewhere. I'll wait, like Zoe said. I will be patient. And I love having friends, like Liv said."

I couldn't help feeling a little smug about me and Simon. It was very good to have my love life resolved, checked off on my list, done, while so many of my friends were still searching and wondering.

Scene 8

The Princesses

On Sunday, we went to a panel on women in the Star Wars universe. It was held in an enormous room that fit a thousand people at least. We stood in line and the Force was with us and we got in—probably because con attendance had dwindled as the weekend came to a close.

The session closed with a ten-minute tribute slideshow of Carrie Fisher as Princess Leia. It had images from when she was a teenager in the original Star Wars, in her white robes with her hair twisted in the double side-buns, all the way to her appearance in *The Last Jedi* in her high-collared jacket, with her graying hair and her lined face and her level, mature gaze. In some of the photos, she was with other characters, talking or in action. But in most of the pictures they selected, she was simply shown alone.

In the background, they played "Princess Leia's Theme" by John Williams.

It was like nobody in that whole entire huge room spoke or coughed or even—it seemed—breathed.

And as one photo after another came and lingered and dissolved to be replaced by another, I realized that something the panelists had been saying was correct. Even as a teenager, there was *opinion* in Carrie Fisher's face. She never fit the old-fashioned storybook idea—sweet, lovely, passive—of what a princess should be like. The panel had discussed whether the director understood this when he cast her—some thought yes, others no—or if instead Carrie Fisher had so imprinted herself on Leia that the princess and the whole Star Wars universe actually developed differently than they would have if another actress had gotten the role.

When the slideshow ended, no one moved, because we'd all been told to stay in our seats. The lights were dim, and got even dimmer.

The actor who plays R2-D2, who had been on the panel, now stood up. He said, "Everyone who is not cosplaying Leia, please turn on your phone flashlight. Hold it ready on your lap, pointing your light downward."

We did this.

"Now, everyone cosplaying Leia, stand up."

There was rustling around the room.

"Flashlight bearers, now hold your light aloft, as high as you can."

We did.

The Leias stood in the light, all genders, all ages, all

races, all shapes, and all sizes. There were hundreds of them. Their faces were full of opinion—and dignity and pride and love.

"Light bearers, continue to hold your light aloft, but also make room for the princesses to file out of your row and into the aisle. Princesses, when you reach the aisle, join hands with the other princesses."

Very low, then, the Princess Leia theme music came back on, and all over the room, the Leias came together. They raised their joined arms.

The rest of us held up the light for them.

The music swelled.

On one side of me, I felt Liv grab my empty hand and squeeze it tight. I squeezed back just as tightly, and I stretched my other arm upward, holding my light as high as I could for the Leias and for us.

The Leias stood there for a full minute.

This feeling rose up in me and stopped up my throat with a weird kind of . . . conviction. I felt the reality of how one particular person can make a difference to the world. This is what Simon believes: that we must all do our small part and that it's our responsibility to do it. I agree.

But I realized that Carrie Fisher's impact on the world was another way, a different way, a more random and weird and inadvertent and mysterious way, a way that was about being genuinely and fully *yourself* and following your own odd particular star, however haphazardly, wherever it might lead you, not even knowing where it might lead you. Just trusting.

But maybe that only worked for a really extraordinary

person, a Carrie Fisher. What did it matter if someone like me was fully herself? What did that even mean, anyway?

"Wave your lights as the princesses depart."

The room turned into a sea of moving light.

The Leias marched quietly and ceremoniously from the room.

Scene 9

Ugly Beautiful

Outside the auditorium where the princesses—where all of us—had been held in the light, we handed out flyers and said, "If you like women in science fiction, please watch *Bleeders*," and "New SlamDunk SF show, why not try it?" and "Woman showrunner, mostly female mixed-race cast," and "This show isn't getting much marketing or publicity, but it deserves love."

One of the Leias paused and held out her hand for a flyer. She was smiling, radiant, still floating on the atmosphere we had all created together. I'd noticed her earlier; she was an older fat woman cosplaying as Slave Leia in a gold two-piece outfit with a mesh skirt, but she was also distinctive because she carried herself with obvious assurance.

"Interesting," she said as she looked at the flyer. "It

seems like a cross between *M*A*S*H* and *Firefly* and maybe a little Star Trek, is that right?"

"I don't know *M*A*S*H*," I said. "But definitely *Firefly* and Star Trek."

"You'd be too young for *M*A*S*H*. It was set in a mobile triage hospital during—"

A guy in a rubber Joker mask leaned in behind her, his mouth an inch from her ear: "Ugly fat freak. You're disgusting."

The bottom dropped out of my stomach. Leia's shoulders hunched and her eyes flew wide. The Joker strode away like he owned the earth.

Slowly, Leia straightened her shoulders, her eyes narrowing, on fire.

"Oh my God!" I said. "Bloodies! Did you hear that asshole?" I pointed down the corridor, but I couldn't pick him out in the crowd anymore.

"I heard every single word," said Meldel.

"I did too," said Cam. "That was totally against the code of conduct."

"We'll report him," Meldel said. "White man in a Joker mask, about five foot eight, one hundred sixty-five pounds, brown hair."

I stared at her.

"What?" she said. "I'm observant. Leia, did he touch you?"

The Leia shook her head. "No. I didn't actually see him, either. And yes, we should report him, for all the good that'll do now. But it's good to have backup. Thanks." Her lips compressed. "Of course he was here to see skinny, sexy, young Leias. Well, I'm happy to have disappointed."

"White Leias, too," another voice said dryly. "With big breasts." This was a different Leia, brown-skinned and middle-aged and small, wearing the military jacket and pants of the older Carrie Fisher from *The Force Awakens.* "He said something to me, too."

Our original Leia's expression softened. "I'm so sorry. Well, to hell with him and whatever he thought he was going to get here. I cosplay for *me.* Not to please anybody else."

"Exactly," said military Leia.

The two Leias and Meldel went off together to report what had happened. Numb, I kept handing out *Bleeders* flyers, mechanically hawking the show.

The crowd thinned around us. Without speaking, the remaining five of us slipped back into the abandoned ballroom, collapsing on some chairs. Todd looked up from his phone. "Meldel will meet us back here in a few."

The Leia incident had not taken long. A very small amount of time compared with the whole con. One rude asshole was involved. One.

It shouldn't overshadow everything.

We were silent.

Finally, Sebastian said conversationally, "In high school, Meldel and her friends used to say stuff to me, stuff that let me know they didn't think I was worth anything. Wasn't even human to them."

"People say shit to me, too," said Cam. "And to Liv."

Liv nodded. "Or they say stuff about other people in front of me. Sometimes that feels worse. Do you respond?

Do you keep silent? What happens if you do say something? What do you say? What will be the consequences? It's exhausting."

I nodded silently, remembering freshman year, when I'd stumbled on three boys covertly examining a manufactured (manufactured!) armband with a swastika on it. One of them had noticed me. Cold eyes fixed on mine, he'd drawn a finger across his throat and mouthed *Jew*. It had changed something in me. Oh, I'd told my parents, who talked to the principal, and there'd been a big deal including an apology—and I even believed one of those boys was sincere in his apology. But the damage inside me stayed. And that was only one incident, to one person . . . only kids . . . nobody died. "It seems like hate pops up everywhere," I said. "Like whack-a-mole. So what do we do?"

"Okay, question," Sebastian said, raising his hand like he was in a classroom. "I started talking about me and Meldel and high school and I really thought I had the floor. Did I give some social signal to start a group discussion of how everybody has experiences like that? Because I'd like to know what the signal is."

There was a beat of time.

I said, "As far as I know, there is no such signal, Sebastian. You didn't do anything wrong."

"I fucked up," Cam said promptly. "Me. Sorry. I missed your totally appropriate social signal that you wanted to talk, and I barged in."

"And me," said Liv.

"And me," I said.

"Not me. I didn't interrupt Sebastian," Todd remarked.

I narrowed my eyes at Todd. "The floor is now yours, Sebastian," I said.

There was another beat.

"Joke," said Sebastian.

We all stared at him.

"I was making a joke," he explained. "About a social signal to start a group confessional. I know there's no such thing."

"But you do want the floor," said Liv. "You have more to say, right?"

"No," said Sebastian. "I already said what I wanted to say. So it wasn't funny? My joke? I was just … hoping to get back to all of us having fun. I didn't want to veer off forever into talking about hate. We don't have much time left this weekend."

Cam snorted. "I wish there was a signal for going back to fun. Can you imagine?"

We all began to laugh then. It was slow, rueful laughter at first, maybe even forced to please Sebastian. But wherever it came from, and whatever it meant, somehow the laughter grew until we were all bent over, roaring, moaning, practically convulsing, eventually even pounding the floor with fists. There was even sort of a laughing group hug toward the end that involved jumping up and down.

Mine was the kind of laughter that gets all mixed up with tears.

When Meldel came back, we had calmed down. There was the sad feeling of things ending. I wiped my eyes and knelt to pick up the flyers that had dropped to the floor during the laughter-tears group hug. I gathered them in my hands, tapping their edges straight.

"Time to go," Liv said.

"Just a minute," said Meldel. "I was hoping . . . well, there's a con next month in Austin, called Weird World. If you can all get there, Todd and I can put you up. So there'd be like no other expenses. Except food, I guess. And memberships to the con." She paused. "I don't want to lose our group. And we still have so much work to do to save *Bleeders*. We can do better than we did this time. I can do better."

I looked up from where I was kneeling on the carpet. I didn't want to lose the group, either.

Or *Bleeders*.

"I hate Texas," Sebastian remarked.

"Give it another chance," said Todd.

After a moment, Liv turned on the flashlight on their phone. Silently, they held it up.

Cam turned on his. He held it up.

The rest of us scrambled to do the same.

"To Bloodygits," Liv said. "To us."

"To Bloodygits," the rest of us chorused. "To us."

"Next month at Weird World?" asked Meldel.

"Weird World!"

EPISODE 3

November 2018 @Weird World

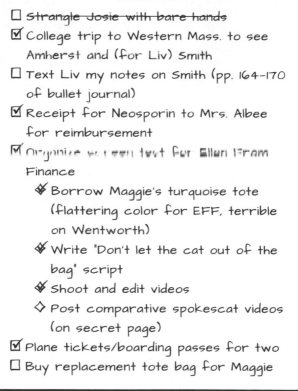

From Zoe's Bullet Journal

TO DO:

- ☐ ~~Strangle Josie with bare hands~~
- ☑ College trip to Western Mass. to see Amherst and (for Liv) Smith
- ☐ Text Liv my notes on Smith (pp. 164-170 of bullet journal)
- ☑ Receipt for Neosporin to Mrs. Albee for reimbursement
- ☑ ~~Organize screen test for Ellen From~~ Finance
    - ☑ Borrow Maggie's turquoise tote (flattering color for EFF, terrible on Wentworth)
    - ☑ Write "Don't let the cat out of the bag" script
    - ☑ Shoot and edit videos
    - ◇ Post comparative spokescat videos (on secret page)
- ☑ Plane tickets/boarding passes for two
- ☐ Buy replacement tote bag for Maggie

Scene 1

Enter Josie

Why me? I thought as Josie settled herself into our row's window seat, breezily assuming I would take care of stowing her carry-on in the airplane's overhead compartment. Which I did.

I needed this complication like a hole in my head. Just when I had effectively minimized my own risk, too! My parents knew about my new fannish friends now. My mom had actually even "met" Liv one day while we were FaceTiming, and—since my mom was active in her alumnae association at Bryn Mawr—they'd ended up having a long talk about how women's colleges were and weren't changing because of admitting nonbinary and trans and gender-nonconforming students, and what the issues, if any, might be for Liv. Liv thought my mom had made some helpful points. My mom thought Liv was super-nice and smart. And I'd felt smug about the introduction until my mom said afterward (with a nonchalance that did not fool me for a microsecond), "I love how your enby friend Liv is open to considering the educational benefits of a nonmale atmosphere."

Gritting my teeth at the memory, I settled into my cramped plane seat. Josie promptly elbowed me, which did not improve my mood.

"I'm so excited! A real con! And I'm actually going to meet Melisande Du Lac!"

I withdrew my arm from our shared armrest and silently fastened my seatbelt.

"Don't be like that, Zoe."

"I'll be however I want." I fished out my phone. "Leave me alone. I have things to do to cover our asses. Such as lie to your mother and brother."

She smirked. "I'm just doing what you did."

"I'm a bad influence!" I snapped. "You should know better!"

Infuriatingly, she giggled. "Simon doesn't even really know you, does he?"

"Simon knows the *best* me!" I hunched my back to her.

My entire future happy life hung in the balance, so I had to bring the little blackmailer along for one glorious, secret con weekend. It had been a tremendous shock. But once I'd put my mind to the logistics, I'd had to admit it wasn't impossible. It had just required—to use Todd's term—some balls. But there was no question that the risk was nonzero.

I sent a carefully worded text to Simon, a breezier, easier one to my parents, and a final note to Maggie.

ME: I owe you my firstborn child.

MAGGIE: What if I don't want your firstborn child?

ME: Of course you do. My child will be delightful.

MAGGIE: I like the name Ravioli. Ravioli Kwan.

ME: No!

MAGGIE: Yes. You gave me your child and I get to use whatever name I please.

Simon probably wouldn't respond to my text for hours, if at all. That was actually part of my plan. Simon was likely too busy to notice much of anything. The election was Tuesday—four days away! He was flat-out frantic at Alisha Johnson Pratt's campaign headquarters and ecstatic to be that way, too.

My parents knew I was in Austin for the con, and to check out UT Austin. So far, so aboveboard. But they certainly didn't know Josie was with me. As for Simon, UT Austin wasn't on our college list, and besides, with the election so close, he could not conceive of my being concerned with anything else. So he thought I was with Maggie, going door-to-door on behalf of a national congressional campaign up in New Hampshire. My parents liked that I was looking at a college that Simon *wasn't* applying to. Deep breath over that, but they had agreed to secrecy. As for Josie's mother, well, there was a whole different plan for her.

It was complicated enough that I'd put together a spreadsheet (which you'd better believe was password protected) specifying exactly who knew what. I was also getting into the benefits of yogic breathing.

I sent Maggie another text.

ME: I use my superpower for good, right?

MAGGIE: Feeling guilty?

ME: A little sick to my stomach.

ME: Josie is sitting here like the cat who got the cream.

ME: But I really had no choice.

ME: And it's not like anybody gets hurt here.

MAGGIE: Agreed, but when you become an Evil Overlord, be warned, I won't be your minion.

ME: I'd have stayed home and canvassed if Josie hadn't blackmailed me!

MAGGIE: Yes dear. I know. Have a good time.

ME: You'd never be anybody's minion.

MAGGIE: Why do I suspect that's what you'd say if I were yours?

Our plane lifted into the air. Josie watched out her window. Exhibiting calm maturity, I took out my bullet journal. With a purple Sharpie, I drew a dotted line down the exact center of a fresh page.

"What are you doing, Zoe?"

"Planning."

In thin orange, I wrote down all the stuff I was going to accomplish next week, including working after school on Monday and Tuesday—election day!—for Alisha Johnson Pratt. Then, in purple again, I drew a small square checkbox next to each task. Then I began a sublist about schoolwork, with *Catch up in calculus* at the top. I reviewed the cost of paying for Josie's trip: basically her plane tickets plus her food, so approximately five hundred dollars deducted from my kitty, ouch. And also the cost of Maggie's replacement tote would have to come from the kitty—and it would have to be quality. (Pause to silently direct a few choice words at Wentworth.) As God is my witness, I am going to find a way to nail Wentworth's furry butt to his YOU'RE FIRED pink slip.

Josie stuck her face in mine. "Zoe, what's Melisande Du Lac really like?"

"You'll see for yourself soon enough."

"I know why you're really mad. You thought you were going to slip off without me."

"No," I said repressively. "I wasn't going to go at all."

"Yes, you were. You wrote down all the possible flights." Josie pointed her chin at my bullet journal.

"That was just informational. I hadn't bought a ticket."

"Only because you were still talking yourself into it. Melisande Du Lac says you did that last month too. *No no no, I can't possibly go!* But then you went. Pattern?"

"Twice is not a pattern, Josie."

"Is so."

"Is not."

"Is so. Anyway, you needed someone to cosplay Monica."

"We were doing just fine without a Monica."

"No, it wasn't right," Josie said judiciously. "The *Mae Jemison* has to have the full crew." She giggled. "You look so good as Lorelei. But you have to admit that you were dumb not to realize you could be recognized."

I gritted my teeth. It had never even occurred to me

that anyone I knew would look at New York Comic Con photos. But Josie had caught me. Fair and square, as my dad would say.

"But you forgive me," Josie said. Her voice got very small. "Right, Zoe? Bloodygits together?"

I didn't answer.

"And now that you've done this for me, which I truly, truly appreciate, I will never tell and I'll love you forever. Even if you hate me."

I relented. "I don't hate you."

"Really? Promise?"

"Yeah. I get why you wanted to come."

She beamed at me. Reluctantly, I smiled back.

I remembered being fourteen like Josie. I'd had one special, secret weekend then, too.

Scene 2

What If

It was the green sign featuring the wide-open mouth of Janice the Muppet that drew me in. It was the second day of my freshman year of high school and dozens of the signs were taped up in the halls. There was even one on my locker:

CAN YOU SING? DO YOU HAVE A WORKING RIGHT OR LEFT HAND? LEAD FEMALE VOCALIST WANTED FOR OUR PUPPET ROCK BAND. WHY NOT TRY OUT? WE'RE DESPERATE!!!

In smaller letters at the bottom, it said COME TO BAND ROOM ON FRIDAY BETWEEN 3 AND 4.

I had not darkened the door of a school music department since I quit orchestra in middle school. Violin had been something my parents wanted me to do and I didn't love it, and once I realized my parents would accept it—I explained that I needed more study time—I quit. Huge relief.

But approaching the band room still felt familiar, even navigating with my school map while half wanting to turn back (but it was just an audition, ten minutes of my time, I had all weekend to do homework, I could have a little fun, it didn't mean I wasn't smart). You could always hear music as you got close to a band room, even if it was just kids blowing softly into clarinets or tapping drumsticks. At three forty-five in the afternoon on that particular Friday at my new school, what I heard was an electronic keyboard, accompanied by a high warbling soprano.

Ever since seventh grade, I've hated you—ooo—ooo—

The voice jumped off-key and stopped. My stomach twisted on behalf of the soprano. As I looked in from the doorway, the singer said to the keyboardist, "Sorry. Can I try again? I don't know this song. It's not really fair. Can't I try, like, something by Adele?" The singer's hands—one of them encased in a brown paper bag—went out in a half-pleading gesture.

The keyboardist's back was to me. He tilted his head questioningly at an Asian girl with a guitar and at a white guy holding a Barbie doll. They looked back with impassive faces. The Barbie shook her head slightly.

"We're looking for a grittier sound," said the keyboard guy to the soprano.

"Oh. Okay, yeah." The soprano pulled the paper bag off

her hand. It fell to the floor. Just after she brushed past me in the doorway, she whirled back. "It's a really stupid song!"

"Shoot me now," said the keyboardist to the other two when she was gone. He banged his head softly on the keys, a smash of discordant notes. "I hate this. Do we really need anybody else? Jordan, tell me again why you can't do lead vocals?"

"Because I don't want to," said the Barbie-wielding guy in a patient bass voice. "I want to bang on the drums with my Barbies."

"But—"

The girl with the guitar nodded her chin to me. "How about we hear her?" She met my gaze directly. "You came to audition?"

"Yes," I said. I was feeling more confident simply because, and I hoped this wasn't mean, the soprano had been *just that bad*.

The keyboardist swiveled on his piano stool. We looked at each other.

So.

So there I was in my black leggings and gleaming white New Balance sneakers and pink tank top from Lands' End, with my hair in a smooth ponytail and zero makeup, with my backpack, everything about me screaming SERIOUS and STUDIOUS and also FRESHMAN. And there he was, keyboard guy, with his ragged gray hoodie with the sleeves pushed up to reveal a tattoo on the inside of one tanned forearm, and eyeliner, and everything about him screaming ARTSY and WEIRD and SENIOR.

He smiled at me. "I'm Henry Ferlinghetti. That's

Marina Liu on lead guitar, and Jordan O'Halloran on the Barbie."

"By the way, I identify as nonbinary and my pronouns are they/them," said Jordan.

This was the first time I'd ever experienced someone saying something like that, directly, to me. I froze for a second, unsure what to say that wouldn't be wrong. Luckily Henry gave me time to recover.

"Right, sorry," he said. "I guess I should have said everybody's pronouns. I'm he/him."

"Apologies kind of make things worse," Jordan observed.

"I don't get that and also—"

Marina held up a hand. "Stop! Now isn't the time." She looked at me. "Don't pay any attention to them. Henry and Jordan bicker about everything. Oh, and my pronouns are she/her."

I nodded. By now, I'd had time to adjust. "I'm Zoe Rosenthal," I said. "She/her. Hi."

"Hi."

"Hi."

Marina said, "So, back to business. The idea is that you'd share front-woman lead vocals with a puppet. Just pretend with a paper bag for now. I'll sing for the puppet, you sing as you, and also you operate the puppet. Make sense?"

"Sure." I stooped for the abandoned paper bag. It was a little torn but workable. I smoothed it out.

"Also, we have original music. Can you read music?"

"Yes," I said.

As I looked at the music, I felt something strange take over inside me. A sureness. They wanted a lead vocalist. They wanted a gritty voice. They wanted someone who could sing with a puppet. I'd never even dreamed of being those things. But my singing is okay even when I'm not by myself in the shower, and also, well, in that moment, I absolutely believed—and this is embarrassing to admit— that I could *become* what they were looking for. That my right place was in their puppet band ... making goo-goo eyes at my puppet ... tossing my hair in a dance frenzy ...

It's like I totally forgot that I am a serious person.

I pulled a Sharpie out of my bag and drew lips and long-lashed eyes on the brown paper bag. I slipped my hand inside and moved the bag's mouth experimentally.

"Janice and I are ready," I said recklessly. "Let's go!"

And then.

It was like we were all in the same movie, where the absolutely right one arrives at the audition, just when the band has given up hope, and everybody knows it's going to work.

Keyboard guy Henry swiveled back to his instrument. He flexed his fingers, played some opening chords. Marina sang. I moved the brown paper bag as if it were singing too:

Ever since seventh grade, I've hated you
But I saw you crying in the bathroom
And I only have one thing to say:
Girl, they're not worth it! They're not worth it! They're
*   not worth it!*
Girlfriend turn your back! Girlfriend walk away!

Second time through, I sang along too, into my fist as if it were a microphone. I waggled Janice the Paper Bag and we swayed together in time to the music. Henry and Jordan came in with Marina and me to shout *Not worth it! Turn your back! Walk away!*

For the next number, I was upgraded to a (clean, I hoped) sock. I ripped my ponytail out and tossed my hair around. Five original songs later—some of them needed work—we exchanged cell numbers and made plans to have band practice Sunday afternoon, in Henry's garage. Also Tuesday, Thursday, and Friday afternoon next week. Lots of practice, because we needed to work on music *and* puppeteering. Plus, we still had to make our puppets.

Henry said, "We have polyurethane. Yarn. Eyes. Felt. Glue. What else do we need?"

Which was when I came down—*thump*—to planet Earth.

I was taking algebra, both biology and physics, English, European history, and AP American history. I'd had to petition to get permission for the sixth class.

So: no.

No. No time!

But I nursed the puppet-band fantasy all weekend. I killed myself to get my homework done by Sunday at noon. Then I had my mom drop me off at the library, which was walking distance to where Henry lived.

The band was to be called Polly You're Insane. My puppet would be operated visibly, by me, but there'd be other puppets dancing and singing on top of a screen, operated by Henry's brother Josh and his friend Jesus. Henry was planning a puppet to sit on his head, operated by strings attached to his upper arms and piano-playing fingers. Jordan had their Barbie drumsticks. I failed to understand Marina's idea for her guitar puppet but believed she would make it work.

We talked, and jammed, and talked, and jammed some more. In the middle, I texted my parents that I'd run into my new friend Maggie at the library. I said we were now studying at her house. Then the band had microwave burritos for dinner.

I had only one bite because of anxiety.

I wanted to stay in the band. I'd been having such a good time! But the all-wrong anxiety feeling grew in me and I knew, inside, that I was doing a bad thing for the band as well by staying, and that it got worse every moment I lingered. They liked me now, but they would hate me soon, when I let them all down.

For a little while longer I told myself maybe I wouldn't let them down.

Henry had said earlier that he'd drive me home, which was a relief because otherwise I would have had to use Lyft, and the charge would have shown up on my parents' credit card and they might have asked about it and then I would have had to tell them where I'd been and why. Which would have been *fine*, because I wasn't actually going to be in the band after all. But that meant there was no reason to tell them; it would only confuse them and they'd ask questions about why I'd auditioned for a band of all things, a puppet band at that, and they'd point out stuff I already knew and agreed with, about time management and priorities and making wise choices. Then they would say with very caring faces that I could go back to violin if I wanted, if I missed music, because music was important and wonderful, and also it certainly wasn't too late to drop a course and take it easier at school. And if I did that, they would then have pretended very hard that I wasn't disappointing them, and very possibly I *wouldn't* be disappointing them, if I were to exchange, say, violin for physics. So there was really no point mentioning anything to them.

It never occurred to me that I might tell them that I wanted to be in this band.

At eight thirty that night, I explained to the band that I needed to go home. We confirmed practice times for the week. I should have told them then. Instead, I thought about those stories of awful cowardly people who break up with other people by text or who ghost them.

I understood now why that happens.

I did one more un-Zoe thing, though. In Henry's car, I touched his right arm. My excuse was his tattoo. I read it out loud: "'You're braver than you believe, stronger than you seem, and smarter than you think.' What's that?"

"From the Winnie the Pooh movie," said Henry. "Do you think that's dumb?"

"No," I said.

We were in complete eye contact.

"I got it to provide myself with constant reassurance," Henry said.

"Does it work?"

He said, "Sometimes. Sometimes it helps me go after what I want."

I was still touching his arm. Flirting. Me. Flirting with the edgy puppet boy! Slowly, very slowly, his eyes on mine the whole time, Henry leaned in. His mouth was a breath away. Then he stopped. "You're sixteen," he said. "Right?"

My skin was quivering. I knew why he was asking and I wished desperately that I was sixteen, like he'd thought. "Fourteen," I confessed. "Fifteen in January."

Henry closed his eyes. When he opened them, he'd moved away. My hand fell from his arm.

"I'm eighteen. Zoe?" He looked serious. "We need to be friends. That's all, no more. You know?"

I did know.

I nodded. "Yeah."

I moved an inch away, too, to prove I did understand.

It was the right outcome, though, because Henry didn't want *me*. I knew that. He wanted the Zoe I was pretending to be. The Zoe who laughed and sang with the sock on her hand, the Zoe who was going to show up at band practice on Tuesday. Not the Zoe who was going to send a breakup text to the band. And of course, he wanted the Zoe who was sixteen.

I got it.

"You're okay?" he asked. "We're okay?"

"Yes," I lied.

I couldn't be that laughing, singing, playing Zoe Rosenthal, anyway.

It is very important in life to know who and what you are and who and what you aren't, and to stick with that and not try to change, and not pretend, either.

Henry started the car. "Band comes first anyway. We're going to be really good friends this year, all of us. Polly You're Insane is going to be *amazing.*" We arrived at my house. "Talk to you tomorrow, Zoe," he said.

I felt more myself with every step I took toward my house, and away from him and the puppets.

Scene 3

Cons a Specialty

Before I even had a chance to look for my friends at baggage claim, I heard "Bloodygit!" Liv ran at me across the airport in exaggerated slow motion, arms flung out theatrically and the frying pan waving in one hand, an enormous Wonder Woman scarf wafting out behind.

I ran at Liv in slow motion too. We hugged and I got gently thumped on top of my head with the frying pan. Luckily it was the aluminum one. Then I turned to Cam and Sebastian and we all jumped up and down together and there was more hugging.

Sebastian was dressed as a bleeder already and totally unselfconscious about it. He wore white pajamas that fit tightly from neck to ankle, along with a red cap, red socks, and red felt slipper-shoes. He had rubbed his exposed skin with a treatment called Luminous Healing Clay, which he had praised ecstatically in a previous text. *It looks just like dried blood! I can keep it on the whole time I'm in cosplay, and then when I wash it off, my skin is soft!*

It all made for a candy-cane effect. People did double and triple takes. I was relieved that his new bleeding machinery—whatever it was—wasn't also on display.

I was conscious of people looking, but in the company of my Bloodygits, it only bothered me a little. We beamed at one another and they told me catch-up stuff about Meldel and Todd, who were already at the convention center.

Belatedly, I remembered Josie. She stood off to the side. I pulled her forward. "This is Josie, she/her, our Monica!"

My reward was Josie's shy smile. "Hi." Her voice came out in a squeak.

Sebastian said, "Good, hello," and Liv said, "Welcome!" and Cam said, "We meet at last!"

He added, "I have a story for you to read later, Josie, if you have time? I'm not sure if it's any good."

Josie said, "Sure, what's it about?"

"Pure invented backstory, how Captain met her husband not knowing he was a spy."

"Wait, you have him betraying her right from the start?"

"Yes. I wonder if I went over the top. I invented this whole other character that the husband is involved with, kind of a Rasputin-like person, and I spend maybe way too much time on them."

"Did you show it to . . ." Josie paused for a reverent moment. "Melisande Du Lac?"

"I really want to run it by you first."

"Oh, okay!" Josie's whole face glowed.

I was surprised. I knew that Cam and Josie had been talking online about fanfic; Josie was critiquing his stuff and Meldel's. But I hadn't realized they were this friendly. It was lovely to learn that Cam respected Josie's opinion. Maybe also he was going out of his way to help her fit in? He'd done that for Sebastian, I realized. Oh. And for me, too. And Meldel and Todd! Huh. In his quiet way, Cam was maybe the social glue of our group.

While we waited for the arrival of our cosplay-crammed suitcases, Sebastian ceremonially presented me and Josie with gift tubes of Luminous Healing Clay ("Your skin will thank you"), and Liv read aloud the description of the first session we were going to at Weird World.

A meticulously dressed woman waiting near us caught my eye and said, "What are you kids getting up to here in Austin?"

"Just a con," I muttered.

The woman smiled. "Of course! I get it. Keep Austin weird! You all have fun!"

I smiled back weakly.

It was humbling to see how quickly my self-confidence faded just because of a little maybe-smirk from a perfect stranger. I'd be okay once we weren't out in public with the Muggles, I thought. I'd be able to put my regular life and my regular self aside, and just be me.

It wasn't to be quite so easy this time, however.

In the shuttle van, Liv said, "I'm dying to know how you two convinced Josie's mom and Simon to let Josie come."

Josie answered before I could. "Zoe didn't tell you?

They don't even know! There would have been a great big fuss and I wouldn't have been allowed. So I told Zoe that she absolutely had to make a secret plan for me, like she did for herself. Or I'd tell Simon on her. Because I just *had* to come!"

In the silence, I watched the Bloodygits put two and two together.

"I feel the judgment," I said. "I feel the judgment!"

"So what was this secret plan?" asked Liv at length.

Details spilled excitedly out of Josie. How she and I had engineered an invitation to Josie's mom from Josie's mom's college roommate, so she'd be away this weekend. How we were betting that Simon wouldn't even notice that Josie was gone.

Cam said incredulously, "What do you mean, he won't notice?"

I said, "It's the last weekend before the election. He's got so many things to do for the campaign, he'll be flat-out, 24/7, between now and Tuesday night. He told me he'll sleep when he's dead."

Liv said, "But after everything you said about how responsible he is, won't he at least check on Josie?"

"Yes. But he'll check by text. And Josie will answer those texts." I gave Josie a stern look. "And I will help her word those texts."

"Meldel might help you out," said Liv. "With the texts."

I gave them an injured look. "I can handle it. Meldel is a little too creative."

"My brother's been mostly forgetting to bug me lately, anyway," said Josie. "Thank God, because he was always trying to catch me doing something he doesn't like, so he can explain to me how wrong I am and how I'm worrying Mom. Even if she says I'm not! He makes me *want* to be bad."

"How could you afford your plane ticket and registration, Josie?" asked Cam.

"Oh." Josie squirmed for the first time. "I'll pay Zoe back. She knows I'm good for it."

There was more silence in the van.

"Ooookay," said Cam.

"Out with what you're thinking," I said. "I should have refused to let Josie come and let whatever happened happen?"

"No, no, of course not!" Sebastian said. "Josie is safe with us. We all had to be here to try to save *Bleeders*. Simon doesn't understand about *Bleeders*, you always said so. I like the secret plan. Actually, Zoe, you're getting very experienced with secret plans." He paused, then grinned. "Zoe Rosenthal: Cons a specialty."

Cam choked. Liv cracked up. Even Josie giggled.

Sebastian looked very pleased with his joke's success. Good for him.

"Hey," said Liv. "Zoe, what happened to your arm?"

I winced, remembering. "Cat scratch. Freaking Wentworth!"

"That thing is six inches long!"

"Six and a half. Not that I measured or anything."

The van driver said, "Convention Center."

As we scrambled out of the van, I found myself next to Liv. We lingered behind the others. "Josie had me boxed in," I said defensively. "I am not some . . . some con man. Con woman. Con person. I am a well-intentioned victim of blackmail who is doing the very best I can."

Liv said, "Do you want to talk about it later? You and me? Alone?"

"Not really!" I said frankly. "Is that terrible? It is what it is. I'm just praying I get away with it." I held up both hands to show them my crossed fingers. "Simon is totally into his politics. And he's right to be! I was supposed to be out there, too, because it *is* the last weekend. But here I am. Instead."

I laughed. A little hysterically.

"Are you *sure* you don't want to talk it out?" said Liv.

"I just want to be here now." I waved toward the Weird World signage. "Really."

To Fight For

At Weird World, we all got into our cosplay. For Sebastian, this meant snaking tubing under his white pajamas; the tubes connected to larger packets positioned under his arms and at his hips. Liv put on a lab coat and looped on another scarf with the stethoscope-garrote. When I gave the new scarf the side-eye, they said airily, "I'm certain Torrance likes leopard print."

"Will leopards be extinct in the future? Reduced to patterns on clothing?"

Liv said, "Stop."

"Sorry," I said. "It's just that I can't always forget what a mess we're in. Even when I want to. Sometimes it just . . ." I shrugged.

We were standing together, apart from the others. Liv said, "I do get it, you know. About Simon's social-justice warrior principles and how you agree but can't live in that space all the time. I sometimes think I shouldn't even be planning for college and my personal future but instead learn farming and hunting and basically, you know, prepare for world disaster. I wonder if everything else is a waste of valuable time. So I'm kind of like Simon, only . . . less optimistic that politics will save us."

Our eyes met, mine startled. Liv smiled crookedly. "And then I think, I'm only one person, so carpe diem, tomorrow we die anyway, and all that. Let the earth take us down if it must."

"I didn't know," I said finally. "That you felt that way about college. So does my friend Maggie."

"Only sometimes," said Liv. "Not always. Sometimes I go to cons and play basketball and things and think it'll all be okay and I might have a future and the right to personal happiness."

"I keep hoping it's okay to search for a middle way," I said. "I want there to be joy in my life."

"Well, me too, obviously. The middle way. The non-binary way!" We both laughed. "Do you think there is one?" Liv continued.

"Simon's very binary. *You're either with us or against us.* Hey, do you know this meme: What's your justice warrior name?"

"I'll play. What's my justice warrior name?"

"Your first name and your last name," I said. "So, Liv?"

"Yes?"

"Don't think I didn't notice that you managed to trick me into talking."

"No tricks," said Liv soberly. "I'm just saying what I think. You're not the only one trying to figure life out, and how to be." A pause. "Even if you always phrase it as *Simon thinks* and *Simon says*."

I blinked. It was startling to learn how I appeared to others.

"Liv?" *Do you think I made a mistake bringing Josie?*

"What?"

"Nothing. Just thanks."

"You're welcome."

Mistake or not, I had done it. Josie was here. Simon wouldn't approve, but that didn't mean I should substitute Liv's opinions for his. I needed my own.

Oh, for crying out loud. I already *had* my own opinion! Josie was a few yards away, her face alight, looking around, in awe. Why shouldn't she be a Bloodygit, too? She belonged in this community. Anybody belonged who wanted to be here. That was the very point. I hadn't brought her only because I'd been blackmailed. I'd also brought her because I thought she belonged here, too.

I needed to own that.

I went right over to Josie and whispered, "I'm glad you came."

Her transcendent expression was my reward.

"But, Josie?" I added. "Never threaten me again, because the payback capacity of an organized woman is beyond your worst nightmare."

"Um," she said. "You'd destroy me with a spreadsheet?"

"You're fairly clever, so I might need to deploy a Kanban board too."

She eyed me carefully.

"Kidding not kidding," I said with a touch of the manic smile that the actress who plays Monica uses in Season 2, when Monica goes deliberately off her meds. (What Monica is up to, we don't yet fully understand.)

There, I thought smugly. *That will keep Josie nicely under my thumb.*

Child-rearing would obviously be a snap for me one day.

We stowed the luggage, got our badges, and made our way to where Todd and Meldel—Celie and Captain—were holding our place in line. We were planning to attend a panel session about women, race, and leadership roles in science fiction, with Zoe Saldana from Star Trek (who played Uhura in the movie reboots) and Gina Torres from *Firefly* (who played Zoë Washburne). Two Zoes! I couldn't help feeling kinship.

Regarding the panel, my Bloodygits had laid out the history via text, a few days ago—before the conversation devolved, that is.

> LIV: So back in the day of early science fiction shows on TV, women were rare and women in important positions on spaceships were even rarer, and as for women of color in important positions, Uhura was the only one, or at least the only one I know about. We eventually got Captain Janeway on *Star Trek: Voyager*, which was great, but of course she was white. Then women leaders on *Battlestar Galactica*—but again, white. Then Zoe Washburne on *Firefly*, but she's second in command. Basically, it's taken a

long, long time to get to a role model like Captain Paloma on *Bleeders*.

MELDEL: I don't think there's ever been a woman of color in command before, has there?

SEBASTIAN: I'm not sure. I'll do some research.

CAM: Anyway, this means our people will be attending that session in droves, so it'll be a really good place to hand out *Bleeders* flyers and make our case.

TODD: But they won't know that they're our people.

LIV: It's their chance to learn. There's a direct historical line from *Star Trek* to *Bleeders*. It goes through other shows like *Battlestar Galactica* and *Firefly*. I think Zoe Saldana and Gina Torres must know about *Bleeders*. Right? It'll make me really nervous for *Bleeders* if they don't!

SEBASTIAN: I hope they do. Hey, should I add that to the flyer, about the direct historical line?

MELDEL: Yes, great. Only make sure I copyedit.

MELDEL: Also, think about this: The original Uhura, Nichelle Nichols, was forced to dress sexy and wear a miniskirt. In her job! I hope someone asks Zoe and Gina about costuming for women leaders and how it's changed over time. Maybe I will. It pisses me off.

TODD: Personally, I like wearing my Celie miniskirt.

MELDEL: You wouldn't like wearing it on the bridge of your spaceship when you're handling critical communications with some new alien species who might blow you up but you're forced to sit with your legs perfectly positioned when that should be the absolute last thing on your mind. That miniskirt was about pleasing the male gaze.

LIV: Wait wait wait!

MELDEL: Don't you agree?

LIV: Maybe not. I feel like you're on the verge of shaming clothing that shows off the body. Move away from thinking about the viewer and think about the person wearing the clothing. It's about what you want to wear and what makes you feel good, and what's fun. Right? I mean, I love my scarves and I love the floaty femme ones that are totally impractical. I don't care what anybody else thinks.

MELDEL: But costuming is the choice of the designer, not the actor.

LIV: I know what you mean, but at the same time, I feel like it's a very dated discussion. Miniskirts. I mean, SIGH. People should wear whatever makes them feel good about their body and their presentation to the world. Sometimes that might be something that's explicitly sexy. Even on a TV show. Women and men and nonbinary people—everyone.

MELDEL: I get you, but I was talking about then, not now.

LIV: But some people obviously did want to wear miniskirts then, too. Right? In the real world.

TODD: Especially if you had great legs like Nichelle Nicols.

LIV: Not a terrible point from Todd.

TODD: I know right?!

LIV: But I'm talking to Meldel, OK? Meanwhile, though, other people wanted to wear pants. Fashion is not only about looking good but also about what the wearer feels good in. Always! You have to hold both things in your mind as you look around at what other people choose to wear. I imagine costumers think about that a lot.

LIV: Not to shame you, Meldel. Or anyone.

MELDEL: It's OK. I take your point.

LIV: Thanks. Good.

MELDEL: It's true that I have been known to enjoy wearing a
short skirt.

TODD: That's what I said!

LIV: Yes, and fashion is an incredibly complicated subject! We
can't just say miniskirts bad, pants good. Even for a TV
show set in the 60s.

MELDEL: I'm seeing what you mean. Let's talk in person
about it.

LIV: There's a lot to unpack!

SEBASTIAN: That's a joke right?

LIV: Yes. Do you like it?

SEBASTIAN: I like it. But are we done talking about clothing?

MELDEL: Yeah.

LIV: Yes.

SEBASTIAN: Good. Zoe, I'll send you a list of stuff to watch
so you'll be ready for the panel. You need to catch up on
your history.

Sebastian sent me the list, which arrived in admirable
historical order, and included annotated links to fan dis-
cussions that he thought were required reading and clips
from several different SF shows. (I went down one rabbit
hole about a character called Starbuck on Battlestar
Galactica who started out male and got reimagined as
female in the reboot.) At first I thought I didn't have time to
watch anything, but somehow Josie and I ended up watching a lot of it together.

And actually, this was why I was now behind in calculus.

(I have a generally decent relationship with math, but it hinges on our spending quality time together.) But SF history had felt as important to me as calculus right then—I needed to prep for the panel. I wanted to fully appreciate the discussion. Fully appreciate both Gina Torres and Zoe Saldana when I saw them. We owed them, like we owed Carrie Fisher. We owe *all* the dream makers who fire our imaginations. They don't have to have been perfect to have given us something to imagine, something to hold on to, something to aspire to, something to fight for.

Meanwhile, in Season 2

Todd and Meldel were in line for the panel, behind three middle-aged guys in red-shirt unitards (yes, really) who let us into the line with an amiable wave. Meldel's costume for Captain hadn't changed, but Todd's cosplay was new and based on Celie as of Season 2, Episode 4, when Celie is outside the ship; Todd had made her space suit. He had on heavy khaki coveralls and a tool belt. He had twisted his hair into a dozen tight, small pigtails all over his head and tied a hairnet over them to approximate Celie's helmet. His breathing apparatus was a clear plastic mask over his nose and mouth that was attached via duct tape to long black hoses wrapping around his neck and snaking down to his tool belt.

"It's from a vacuum cleaner," Todd said when I admired

the hose construction. He turned so I could see two large metal spiders on the nape of his neck. (In the episode, they fasten themselves to Celie so they can burrow to her brainstem.) "Brooches," he said. "I superglued them on."

"How are you going to get them off?" Cam asked.

Todd mimed ripping them off with his fingers.

Liv pointed out, "You might take away a lot of skin."

Todd shrugged. "Razor, then."

The twins exchanged a look.

"Sure, go on, slice through your neck," murmured Liv.

"So there's some blood. Who cares? I'll tell Sebastian not to watch." Todd thought some more. "Or, you know, I can keep them on as permanent jewelry. Evidence of how totally secure I am in my masculinity."

"Nail polish remover," advised one of the Star Trek cosplayers from in front of us, over his shoulder. "It's the kryptonite of superglue."

"Thanks!"

The line shuffled forward.

"Speaking of blood, don't you Bloodygits want me to demonstrate how I bleed?" Sebastian patted a bulge under his arm. "I've been waiting for you to ask. My new technology is foolproof. Third time's the charm."

"Of course we want to see you bleed," I said. "But maybe after the panel?"

"Oh. Of course."

"And we need to be ready to catch you if you faint," I added anxiously. "And maybe a trial run in private is a good idea. Is it ketchup again?"

Sebastian shook his head. "No. I'll tell you after you've

seen it in action. I've already handled it a lot, so that's why I know I won't faint. I just needed to know for sure it wasn't human blood. I think that was the problem."

He had said this before, but I kept my peace. Meldel and Todd were finally greeting Josie, who'd been almost hiding behind me, waiting to be recognized rather than stepping forward—an atypical shyness that I attributed to her awe of Meldel.

"Monica!" said Todd genially to Josie. "There you are. At last!"

"Hi."

"Let's see your cosplay!" said Meldel with a kind smile.

I relaxed, happy at how nice they were being to her, while Josie twirled shyly in her lab coat with the ship's insignia and yellow-and-black striped leggings and her mother's hiking boots. She also had on a pair of heavy black glasses which I recognized as Warby Parker samples. "Is it too simple?" she asked. "I had to pack light."

"Simple's good," said Todd.

"Yours isn't simple," Josie pointed out. "Or . . ." She glanced anxiously at Meldel.

Meldel smiled generously. "Your Monica is fine. Listen, I'm having an idea about a skit based on Monica and Captain. Can you act, Josie?"

Josie was thrilled. "Wow! Yes! I mean, I haven't ever, but I'm sure I probably can."

Meldel waved an arm grandly. "The flow for it has been, like, streaming into my head. I want to expand on what just happened in Monica's lab. What if I have Captain come in and catch Monica injecting herself?"

"With the stuff that's keeping her in manic-genius mode?" Josie asked.

"Yes!"

Josie nodded. "I feel like that might happen for real, don't you? I mean, it *has* to. This can't go on. Monica has to get caught. Plus, how long can she stay manic?"

"It might be that someone else will figure out what Monica's doing," Cam said. "Not Captain. Like, I think Tennah is worried."

"The problem there is that Tennah isn't ever going to tell Bellah anything," I said. "And Bellah is the one who reviews Monica's lab results."

"In my *skit*, it's going to be Captain who notices," announced Meldel. "Because we need a big scene with Captain and Monica together. Emotions need to run high. The fan base is absolutely dying for them to be together, am I right? So at least there needs to be some big drama. Fan service!"

"That's so, so right," said Josie eagerly. "Monica is dying for a word, a sign, from Captain! Anything but indifference! Even anger!"

"Yes. I see Captain as absolutely enraged in my skit. In her soft-spoken way, at least to start with. But then maybe she breaks, too. She's been under so much pressure. Maybe she should be drunk. Should I write a fanfic, too?"

"Yes! It would be awesome! Can they—can they kiss?"

"Too much at this point, I think. But they can come close."

"Oh. Okay."

"But I see Monica collapsing alone, in a puddle of unspoken desire, at the end of my skit."

Josie started to collapse to the floor then and there, but I caught her firmly under the arms. "We're walking," I said sternly. "As part of a line that would like to attend the panel."

She gave me a look. I revised my view that Josie would be easy to manage.

We finally got seated, a third of the way from the front. Not bad. I craned my neck to see if Zoe Saldana and Gina Torres were visible yet. Nope.

"Speaking of *Bleeders*," said Liv. "Did Monica discover a possible Bleeder vaccine? Or didn't she? I know I was confused."

I sat up straight. "There was definitely something happening in that petri dish!"

"But nobody saw it, not even Monica. It's like when the tree falls in the forest. If nobody's there, does it matter?"

"The camera saw it," I said. "Fans saw it. So it exists! There's a treatment that makes the virus shrivel up. Why couldn't they just let Monica see it? The writers, I mean."

"Because Monica's totally losing it," Josie pointed out. "Between unrequited love and her extra medication. Did you see how her hands were shaking?"

"She might see the results later," said Liv.

"Or she might not," I countered. "Because why would they let her come up with a cure? Wouldn't that like end the whole series?"

"Not necessarily," Todd said. "We don't actually know

what she'd *do* with it. I don't trust Monica one bit. We know *nothing* about her background."

Cam said, "Ahem. If I may interject a clarification. A treatment isn't the same thing as a vaccine. Given how quickly the virus kills its host, this thing that makes the virus shrivel would need to be given super-fast. So it would hardly help at all. They need a vaccine to cause the body to resist the infection in the first place."

We looked at him.

"Basic science," said Cam.

"By all means," said Todd. "Let's keep our TV science accurate."

"That's what I'm talking about."

"Anyway!" I said.

Some background on Monica. She's a medical doctor; everyone on the *Mae Jemison* is. And Monica is also a research scientist, so she's incredibly important to their search for a vaccine (not a cure, thank you, Cam). The thing is, she's no longer reliable. This season, Monica started tweaking her own medication—the stuff she takes because she's bipolar—to remain manic so that she can work harder and longer. And then she started taking something *else* to increase her concentration. And let me tell you, there's nothing like watching a character secretly shoot up to make you nervous.

So far, Monica's gotten more and more twitchy and more and more brilliant. (Personally? It's a little too much like clichés of a mad genius for me. And Josie says flat out that she doesn't find the storyline credible because "six doctors living in close quarters and you ask me to believe that people wouldn't notice Monica's personality change?" But I maybe disagree with that; I think people are basically self-involved enough to miss what isn't directly in their face. Doesn't matter how smart they are. I have proof of this in my own life.)

Anyway. After the episode where Celie was floating around outside the ship fighting for her life and sanity against the invasive space spiders, Monica wasn't paying attention to what was happening in her experiments, for once, because *Captain* was in the lab. And *that* was when viewers saw a test sample of infected tissue react to her latest compound and sort of wither. Which means Monica is finally on the trail of a viable vaccine. Only she doesn't know it.

The other question is about trusting Monica. Her background is mysterious and potentially suspect. Was she part of the team that concocted the original virus to begin with? Does Captain know this, if so? Is Monica a double agent of the government who's being tempted to the side of good because she's in love with Captain? But Captain is still in love with her piece-of-crap (as far as we know, but some fans hold out hope) husband. Who has *got* to show up by the end of Season 2, am I right? I understand about the dramatic effect of an offstage character (Meldel has made sure we all do). But at some point, if we don't meet them, it just feels like a pointless tease.

We were back into a detailed discussion of all of this when the audience exploded into applause for Gina Torres and Zoe Saldana.

Squirrel Girl

"But there were no questions of substance!" Liv said afterward. "The moderator led a good discussion, but after that it was all 'Gina, how terrible was it when they killed off your husband on the show?' and 'Zoe, how do you feel about taking up the mantle of such an iconic character?'" Liv used their scarf in a mock stranglehold.

Meldel added, "And 'What does the original Uhura think about Spock versus what Zoe's Uhura thinks about him?' I mean, does it *always* have to be about the boy?"

"Lots of wasted opportunity," said Sebastian. "And no questions about race! Like, at all!"

From behind me, a girl's voice said, "I know! I agree! A total waste!"

We all turned to see who'd spoken. She was all brown: bodysuit, skin, hair, and leggings. She wore a headband with triangular furry ears, her arms were covered by leather gauntlets, and she wore brown flat boots with fur edging the tops. A stuffed squirrel rode on her shoulder. She'd somehow attached an enormous furry squirrel tail to herself using a belt. Her cheeks were slightly chubby, as if there might be an acorn stuffed in each one. She'd painted round red circles on each cheek and wore lipstick to match. She actually made me wonder if I should make a kitty soap video with a human dressed as a cat. But no, no need; I wouldn't be suffering with Wentworth much longer. And Ellen From Finance took direction.

Sort of.

"Squirrel Girl!" Cam exclaimed happily. "You look marvelous!"

Squirrel Girl laughed. "Thanks." She looked our group over with interest. "So, who are you all?"

Liv said, "We're from *Bleeders*. New show last year, on SlamDunk? In its second season now."

"I haven't heard of it."

"Well, for one thing, there's a woman of color as Captain," said Meldel.

"Oh my God, I definitely need to know this show," said Squirrel Girl.

I was only able to pay partial attention to this because Sebastian had stopped breathing, although nobody but me seemed to notice. I wanted to be ready in case he fainted.

Finally, beside me, Sebastian exhaled in a great big huff.

"Yes, me too!" Liv was now saying, in response to I-would-never-know-what. "But what questions would we have liked them to answer instead? And why didn't we get up and ask them? Why didn't I? We have to take personal responsibility."

"There is that," Squirrel Girl admitted. She came alongside Liv, and we continued walking together. Sebastian was able to move, if somewhat robotically. I remained at the ready to grab his elbow if need be. "I had some ideas, but honestly? I felt too shy to ask," said Squirrel Girl.

"There were already so many people rushing the microphones," said Cam gloomily.

"Including that one guy who got in line and then didn't have anything to say when it was his turn," I said.

I nudged Sebastian—*say something, you fool!*

"I actually felt sorry for that guy," Squirrel Girl said.

"I didn't," I said. "Because I have a cold and tiny heart."

Squirrel Girl laughed, turning to look at me and, perforce, Sebastian. I elbowed Sebastian again, discreetly. He cleared his throat, but no words came out, and then he lost his chance because Squirrel Girl turned back to Cam.

I leaned closer to him.

"Who's Squirrel Girl?" I whispered.

He cleared his throat again. "Marvel. Marvel Comics. Her name is Doreen."

"You *know* her?"

"N-no, I mean, Squirrel Girl's alter ego is Doreen Green."

"Oh," I said.

"I've never seen *her* before." An expression of pure wistfulness filled Sebastian's face as he gazed at Squirrel Girl's back. She and the others were strolling the hallway ahead of us. Sebastian finally croaked out words in an attempt to join the conversation. "It's hard to think of good questions, I guess."

But I was the only one who heard him.

It's all very well to roll your eyes about insta-love as a plot device in a show or book. But when you've seen it strike one of your real-life friends, well, you have to believe. Insta-love, insta-lust, insta-attraction, whatever it is.

It happens.

It hurts.

Squirrel Girl was now using the kind of body language—stepping away, smiling, starting to turn—that meant she was about to leave. I saw my duty as Sebastian's friend.

"Squirrel Girl! Are you a big fan of Star Trek?" I asked.

She turned to me. "Yes, and I'm excited about *Discovery!*—"

Todd cut in right on top of her. "Bloodygits! Want to know my big disappointment? No miniskirts! That was a bust. Hahaha! See what I did there?"

Squirrel Girl compressed her lips.

"Todd, Squirrel Girl was talking," I said pointedly. "About *Star Trek: Discovery.*" Which I had not had enough time to watch, but my mother was watching.

"No problem, I've got to go," said Squirrel Girl easily. "Another panel. See ya!" She waved and thumped off in her boots.

I watched Sebastian watch her go.

Maybe someone else, someone not Sebastian, would have been able to go after her. Say something like, "Wait, I really want to get to know you, would you be willing to hang out later?" Or, "Wait, what were you going to say about *Discovery*? I'm really interested." Or even, "What panel are you headed to next?" Saying anything would have been better than saying nothing.

But that's easy to say when you're the observer, not the actor.

Scene 7

Insta-Heartbreak

I kept a compassionate eye on Sebastian as the day waned and turned to night and the next day dawned. We did our con things—attending panels, handing out flyers, posing for photos as a *Bleeders* group. We stayed up nearly all night talking about *Bleeders*. The other Bloodygits didn't seem to notice Sebastian wasn't completely himself.

But I did.

He didn't even ask us to see him bleed!

Everywhere we went, his head turned, his eyes scanned. His chest rose and fell with the rapidity of his hopeful breath. But we didn't see Squirrel Girl again.

I felt terrible for him—and not just because he didn't find her. I was also imagining what would happen if he did find her. Doom. That was what. Heartbreak. Disaster. Fantasies crushed to gravel!

I cherished Sebastian. He was quirky and sweet and earnest and unique and smart and caring. But Squirrel Girl was out of my dear friend's league, I had decided. All I could do was hope that—if he did find her, if he did manage to express his interest—she'd be kind. Reject him in a way that wasn't personal. Maybe she wasn't interested in boys. Maybe she wasn't interested in white boys. Maybe she was with someone else. Something, anything!

Things got even more depressing in my head from there, because I doubted Sebastian had the skills to get *anyone*. He'd have to *get* those skills, somehow, and it would be hard for him. Then I wondered, how did *anyone* get romantic skills? We weren't born with them. I hadn't been. And who was I to think I was such an expert now? I had one boyfriend who luckily liked me. Simon and I had been clumsy *together*. That was why it had worked out.

So how was it that you could have a boyfriend and be totally and completely and utterly happy with him, but also realize that you had no idea really how it all worked, and that if you ever had to start all over again, which please God forbid, you wouldn't have a clue and you'd be in as bad a shape as Sebastian, or nearly?

In short, I spent hours secretly making myself miserable and insecure about the nature of love, because Sebastian had fallen in insta-love. I knew it had nothing to do with me, and yet I was reduced to a simple selfish prayer that Sebastian not see Squirrel Girl again. Please. How lucky, lucky Liv was that they didn't care, I thought.

I had basically exhausted myself emotionally by the time Sebastian actually did find Squirrel Girl.

It happened late Saturday afternoon. We were browsing the show floor. The stuff on the floor is largely for sale: art, posters, comics and books, jewelry, clothing, games, toys, and fixings for cosplay. The vendors tended to be independent artists scrabbling a living, with some big companies representing, too. Most everything is themed to fandom, so, for example, you wouldn't find cat posters; you'd find cats dressed as Captain America, Spiderman, and so on. Of course, my own personal favorite was Catwoman, because what could be better than a cat dressed as a person dressed as a cat? (It made me wonder again if I could or should do something with cosplay for Mrs. Albee's kitty soaps. If I were allowed.)

Our group mostly stuck together even though we had very different browsing interests. Liv was, as usual, on the hunt for distinctive scarves. Todd checked out medieval weaponry: swords, axes, war hammers—most of which looked alarmingly real to me (because they *were*, it turned out). Cam wandered off and came back, wandered off and came back. When I wasn't brooding about doomed love, I was searching for something for Maggie, in case I couldn't find her just the right turquoise bag. Maggie likes to wear only black, and she accessorizes with turquoise. Period. You would think this makes her easy to shop for, but I could write a college application essay on the difficulties. (Yes, I have been torturing myself with bad essay ideas, and the deadline is next month and it is not like me *at all* to wait until the last minute.) Meldel walked silently alongside us, entering no booths because she was, she said, writing in her head. This meant she alternately grimaced and smiled randomly at nothing, while Josie humbly handed her a water bottle whenever Meldel gestured for it. (Josie's worship of Meldel definitely contributed to my irritation. *Who* had brought Josie here, might I just ask? *Who* had paid for it? *Whose* kindness and inclusivity should be at least appreciated? *Who* had risked basically her whole life to do it? I am simply asking these humble questions.)

I made the ungrateful little pip-squeak Josie send Simon a reassuring text. He sent back a thumbs-up, and I breathed a little easier then. I was just checking Simon off (for now) on my mental checklist as we entered a specialized, roped-off, expensive area called Original Art.

Todd held up a jeweled dagger right out of Tolkien. He made a surprisingly skillful wrist twist with it. (Did he play with knives at home? Ugh.)

It was then that Sebastian spoke. In an outdoor voice. "Bloodygits! Don't you want to see me bleed?"

I now must provide some essential background on the Original Art area of the con floor and what you will find for sale and display there, namely:

Masks.

Sculptures of elves.

Handmade lutes, artisanal swords, silvery gauntlets.

Necklaces and earrings. Intricately wrought diadems and tiaras and crowns set with semiprecious stones.

Exquisite dragons with scales of hammered silver and jewels for eyes.

An entire tray of One Rings to Rule Them All, and another of rings with secret compartments ("For poison," said Cam appreciatively).

A life-size TARDIS for seven hundred and fifty dollars. Total bargain, because the price included shipping.

So, basically, Original Art is not the right place for a spontaneous demonstration of bleeding. I opened my mouth to (gently) make this point to Sebastian, when I saw Squirrel Girl.

Squirrel Girl stood, and this is important, near an enormous, realistic oil painting of Aragorn (or maybe I should say, Viggo Mortensen as Aragorn). She caught sight of our group, smiled with recognition, and started toward us.

Sebastian had seen her too. Already. Of course. That was the whole point. So what happened next was like the ritual dance a male bird does in an attempt to impress the female. (Google "Bird of Paradise mating dance" and watch the video right now. I'll wait.)

Sebastian bellowed: "EVERYBODY! IN SUPPORT OF THE BEST NEW SHOW THAT YOU'RE NOT WATCHING! *BLEEDERS* ON SLAMDUNK! I AM A VICTIM OF THE BLEEDER PLAGUE! BEHOLD! BEHOLD HOW THE BLEEDING MECHANISM OPERATES!"

He unbuttoned the front of his white pajama top and tossed it to the floor. He stood half-naked in his red cap and white pajama bottoms. Tubes ran all over his torso and down his arms and legs. The tubes were attached to a few large, bulging plastic bags duct-taped to his wincingly white skin.

Of course, people other than us and Squirrel Girl were watching by now. If I could have stepped into the TARDIS and disappeared—say, to New Hampshire, where I should have been working in advance of the election—I would have done it. Believe me.

Sebastian made a sweeping gesture over his chest. "FANS! THESE BAGS ARE FILLED WITH ACTUAL CHICKEN LIVER BLOOD! IT IS FORCED THROUGH THE TUBES! IT SEEPS OUT THROUGH A SERIES OF PINHOLES WHEN—I—DO—THIS—"

He mashed both of his fists into two of the bags. But his bag-tube-pinhole system did not work as designed.

Let me explain. No, there is too much. Let me sum up:

- The bags exploded
- Blood rained through the air
- Landing on people
- And on many small things (cost: $445, split evenly by hasty agreement among the Bloodygits)
- And on the oil portrait of Aragorn (cost [gulp]: $1,250)
- And finally, on Squirrel Girl (cost: incalculable)

Cards Against Humanity

At 1:32 a.m. on Sunday morning, Cam, Liv, Josie, and I were part of a bigger group playing Cards Against Humanity. Actually, Josie was snoozing, with her head pillowed on her arms.

We were forbidden to return to the dorm until Meldel and Todd told us Sebastian was doing better. The idea was to create an atmosphere of calm for him. Basically, they were babysitting while Sebastian sat in Meldel's closet. Also present, leaning against a wall, was the giant portrait of Aragorn. Perhaps I should say, *my* giant portrait of Aragorn. The vendor had literally hefted a pitchfork and started toward Sebastian's prone body. (The pitchfork had a silver-coated blade and was suitable for the arms-length killing of vampires or, I supposed, orcs.) I'd stepped in his way and blurted, "I want it! I'll buy it!"

"PayPal, Venmo, or debit card," snarled the vendor. "And you wait right there while it clears."

"No worries," I said weakly.

"Zoe, you are awesome!" Josie exclaimed while I anxiously double-checked my bank balance on my phone.

Now, at the Cards Against Humanity table, Cam said quietly, "Let me say just one thing. I am never, ever going to forget the look on Sebastian's face right before he fainted. It will haunt my dreams."

"Me neither." Liv had on their new scarf. It was not to their usual taste, but it had been only slightly chicken-blood-spangled, and the spots had come out with cold water.

Heartlessly (she is yet young), Josie snorted her snort laugh. (Neither Josie nor Simon can laugh without the snort. The first time Simon snorted in front of me, he was so appalled, he turned pink. It was adorable. Oh, things were simpler then.)

At least I knew Simon would never ask me what had become of the chicken-blood-spattered top I'd thrown out, or where and why I'd gotten my brand-new "Do You Know the Way to Hobbiton?" T-shirt. Simon doesn't usually notice my clothes. In any case, I wouldn't wear this new T-shirt at home, where Simon could see. And I would hide Aragorn from him. Somehow.

I didn't think he'd fit into my bedroom closet.

More or less simultaneously, our phones pinged.

MELDEL: Sebastian spoke at last. He asked for pizza.

MELDEL: Another $20 on my charge card. Hahaha. Why not?

Pile it on!

CAM: So he's come out?

TODD: Not exactly. He wants us to crack the door and hand it to him.

TODD: Slice by slice

MELDEL: In silence.

CAM: So can we come back now?

TODD: Negative

MELDEL: Patience!

MELDEL: I'm going to chant him a meditation that I learned recently.

MELDEL: It's to promote inner peace.

Cam and Liv and Josie and I put down our phones in unison. Josie returned to napping.

"Are you folks playing or not?" asked the current card czar.

"We're in. Except Josie."

"Good." The czar put a black card down on the table. *What's there a ton of in heaven?*

I considered the ten white cards in my hand and went with *Sweet, sweet vengeance.* There were ten people playing, but the card czar awarded me the round. Yay.

On impulse, I looked around the table and said, "Can I ask everybody a question? Have any of you ever screwed up big time in front of someone you really wanted to impress?"

There was general laughter. A bunch of yeses, a couple noes. The man sitting across from us, middle-aged, in Harry Potter glasses and with temporary tattoo of a lightning bolt on his forehead, said, "My story is a record breaker."

A woman cosplaying as Ursula the Sea Witch asked him, "Well?"

"You really want to know?" We nodded. "Okay. Brace yourselves. I was with my then-boyfriend, now-husband. Meeting his family, right? We're there for the weekend."

He paused. "So, I should back up and say that my husband's white and comes from this very religious family, and they're freaked that he wants to marry a man. But you know what? They're *trying*. We're all *trying*. So, we're in the dining room and it's the good china and this elaborate meal that Seth's mother spent hours on. Only it's meat and I'm vegan. So is Seth, but it turns out that when he's home, he eats whatever his mother serves. Which, by the way? He didn't bother to mention to me beforehand.

"So, the platter goes around, and Seth gives me this pleading look, like, 'Take the ribs, Ali. Please, just take the ribs.' What can I do? I'm horrified, but I take a rib."

The new card czar for the round interrupted. "Can we play and listen at the same time? This card is actually relevant." She put down: *What ended my last relationship?*

We all groan-laughed.

The storyteller checked his cards, put in his choice card, facedown, and continued. "So, I've got a barbecued rib on my plate, which I am trying to hide under my creamed corn, which I actually don't want to eat either, if you know what I mean. Meanwhile, there's, you know, polite conversation about people I don't know, including a whole lot about Seth's high school girlfriend." He articulated carefully. "Ka-trin-a. Who, guess what? Is still *available*."

Josie snorted again. We all looked at her. She cracked

one eyelid and then closed it. "I'm awake," she said. "I'm listening. I just can't keep my eyes open."

The storyteller laughed and went on. "But, like I said, Seth's family really is trying. In their way. That's what I tell myself. But I'm also feeling kind of pissed off. Only then." He paused. "Then, I start to notice this *smell*. This really bad *smell*. Which is getting stronger and stronger." Another pause. "And *stronger*."

Several players have also put down cards in response to *What ended my last relationship?* I added mine, face-down: *Judge Judy*.

"Everybody starts to notice the new smell. The family's shifting in their seats. They're exchanging glances. Seth's mom sniffs. But nobody says a word. They go on with the stupid small talk. Now they're discussing their family history.

"And I think: *Why is everyone ignoring the smell? That's crazy!* And you know what? I'm not the kind of person who *ignores* things. I'm the kind of person who *confronts* things. That's my *personality*. So. I do it. I take charge. I sniff the air ostentatiously. 'What's that awful smell?' I say.

"Now, I should mention that there are a couple of family dogs. And that before dinner, I was out in the yard playing with them."

"Oh no," murmured Cam.

"Oh yes. Oh yes, my friends. Yes, I have *stepped* in it. Yes, I have tracked it into the house. I have tracked it over the rag rug that was handmade by Great-Great-Grandma Matilda when she was crossing the prairie in a covered wagon powered by true grit—or true sin, depending on your understanding and interpretation of so-called American manifest destiny and the takeover of Native American lands. My understanding of history is just a little *different* from Seth's family's, let me just say that, so I wasn't quite ready to worship at the shrine of Great-Great-Grandma Matilda. But none of that mattered right then, because what everybody at that table, including me, suddenly did understand was that it was on my shoe, underneath the dining room table, mixing with the smell of the barbecued *ribs*." The storyteller paused. "And that, my friends, is when I threw up my barbecued ribs-flavored creamed corn. On the table. And the rug. Where I had already ground in . . . well, you know."

We stared at him. Liv was the one who started the slow clapping, but we all joined in. The storyteller, Ali, stood up and gave a sweeping bow. When we finished laughing, this round's card czar read all the entries but said the winner was Ali, no matter what card he'd put in.

I turned to Ali. "And your relationship actually *survived*?"

"It did."

"Your boyfriend wasn't mad?"

He grinned. "Once we were safely alone? Seth laughed until he cried. He proposed the next week. On bended knee."

"And has his family forgiven you?" I pressed.

"We have—uh—swept it all under the rug."

Everyone at the table groaned.

"And what they say behind my back is none of my business."

I was the card czar next, and after I put down a black card, I told everyone the story of what had just happened to Sebastian and how I'd recognized that he was in insta-love. "What do we do to help him?" I asked. "He's like freaking dying in that closet right now."

"Not dying. He's eating pizza," Cam reminded me.

"This is Sebastian. He'd be able to eat pizza on his deathbed."

"True."

Cam said, "So, is there a way we can make things right between Sebastian and Squirrel Girl?"

"That's not what I meant when I asked—" I started.

"Wait, what? You're trying to fix his love life?" said Ali the storyteller.

"No!" I said, but Cam said, "Yes, why not?"

"Oh, dear naive one." Ali shook his head. "Everybody has to find their own way. It's like a law of the universe. The good news is that with every mistake you make, you learn and you do better the next time. Don't butt in for your friend. Please. Interfering in love always backfires."

Ursula the Sea Witch shook her head. "I totally disagree! Listen, I've matchmade for people—"

"There's a difference between matchmaking and interfering—"

"But it's good to try—"

A contentious discussion about love and life and friendship went on as we played. Josie snored through the whole thing, but I listened and eventually pulled out my bullet journal and took notes of the adult advice:

☐ Don't interfere.

☐ Matchmaking can work, but you have to make the introduction and step away.

☐ Give your sweetheart room.

☐ Stand up for yourself.

☐ Watch for red flags like when they don't introduce you to their friends.

☐ Set expectations up front.

☐ Fully disclose all allergies.

Then Liv said, "Zoe? You're so busy taking notes. Do you want to ask for specific advice about you and Simon?"

Scene 9

Lawful Good Again

Horrified, I glanced at the sleeping—I sincerely hoped—Josie and dropped my voice. "No!"

"You have this great opportunity to get experienced adult opinions," Liv said coaxingly.

"I don't need any!"

"You're having love problems, too?" said the current card czar. "Like your friend in the closet with the pizza?" She was a compact white woman in her twenties, wearing antlers strung with lights.

I tried to make eye contact with Cam, but he kept his eyes stubbornly on his cards.

"My boyfriend is a totally great guy," I said firmly to Antler Woman and Ali the storyteller and Ursula the Sea Witch and a man in a Captain Hammer T-shirt. They all looked back at me with enormous interest. They comprised all the players at this point, plus us.

"What's this Simon look like?" said Ursula the Sea Witch.

I saw no harm in that. Au contraire. I showed her on my phone. She passed it around.

"Nice," said Antlers.

"The intense type," diagnosed Ali.

"Yes, he is. How'd you know?"

"It's in the eyes. Is he here at Weird World?"

"No."

"And he doesn't know that Zoe is," Liv put in. "She keeps her fangirl self a complete secret from him."

Ali raised his brows.

"Why is that bad?" I demanded. "Do you tell your husband everything? I mean, he didn't tell you that he ate meat at home, right?"

Ali made a dismissive hand motion. "The important, real-world things, we share." He paused. "Yes, Seth should have warned me he ate meat at home, and told his mother I was vegan. He should've, and he knew he should've, but I get why he didn't. He was afraid. We talked it out. It's not like I'm perfect, either. It's a work in progress, but the goal is that there's no actual lying or deliberate evasion. That said, I don't share everything that I *think*, and I don't expect him to do that, either. I guess that's the line." He looked around the table. "Other knowledge in this area?"

Ursula the Sea Witch and Captain Hammer nodded. Antler Woman said, "I'm single. But yeah, it's worked that way when I'm with someone. There is a line of discretion, I guess, but you shouldn't cross over into dishonesty."

Cam asked, "So how do you know when to say something and when to keep your mouth shut?"

"Experience is your teacher. And good sense, I guess. And fairness." Ursula the Sea Witch shrugged. "But there are just some things you learn not to say, either, because it won't do any good or it hurts their feelings or you know it'll pass, it's not important."

"Or you don't want to have that argument right now," said Captain Hammer. "Or ever."

"Or there's no point, because this is just how it is," said Antler Woman. "Like, I know better than to say, 'You were the one who said we should go I-95 and now we're sitting in traffic and we should have used Waze to check the route like I said.'"

Ursula laughed. "Or, 'Why didn't you pack a snack for the kids? You know what it's like when they have a meltdown and I explained three times where the granola bars were.'"

Captain Hammer said, "'How come you can't just tell your sister that where we're going on our vacation is not her business and neither is how much we spent on it? What's so hard about that?'"

They were on a roll.

"'You've told that story before like twenty times! Nobody wants to hear it again.'"

"'Why did you order the marinara? You'll be up all freaking night.'"

"'I can't stand your best friend.'"

"'I told you not to have that third martini.'"

"'Why can't you be open to a little simple feedback?'"

I was nodding and scribbling notes as Liv cut in. "But wait, everybody. All your partners? They all know that you're at Weird World being a fan? Even if they're not here, too?"

"Yeah," said Captain Hammer.

The others nodded.

Liv leaned in. "See, Zoe's boyfriend thinks she's in New Hampshire right now working on a political campaign."

"Democratic?" asked Ursula.

"Of course!" I said, stung.

"No politics here," said Antler Woman plaintively. "Please."

"Okay, sorry, yeah. Getting back to love," said Ursula. "Zoe—that's your name, right? Zoe? Okay, so—"

"Wait," I said, and held up a defensive hand. "Look. I'm not *married* to Simon. And it's healthy for people in relationships to have separate interests."

"Now, that's true," said Ursula. "You don't want to be attached at the hip."

"Thank you," I said, and slid Liv a triumphant look.

Liv wouldn't quit. "Isn't this different?"

Ali shrugged. "Maybe. But remember what we said, up at the top? About not interfering in your friends' relationships?"

"Yes," Liv said warily.

"Unless there's something *really* wrong that you suspect or know," Antler Woman put in. "You know, like abuse."

Everybody suddenly looked at me.

I blanched, shocked. "Liv, you don't think—?"

"Oh, no," Liv exclaimed. "Nothing like that! Just—just . . . okay, I'm sorry. I was out of line. Forgive me, Zoe."

"Doesn't anybody want my opinion?" said Josie, in a slurry, sleepy voice. "About my own brother?"

All heads swiveled to her end of the table.

I had actually forgotten she was there.

She didn't lift her head or open her eyes. "Zoe's lying to my brother about being a fan and about being here, but so am I, and we have to, because, and this is politics, sorry, but you can't talk to Simon about practically anything fun. He thinks it's almost, like, evil to not be serious and intense all the time. He wants to save the country and the planet and everything."

"Social-justice warrior?" said Ursula.

"Yes, always, but he used to laugh more. Zoe doesn't know that. She didn't know him then. But it doesn't matter because now he has to save the world all the time."

"He'd dump me," I said. The words burst from me. "Which I don't want. Also, he's right about—this is more politics, sorry—but see, I'm Jewish. I understand what happens in the long term if you don't fight back against hate. So, we have to resist. I'm on board for that, and I'm glad to have a boyfriend who understands this stuff, and not someone who—who plays the piano and sings all day like a grasshopper or whatever. It's just that I need a vacation from it sometimes.

"I love my show!" I said. "I love my Bloodygits." I swept my hand toward them. "My fan friends. But I also love my boyfriend. He's—he's *lawful good*! Who doesn't want that in their life?"

Everybody was quiet then, and finally Liv nodded and said, "Sorry, Zoe. This is your business and not mine."

Ursula the Sea Witch said to Liv, "She'll turn to her friends when and if she needs to. I can tell she will. Don't worry. Meanwhile, she'll work out her relationship and her feelings on her own as best she can."

"Which is what we all have to do," said Antler Woman. "Work our problems out."

"No! I don't need to work out anything," I said. "Everything is fine. *Fine!* There are no problems. This is one of those things like you talked about, that you don't need to say. And I'm getting away with it, anyway."

There was silence until Ali the storyteller said, "We hear you. Whose turn is it next?"

"Me," Cam said, and dealt a card.

EPISODE 4

December 2018 @Bloodygit
Video Chat Meeting

From Zoe's Bullet Journal

<u>TO DO</u>:

- ☑ Simon new job congratulations gift
- ☑ College application essay
- ☐ Hanukkah, Christmas gift list p. 253
- ☐ Improve financial situation, ideas p. 255
- ☑ Send college applications!!!
- ☐ ~~College app celebrate w/Simon Fri Sat~~
- ☑ *Bleeders* binge: Fri night
- ☑ Read/critique Meldel and Cam's new Lorelei fanfic: Sat night
- ☑ Strategize with Maggie re electrical apprenticeship: Sun night
- ⟼ ~~Spokescat comparison presentation~~ (postpone to January)
- ☐ Aragorn ???

Scene 1

Thrift

The last weeks of December meant vacation for the college Bloodygits. We'd scheduled a group video chat—our substitute for attending a con. It was terribly disappointing not to get to hang out with everyone in person, though.

The upside was thrift. Belt tightening was desperately necessary. My savings had taken serious hits lately (wince—travel for two; double wince—Aragorn).

I'd turned down reimbursement for Aragorn. I was still kicking myself, maybe. Or maybe not. Sebastian had offered to pay me back on a monthly installment plan. Only I just couldn't let him. Yes, it was a giant chunk out of my savings, nearly half of what had taken me so long to accumulate, but I *did* have those savings, not to mention the ability to ask my parents for help in situations where I really did need money. And Sebastian was so woebegone.

This was something I could do for him and it was a privilege to be able to help, really. I had told him that instead he should pay it forward one day to another friend. I'd even assured him that I liked Aragorn, had him on the wall, and planned to take him with me to college. Sebastian had been transparently relieved. Fortunately, he did not ask what Simon thought of Aragorn.

Soon I would be doing better financially. Surely! I had a plan. There would be Hanukkah money from Aunt Kath and from my bubbe on the Rosenthal side. And then, after I had Ellen From Finance installed as spokescat, we'd have an enormous influx of new customers and, therefore, Mrs. Albee would give me a raise. I wondered how much to ask for. I wondered if the raise could be retroactive to when I'd begun ~~scheming~~ working on the Ellen From Finance plan. Once I figured out the exact right approach for persuading Mrs. Albee about Ellen From Finance.

I had made the mistake of mentioning my desire for extra pay to Simon. He'd leapt into fix-it mode, offering to try to get me a job doing something "more socially meaningful." Now that his job with our new state senator was permanent, he had "connections," he said.

Since I didn't actually *want* a new and more socially meaningful job—no matter how much I complain about Wentworth—I'd been forced to ask if it wouldn't trouble him to use his privilege that way. Ten seconds later, he'd thanked me for my insight, for understanding his situation, and for putting him first and sacrificing my own best interests for his.

I teetered between being pleased with myself for my

deft handling and wondering if I was being manipulative. If only I had never learned about character alignments!

On the bright side, Mrs. Albee was exploring my other idea, the one that had *not* required any sneaking around, involving packing her soaps in yarn for shipping. It would be cute, it was reuse-recycle friendly, and it would make our product appeal to cat people who knit—like Aunt Kath. I had already set up baskets at two local yarn shops to collect scraps.

Purr-fect!

Scene 2

Competition

Josie and I sprawled on my bed with my laptop open. We had just taken the Bloodygits on a virtual Rosenthal house tour, mostly so that they could view Aragorn in our family room.

> **MELDEL:** (Approvingly) He dominates the space.
>
> **TODD:** A masculine man! It's good to see him situated where all can worship.
>
> **ME:** Yeah, well, my mother was here when the package came, and she was desperately curious because it was so huge. I had to open it in front of her.

I could not, in front of Sebastian, say that my original plan had been to loan Aragorn to Maggie. She could have used the distraction. Maggie was in the fight of her young life over what her parents were insisting on calling her "gap year" plan.

ME: Then my mother told me it was a lovely gift for her, and told my father she wanted it in *their* bedroom. At first I didn't realize she was joking!

LIV: Too much information, Zoe.

CAM: So your mom didn't notice the bloodstains?

TODD: What bloodstains? I did a really good job cleaning before I shipped it.

MELDEL: It's true.

TODD: I want credit for taking it to be shipped too. It's heavy! But of course, I'm strong like bull.

ME: Long story short, he ended up in the family room. An heirloom, my mom says.

CAM: A fairytale ending.

ME: Well, it's not quite exactly the end.

JOSIE: Right, because now Zoe has to keep my brother out of the family room when he visits. Because what if he asks and then Zoe's parents say it's hers and it got shipped to her from Weird World by some guy. They were very interested in you, Todd, by the way. Zoe's parents, I mean.

CAM: Oh, what a tangled web we weave, when first we practice to deceive.

TODD: Why are they interested in me? Not that I'm not fascinating. I get it. But they haven't actually met me.

ME: Actually, Simon's been so busy lately that he hasn't been over much, so it's a nonissue. Did I tell you Bloodygits that after Alisha Johnson Pratt won, she offered him a permanent job at the State House?

TODD: Artful change of subject by Rosenthal! Two points!

MELDEL: You may have mentioned this new job, yes.

SEBASTIAN: You've told us. Bloodygits, please, can we talk about something other than Aragorn? I am still very sensitive.

CAM: You're doing better, though. I can tell.

MELDEL: You smiled about Zoe's mom.

SEBASTIAN: I may no longer lie awake in an agony of remembered humiliation, or at least not for more than an hour a day. Still, I would prefer to change the subject.

ME: I was trying to.

CAM: But first, what's this about Zoe's parents and Todd?

TODD: I am strangely curious myself!

JOSIE: Oh, just that after Zoe's parents saw Todd's name on Aragorn's return address, they asked about him.

ME: (Sarcastically) Were you there, Josie? No, you were not.

JOSIE: You told me. You were like vibrating with anxiety.

TODD: Ooh la la! Am I now viewed as potential competition to Simon for the fair Zoe? Intriguing!

ME: Shut up, Todd.

TODD: I feel sure I could destroy Simon in single combat.

ME: In a video game? Possibly true.

TODD: The lady is scornful! I would try to win her from Simon the Undeserving, were my heart not pledged to another.

ME: Shut up, Todd.

JOSIE: The point here is that Zoe's parents *want* my brother to have competition. Even someone like Todd, not that they know you, Todd.

TODD: What's that supposed to mean? I feel injured.

ME: Josie.

JOSIE: What?

ME: Bloodygits? Excuse us. Josie and I need a minute to talk.
Alone.

The Tangled Web

I muted my laptop and scowled at Josie.

"It's true," Josie said defensively. "I know it."

I pushed my hand into my hair. "Yes. But . . ."

There was no denying it any longer. My parents had summoned me to a family discussion about my college applications. At the last minute, they'd wanted me to add two or three more schools—at their expense, even. Places that Simon and I had ruled out. Or a women's college.

Like your friend Liv, said my mom.

Where's the harm? my dad said. *Give yourself more options!*

I have tons of options, I said.

Nothing wrong with more, right?

To shut them up, I had finally agreed to add one extra school to my list. Just one.

I was trying not to think about it.

I hadn't told Simon and I felt awful. It wasn't like sneaking off to a con. This was a completely different order of sneaking. I knew it even if I wasn't lawful good. I shouldn't have applied to that extra school behind his back. And having done it, I should at least tell him I'd done it.

But maybe he'd never need to know.

I asked Josie, "How'd you find all this out? I told you about Aragorn, but not about my parents."

"Your mom called my mom the other day. I . . . happened to hear what my mom said."

"What?" I sat up. "What is this, a conspiracy? Why are they getting all Capulet and Montague? I don't understand! There's nothing wrong with Simon! There's nothing wrong with me! Or us! We're just young, that's all! And my parents met in high school, too. They should talk!"

Josie shrugged. "Why ask me? All *I* wanted was to be a Bloodygit! I don't care whether you're with my brother or not. That's not my business."

I refrained from saying that for something not her business, she certainly had been eager to eavesdrop. And then to tell me what she'd heard.

"Well," I told her. "It's not like my parents can or would force me to break up with him. They said so. My life, my decisions." I crossed my arms. "Does Simon know about this conversation, too? Between our moms?"

Josie looked resigned. "He wasn't home when it

happened. I guess you need to talk to him and ask if my mom talked to him."

"*You* didn't tell him?"

"No. And I don't think my mom would have. She said something about him being an adult."

"You shouldn't have been eavesdropping anyway!" I took a breath. I reminded myself that I was hardly a model citizen. Still, everything would be all right in the end. Simon was really happy right now; that was what mattered. We were now focused on getting accepted to a close-to-Boston school so he could keep his job with Alisha Johnson Pratt.

"If your mom didn't tell Simon, then I won't," I said. "He's *busy*. And this is nonsense. They're acting like total babies. If she says something to him, then he'll come to me. And we'll talk at that time, if we need to."

"Zoe?"

"What?"

"Something else is bothering me."

I eyed her.

"I don't like lying to my mom. Or even Simon. About Bloodygits and everything. I thought it would be fun, like secret-agent stuff. But it's actually not."

I sighed but said nothing.

"I feel terrible. What are we going to do?"

"I don't know," I said. "I hear you. Lying is bad. I'll fix it. I will figure it out. Soon. In the new year. By the next con. Or the one after that. I have the definite feeling that things will just fall into place once Simon and I know where we're going to college. And we don't want to force the river, if you know what I mean."

"I don't," said Josie.

"Well, never mind. Just trust me," I said.

"Okay. I guess."

We rejoined the Bloodygits.

Scene 4

Hope

SEBASTIAN: Zoe, are you breaking up with Simon?

ME: No.

SEBASTIAN: Just asking. Calm down.

ME: I'm calm! I'm calm!

Awkward silence.

MELDEL: So, to tactfully change the subject, what's the final
word on where you are all applying to college?

As far as I was concerned, this was not a subject change,
but I recognized that Meldel didn't know that.

CAM: My first choice is NYU.

SEBASTIAN: Oh, that's great! Great! I was hoping!

CAM: I really want to be in New York. I love it there. So also some of the CUNY schools. My backup is Georgia.

MELDEL: Zoe and Liv?

ME: Well, my list is too long to go over it all. Simon now wants somewhere close to Boston, so our top choices are Boston University and Tufts. And we have a couple other local schools as possibilities, too.

SEBASTIAN: What about Boston College?

ME: No. I'm not very religious, but I'm just not comfortable with a traditionally Catholic school. Simon said he understood. And we didn't apply to Brandeis in case Simon wouldn't be comfortable with a traditionally Jewish school.

MELDEL: Is Simon Catholic? Josie, are you Catholic?

JOSIE: Yes, we are, but our family doesn't agree with everything.

LIV: Well, who does?

SEBASTIAN: Liv? Colleges?

LIV: I've applied early decision to Smith, and that's it. If I don't get in early, I'll still have time to apply elsewhere.

TODD: Smith? What? Never heard of it.

MELDEL: It's a women's college in Massachusetts, one of the Seven Sisters. They're like the women's version of the Ivies. Nice, Liv! Good luck! Only, will you be comfortable there?

LIV: I think so, yes. I've talked to a lot of people, including the basketball coach and a couple other nonbinary students, and also the head of their program in women and gender, which is what I think I want to major in.

ME: Smith is less than two hours from Boston, so maybe I'll see a lot of Liv.

CAM: Liv hasn't yet visited this palace of perfection, mind you.

LIV: The admissions director talked to me. I'll visit if I get in. Like I said, I'll still have time to apply elsewhere, and they also said they would still let me turn them down if I was uncomfortable, even though I applied early decision. But I have a good feeling. Also, Zoe went to see it for me. We did a campus tour together, sort of, with me on the phone.

ME: I'm just glad applications are over. I only wish I'd written a better essay.

LIV: What did you write about?

ME: (Sighs) Why I love making a to-do list.

MELDEL: Oookay.

ME: Every time I tried to write something else, it fell apart on me.

(Silence.)

ME: Oh, God. Is it really so bad?

TODD: You seem so normal at first, but you are peculiar in your own way, aren't you, Zoe?

ME: But how peculiar is it? It's really about the importance of logistics. Lists are a very helpful tool in life!

MELDEL: I really, really wish you'd asked for my guidance.

ME: Liv read my essay and didn't think it was bad!

LIV: I liked it.

CAM: What did your friend Maggie think?

ME: Maggie has her own problems. I didn't want to bug her with college stuff. She doesn't want to go to college at all. She wants to apprentice to become an electrician. Her parents are not thrilled.

MELDEL: Stop changing the subject. I am a best-selling writer to be, and you didn't even ask me to help.

TODD: She feels hurt. You hurt her.

ME: It was my essay! I just couldn't think of anything else to write, okay? I tried to write about being a media manager, but it just turned into a rant about Wentworth.

SEBASTIAN: Does anyone else find Zoe's vendetta against that cat disturbing?

ME: It's not a vendetta.

JOSIE: I like Wentworth.

ME: What?

JOSIE: He seemed to like me, too, that time I met him.

ME: That's because you just petted him and told him how pretty he was! The fact is, Wentworth can't follow directions. It's not a vendetta. I am exercising good business sense.

SEBASTIAN: You expect a cat to follow directions?

ME: He's a working cat, okay? He has professional obligations!

MELDEL: Todd, you're right. She only seems normal at first.

ME: Bloodygits, Wentworth peed in Maggie's handbag. Which was a critical prop for the video! Not to mention Maggie's property.

SEBASTIAN: Well, that's probably because he just wanted to nap or cuddle or whatever, and you were bugging him to follow directions.

ME: Have you met him? Have you *met* Wentworth, Sebastian? No, you have not! So how are you entitled to an opinion?

MELDEL: Ahem. Zoe, I believe we were discussing your essay, and your failure to seek professional help.

TODD: (Snicker.)

ME: Ellen From Finance is also a cat and *she* follows directions.

Just saying. There are cats and there are cats. I like cats
that do their jobs!

SEBASTIAN: But a cat's job—

MELDEL: Essay. Essay! I don't want to hear anything more
about the cat! We need to focus on Zoe's essay! We can
come back to the cat.

ME: I don't want to come back to the cat.

MELDEL: Good. Let's talk about your essay.

ME: There's nothing to discuss. I did it. I wrote what I wrote.
It's done.

CAM: I wonder if you were trying to sabotage yourself?

ME: What is this, attack Zoe day?

LIV: People. Stop. I read Zoe's essay. It was a fine essay. It was
unusual! I know it sounds like a stupid topic, but it really
wasn't.

ME: Sounds stupid?

LIV: I said it *wasn't* stupid.

ME: Bloodygits, look, I don't have anything important to say.
Simon did. He wrote all about his work with Senator
Pratt, and how he's looking within our immediate com-
munities for kids who can speak out, like Greta Thunberg.
He wants to be the one to help elevate those voices.
Senator Pratt is all about inclusive community voices of
all ages and from all walks of life. She's a sign of politics to
come. She's the kind of leadership we need, and anything
he can do to help—

TODD: Weeping hemorrhage, stop. Just. Please. Stop.

ME: What did you say?

JOSIE: He said weeping hemorrhage. It's just something the

fans are starting to say. You know. Blood-related phrases.
As curses.

TODD: You were having hemorrhage of the mouth there, Zoe.
You're having a day.

MELDEL: Todd.

TODD: What?

MELDEL: Be nice.

TODD: I'm nice. I just don't want her going on about politics.
It's pointless.

ME: Pointless?! You're old enough to vote! Do you vote, Todd?
Do you? Do you use your privilege as a citizen to raise
your lawful voice, or do you trample on that privilege by
ignoring it and calling it pointless?

TODD: It's entirely my own business whether I vote.

ME: Do. You. Vote? I want to know!

TODD: Voting doesn't matter, because the planet is voting
with its feet and it's too late. Everything we do is just
passing the time. My plan is to pass it as pleasantly as
possible and have as much fun as I can. Carpe diem, baby.
Carpe diem.

LIV: I disagree. We can't know whether whatever we do now
is going to be meaningful or meaningless. We have to
try. It's our future at stake. It doesn't mean we can't have
regular lives at the same time.

ME: We need that balance for sanity. Responsibility doesn't
mean no joy.

TODD: Think that if you like, Liv and Zoe and whoever. In my
opinion, humanity is racing down the steep slope to the
apocalypse. No brakes. So let's give up.

JOSIE: Are you okay, Zoe? You look weird.

ME: I'm fine. Just thinking.

TODD: Always a mistake.

I grimaced at him.

They went on talking, but I tuned out for a moment.

I had had a realization when I wrote my essay about planning and lists. Planning helps me feel like I am in control, not only of the details of my life, but also of my own despair. For me, detailed planning *represents* hope. Hope isn't the same as conviction, though. I think hope is inherently a wobbly place. Hope may be the thing with feathers—nod to Emily Dickinson—but that doesn't mean it will fly. Sometimes it's stuck on the ground, like a turkey. Hope is just possibility. And it's not enough! Whereas lists are possibility made action, which is better than hope. For me.

I had started writing the essay and that was where—to my surprise—I ended up. Even if it wasn't great, I was telling the truth. About what I believe. About who I am. About why lists are not a shallow thing. About planning as a tool for survival.

I hadn't shown my essay to Simon, though. I wasn't completely sure he'd like where I went with it, or what I was saying about myself. Anyway, he hadn't asked to read it, not even after I read his.

Scene 5

Capitalism

SEBASTIAN: I think we're going to save ourselves. Not everyone will make it, and things will change, but humanity will go on. How can you be a fan of science fiction and not believe that?

TODD: Believe that science will save us?

SEBASTIAN: Yeah.

TODD: Science is one of the things that's doomed us, man.

MELDEL: Maybe we should—

JOSIE: Change the subject?

CAM: I feel like all we've done in this conversation is change the subject. But fine. Hemoglobin! Fans are saying that now, too.

JOSIE: I don't like that one. Listen, Bloodygits, I need to send you a link—this one guy wrote this whole post, like, with footnotes, about blood swears in *Bleeders*.

MELDEL: I read that. He makes the case that there's an etymological relationship of *Bleeders* phrases to Elizabethan swears like "God's blood" and "God's wounds."

CAM: God save us.

ME: (Trying to sound normal) I'm confused. The crew of *Mae Jemison* doesn't actually swear that way. They use Mongolian-derived phrases.

TODD: Fandom can diverge from canon.

ME: Hello, I know that!

Another awkward pause.

CAM: So, are we going to talk about Episode 8? Like, at all? Please?

MELDEL: I don't know if I can! I'm so horrified—Celie can't be dead! This totally wrecks my fanfic, Bloodygits.

CAM: Always about your fanfic. How about mine?

MELDEL: Wait, you're writing Celie dead?!

CAM: I programmed her personality into the head of the Sanitation Soldier. Remember, the one Celie put in the kitchen to make toast?

TODD: Hey, that's not bad! I can do that cosplay!

SEBASTIAN: But what if she's not really dead?

CAM: I can't stand how the episodes don't come out all at once or at least on a schedule. I hate waiting.

MELDEL: It's about money. I don't understand the details, but I hear AMT is working on finances and she might have a big investor on the line. That will help.

JOSIE: Isn't SlamDunk their investor?

CAM: One of their investors, but I guess more are needed. Or at least one other big one. Or advertisers. Whatever. It's expensive to produce the show.

JOSIE: I hate capitalism.

TODD: What's capitalism got to do with it?

JOSIE: *Bleeders* is art! But it's got to act like a business. That's not fair.

TODD: Listen, if the United States were a socialist country, do you think *Bleeders* would get financed by the state? The answer is no. There would be no artistic paradise. You've been listening to your brother the social-justice warrior too much, if you ask me.

JOSIE: You don't even know Simon!

TODD: I don't have to know him to know that everybody and everything has to find a way to pay their own way in this world. Art is no exception.

MELDEL: Unfortunately, that's true. It's why I plan to be a best-selling author.

TODD: And who says *Bleeders* is art, anyway? It's entertainment. It has to entertain enough people to pay its own way, or it's gone. That's fair.

ME: But not all art is popular. It's still art. It's still good. It's still worthwhile and it has a place in the world even if it's not popular.

LIV: Right. And sometimes good stuff isn't loved or recognized right away. The original *Star Trek* got canceled. Van Gogh wasn't appreciated in his own time. But even when not a lot of people appreciate something, you can't say it shouldn't exist. It's more complicated than that.

There has to be a place for art that isn't about money or popularity. And if just a few people love something, that something is still of worth.

MELDEL: Right. Not everything can be measured in dollars and cents.

ME: Agreed. We love *Bleeders*, we know it's wonderful, but maybe not enough people will feel that way for it to go on. That doesn't mean we're wrong.

TODD: You are naive. Not all good things survive in this world. It's Darwinian law. Right? Van Gogh died. End of story. I will not mention our planet again. Notice my restraint.

CAM: So noted.

LIV: Everyone dies, Todd. But art needn't.

JOSIE: But lots of good art is forgotten. Or is never seen or appreciated by many people. But it still existed. Doesn't that matter?

ME: Yes. It matters.

CAM: It definitely matters. And whatever Todd is saying, we know he loves *Bleeders*, too.

TODD: I do. But it might be doomed. And I'm a realist.

All of us sighed at once.

TODD: But we'll always have Seasons 1 and 2!

CAM: And maybe more. The *Firefly* fans and the *Veronica Mars* fans had the same problem. They ended up getting more, later on. And Star Trek—

LIV: We know about Star Trek. The show that would not die.

ME: Let's just say it straight out, though, okay? We'd better face it. It's looking like AMT is getting ready to wrap up the whole series arc early, this season. Just in case she can't find financing for Season 3. And that's why Celie is dead.

JOSIE: If she's dead.

ME: (Softly) I think she's dead.

LIV: But it's not over yet! We need to redouble our efforts, Bloodygits! We've let ourselves be distracted. We have to get back to doing everything in our power to pressure SlamDunk and show them that *Bleeders* has passionate fans, and we have to work to get more fans. So, since we're stuck with capitalism—Todd is right about that—

TODD: Thank you for flinging me a bone.

LIV: We have to work with the rules of capitalism. Let's go full court press, now that college applications are out of the way.

SEBASTIAN: Let's talk about next month. Where we're going to meet and what we're going to do.

LIV: Any ideas? Anyone?

ME: Actually, yes. Bloodygits, do you know anything about Lilithcon? I've been doing research on it.

We hung up an hour later, with plans starting to form for January.

Josie said, "Should I text my mom to come get me?"

The pleasure of my having talked everybody into Lilithcon faded. All my real-life problems slammed back down on me.

"I'll drive you. Uh. Do you know if Simon is home now?"

Josie shrugged.

I texted Simon. Luckily, he answered right away: he was

at work, as usual nowadays. I decided this was a sign that I should indeed do what I wanted to do, which was not to tell him what was going on with my parents. Yet, anyway.

"Are you ready?" I said to Josie.

"Yeah."

"Josie? Listen, next month will have to be the very last con for me. It's like you said. The lying has to stop. For both of us. No matter what happens with *Bleeders*."

Josie looked stricken.

"I'm really sorry I got you into this," I said.

"No!" said Josie. "No! You'll figure it out for us! I know you will, Zoe! We have to go on! You said before that maybe it would all come right on its own. Maybe it will! Can't we wait? Until after you get into college and everything. Like you said."

I stared into her pleading eyes.

Maybe, I thought. Maybe I could find the perfect, balanced way out, the one where we could have everything. And no lies. Maybe it would really all come right once I knew about college. Many things resolve themselves given a little time . . .

Or maybe I just needed a better to-do list.

EPISODE 5

January/February 2019
@Lilithcon

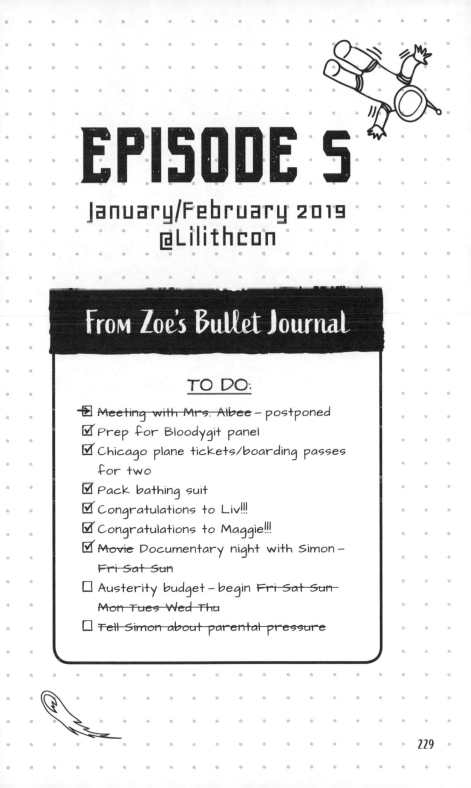

From Zoe's Bullet Journal

<u>TO DO</u>:

- ☑ ~~Meeting with Mrs. Albee~~ – postponed
- ☑ Prep for Bloodygit panel
- ☑ Chicago plane tickets/boarding passes for two
- ☑ Pack bathing suit
- ☑ Congratulations to Liv!!!
- ☑ Congratulations to Maggie!!!
- ☑ ~~Movie~~ Documentary night with Simon – ~~Fri Sat Sun~~
- ☐ Austerity budget – begin ~~Fri Sat Sun Mon Tues Wed Thu~~
- ☐ ~~Tell Simon about parental pressure~~

Scene 1

An Artisanal Con

The Bloodygits stood in the muggy, chlorinated air of the Lilithcon hotel lobby, which was also, incidentally, an indoor waterpark. I swiveled out of the way just in time to avoid a soaking wet little girl in an Octonauts swimsuit, who had almost run into my knees.

Cam said accusingly, "Zoe?"

I pretended not to hear him, which was not hard because of all the screeching little kids.

In hindsight, there had been a clue: the con's low, low price. I had counted that in its favor, like its being in the Chicago suburb of Evanston—site of Northwestern University. Northwestern was no longer highly ranked on our list now that we were targeting Boston. Still, it had made my trip marginally plausible to Simon and also meant my travel costs were underwritten by my parents. (I still had to pay Josie's costs, however.)

Maybe I should put Aragorn up for sale on eBay? If Aragorn were gone, I could fearlessly invite Simon over again. Luckily, he'd been too busy to notice I'd stopped. My father might thank me, too, since my mother had taken to wandering into the family room simply to gaze at Aragorn. She had bought my father a black cape—but I did not want to think about private parental cosplay.

"Zoe?" Cam insisted. Meldel had her hands on her hips, Sebastian had cocked a questioning brow, and the others—except Josie, who was looking at her phone—were giving me the hairy eyeball.

I gave it right back to them. "Don't prejudge. This con is going to rock!"

I had our panel presentation fully organized, including getting everyone to sign the mandatory release for recording, making an awesome PowerPoint with a (Todd-prepared) soundtrack, and basically planning every second. Meldel and Josie and Cam had fanfic to hand out, and we'd all be in our cosplay. We'd start by explaining a bit about the show and introducing the characters, and then I'd planned a discussion about women in science fiction and fantasy and science and medicine, and we would encourage audience participation. Also, I had spotted a Target across the parking lot. We'd serve Twizzlers! That would bring in the hordes! Also—for me privately—it would be an easy app ride from here to Northwestern. I would tour, even though I already knew, from the snowstorm brewing at this very moment, that Chicago winters were not for me. However, they probably explained this hotel.

The Bloodygits must never know that I had thought the hotel looked fun.

"No offense," Cam told me. "But I'm thinking we fire you from responsibility for picking our next con."

"All in favor?" said Liv instantly, and I wondered if having their college plans settled had given Liv a bit too much extra confidence. Meldel and Todd and Sebastian and Josie (traitor!) shot their hands up in the air.

"Although, then again," said Todd, eyeing the Roaming River a few yards away, where a woman in a full wetsuit was handing kids colorful inner tubes before they launched into the water. "Maybe if you had a nice cold brew while you floated in your inner tube?"

Todd was not exactly the ally I would have picked.

"Lilithcon is homegrown," I explained with restraint. "Didn't you read my notes? There's no rich sponsor trying to make a big profit here. It's just the fans putting together programming of interest to other fans who are feminists and who happen to love fantasy and science fiction. The only celebrities coming are, like, YA writers who'd never even *dream* of charging you to take a photo with them! The Lilithcon audience is simply a better fit for *Bleeders* than any big corporate con."

"You might even call Lilithcon an *artisanal* con," Liv murmured blandly.

"We're going direct to the people here," I persisted. "We bypass the corporate overlords and their rules and regulations and money-grubbing. It's those overlords that threaten our show."

"You sound like Simon," Josie remarked. "If he were a fan."

"Well," I said. "Maybe Simon would like this *particular* con."

"No." Josie looked down at her sneakers. She sighed. "He wouldn't."

She had seemed tense all morning while we traveled from Boston. Of course, we were still sneaking around on her family. At least my parents now knew the full story.

I pushed down the guilty knowledge that my parents' approval hinged on their thinking my love for *Bleeders* meant I was losing interest in Simon. Which I wasn't. Oh, and their not knowing I had brought Josie. I planned to enjoy myself this weekend. Time was running out for my fandom freedom. In just a few weeks, we'd get college acceptances (please, God). After that, I'd be so, so good. The goodest. Lawful good. I'd tell Simon everything, once it was safely in the past. He would take my confession well. It wasn't like this was important. Our future was important, not the past.

Last Sunday, Simon and I had watched a documentary about Ruth Bader Ginsburg, the Supreme Court justice. I could easily imagine Simon working for the good of the people until four in the morning every night, like she did.

I wondered what I'd be secretly binge-watching when he was working his twenty-hour days. No, I'd be working just as hard, by his side. Or I'd be doing something to earn money for us while he performed important public service. RBG's husband had been a tax attorney. I'd probably love that because, most likely, spreadsheets would be involved.

At that time, I would watch only educational documentaries. I would never read romances or fantasy or science fiction or celebrity biographies or murder mysteries. I would certainly not make cat videos; that was not an acceptable profession.

"Come on, Bloodygits," I said. "Let's give this con a chance! They're giving *us* a chance! We proposed our panel late and it was still accepted. These are our people!"

"Our people?" Cam gestured to two mothers and a dad trudging by, wet, exhausted, with their toddlers.

"Our people will be here shortly." I had to raise my voice as the Roaming River swirled a screaming clot of older kids around behind the hotel registration desk. "I have had many reassuring communications with the conference organizers. Also, our hotel room only costs eighty-nine dollars a day. Plus tax. Divide by seven, Bloodygits, divide by seven."

"At that price, we could have gotten two rooms," said Meldel thoughtfully.

"No," I said, alarmed. "We'll enjoy being together. We'll take turns sleeping. If anybody does. Who needs sleep?"

"Airfare wasn't bad, either," Sebastian offered.

I was happy for this support but nonetheless winced. I was recovering from earlier anxiety about whether Winter Storm Natasha would cancel flights altogether. We'd all gotten in by the skin of our teeth. Natasha was just getting going now—the weather-folk said it would be totally crazy tonight.

Suddenly there came an explosion from Splish-Splash Mountain.

"Anybody bring a swimsuit?" Liv asked. "In case the con isn't here after all and we all just end up hanging out poolside?"

Cam said, "Liv. Pee."

"No! Nobody would pee in the water!" Sebastian pointed. "Look. There's a sign."

We all read the sign.

"I used to pee in pools all the time when I was a kid," said Todd nostalgically. "What a feeling."

Liv took a step away from him. I decided not to mention that I had brought my bathing suit. The din of splashing and shouting rose and fell, rose and fell.

"I'll go check us in," Meldel said.

Since you had to figure that a hotel—even a "hotel"—wouldn't be happy about seven people (especially teenagers) checking into one room, we'd determined on a methodology involving Meldel and her credit card. While we waited, Todd entertained us with a dramatic reading from the hotel brochure. "The Family-Friendly Slide Will Make You Smile from Ear to Ear! Relax on the Pink Sands of the Beach by the Wave Pool! Or Brave the Twists and Turns of the Tornado Tower! Relax in Your Inner Tube on the Roaming River!"

Meldel returned. "Room 406. It turns out that the convention center area is on the other side of the hotel. There's a totally different entrance. Our people will be over there."

I exhaled in relief.

Meldel said, "We follow the Roaming River, turn left at the Tadpole Pond—"

"—and straight on till morning?" suggested Liv.

"Left at Lily Pad Crossing." Meldel waved a map. "And we're supposed to go up in an elevator at some point. They told me at the desk that this used to be a multibuilding motel, but they built new ceilings and covered walkways to bring all the buildings together."

We dragged our suitcases after Meldel, avoiding puddles. Sebastian fell into step beside me at the back of the group. "Zoe," he whispered. "Top secret! I have a new bleeding apparatus!"

This was the first time I'd focused fully on Sebastian since we all met up at the airport, and he was looking good. His winter jacket seemed new, and it was a great color and style for him. He had gotten a haircut and cleaned his glasses. Even his posture was better. In some mysterious way, had disappointment in love been good for him?

"I thought you were giving up on the bleeding?"

"I thought so, too, after last time, but I changed my mind." He leaned in. "I was talking with my friend—this *other* friend, I mean, not one of us—who had a new idea for how to make it work. So, I experimented and I've got it, I think!" He lowered his voice even more. "I'll need help to set myself up. But only you, Zoe. I want it to be a surprise at our panel for the others."

Sebastian's eyes were eager, trusting. But I thought of the blood-spattered Aragorn in our family room and hardened my heart. "Sebastian, I don't know—"

"Zoe, I want Bloodygits to be proud of me. To see that I'm not a loser and that I can do this bleeding right."

"We don't think you're a loser! What happened at Weird World was an accident. Nobody blamed you."

He shook his head. "You pitied me. I know you did."

I was silent.

Sebastian said, "The thing is? This friend of mine? She wasn't sure, but she might actually be coming to this con. Like, in time for our panel tomorrow!"

I stopped walking and so did Sebastian.

"*She?*" I said.

Sebastian's voice was barely audible, but his eyes were wide with joy. "Remember Squirrel Girl? From *Weird World?* She found me! Online in the *Bleeders* forum! Can you believe it?"

My jaw nearly unhinged. "*Squirrel Girl?*"

"Yes! She's so smart! She helped me! She had this great idea for the bleeding."

"And did you also say that she's coming here? To Lilithcon?"

"Maybe? Her flight was canceled because of the storm, but she got rescheduled for tomorrow, and I'm hoping. She really cares about her design. Anyway, you'll help me, right? Just you, Zoe. I really don't want the others to know . . . and especially I don't want them to know about her. In case . . . well, you know. In case."

Sebastian was very obviously insane. Love will do that.

"Yes," I said. Because what else could I say? "Of course I'll help."

Scene 2

AMT!

The convention center part of the hotel was shabby and dated, and there weren't many people in actual cosplay. (In fairness, we weren't either. Yet.)

But.

The place was crammed with real fans, ordinary fans, fabulous fans, in their fannish T-shirts and hats and pins, fans of all ages, fans of all genders—though the majority were female or gender nonconforming. This was a feminist con, after all. There was a palpable buzz of interest and happiness in the air, which went a long way toward neutralizing the persistent whiff of chlorine. I noticed with enormous interest that absolutely everyone was wearing little ribbons that specified their pronouns.

And my Bloodygits were finally smiling. Cam nudged

me and indicated a coat closet with a hand-printed sign that said TO NARNIA. "I take it back, Zoe. You can organize the next con."

I felt warm and fuzzy as I looked around with renewed satisfaction.

Because this was such a small con, you didn't have to run from one hotel to another. Everything would happen in this one centralized space of meeting rooms and ball-rooms. (I resisted putting mental quotes around the word *ballroom*.) Also, I had been reliably informed that there would be no lines, that you could show up for a panel right before it started and still get in.

The Bloodygits huddled together to consult the printed program, which, let me just say, they had had plenty of opportunity to look at online before we got there because I had sent them the link. I had *also* sent personalized sched-ule suggestions, on which I had expended a certain amount of unappreciated effort. But at least now they were under-standing that here, despite the smaller size of this con—or *because* of it—there were multiple interesting things to do at any one time.

For the first time in our connish lives together, we actually ought to split up to pursue diverse interests. I felt wistful about it, which I hadn't realized I would. But it was only for a short time.

"We'll all meet back here at six?" Sebastian said, a little anxiously.

"Yes. I made a dinner reservation for us in the Con Suite," I said.

"I wish I could be in two places at once!" Meldel said.

"But the writers' workshop, well, I can't miss that. Ramona Freeman and Sandra Wu will be there!"

The fantasy writers' workshop was first choice for Meldel, Josie, and Cam. Todd was going to "Sentient Beasts in Science Fiction," and Liv wanted to roam the ballroom, where there were booths with tarot reading, hair braiding, button making, and a clothing swap.

Sebastian went with me (to my surprise, because I'd thought he'd go to a cosplay creation workshop) to a panel called "Redemption and Revenge: Antiheroines and Villainesses Taking Control." It was about retelling fairy tales to center the experience of the women involved. The major point was that women in positions of power were often unthinkingly coded as evil, and why was that?

As part of the discussion, someone brought up Ruth Bader Ginsburg and also Hillary Clinton, saying that Hillary had been coded like an evil witch, and somehow Ruth Bader Ginsburg hadn't been. And why was that? And how did tropes in fiction influence thinking in real life?

I sat on the edge of my chair and half wished Simon could hear all this. But he would never believe that the kind of thinking that went into fiction (especially the kind of fiction talked about at a con) and fictional analysis intersected with real life. If he were here, he'd be sitting with his arms crossed and a skeptical look on his face. Very likely he'd raise his hand during the discussion and say something devastating yet true and smart that would topple the central thesis, ending the discussion altogether.

It was better to be with Sebastian, who even took notes, which surprised me. He wrote down the names of every book and movie that was mentioned, even nudging me at one point to correct his spelling of *Maleficent*.

Then one of the panelists mentioned *Bleeders*. She talked about how maybe Monica was shaping up as a classic female villain. I was so excited, and she saw it.

"Hey, are you a Bloodygit?" she called out to me. (There were only about twenty people in the room.)

"Yes!" I exclaimed. I pointed my chin at Sebastian. "He is, too."

Sebastian waved his pen.

Afterward, the panelist came over to say hello. Her name was Sheilah.

I said, "But listen, from the beginning, all the hints of potential villainy have been about Lorelei, not Monica."

"Misdirection?" Sheilah raised her eyebrows.

"But it's Lorelei who just killed Celie."

"I'm not so sure that means what we think it means."

"And some aren't sure Celie is dead," said Sebastian. "And it might not matter, because aren't you worried *Bleeders* is going to be canceled? We are."

"Actually." Sheilah leaned in close to Sebastian and me. "I just heard that there's going to be an announcement about the future of *Bleeders*—from AMT herself, *in person*, at Bean Con in Boston. That's in April." She sighed. "Two whole months away."

I froze.

"Boston?" I repeated.

Sheilah nodded. "AMT, and also at least two of the actors." She pulled out her phone. Sebastian crowded in next to me to look at the website.

Just announced!
Special Bean Con guests of honor!
From Bleeders: *Anna Maria Turner, along with Jocelyn Upchurch (Captain) and Hugh Nguyen (Torrance).*

"Torrance and Captain!" Sebastian pressed both hands to his chest. "I may have a heart attack."

Sheilah grinned at us. "You Bloodygits are going, then?"

"Of course!" Sebastian said. "Zoe lives near Boston, and so does our friend Josie! We'll be there for sure!"

No, no, no, I thought frantically.

The next thing I knew, I was walking down a corridor beside Sebastian as he nattered on about Boston and how great it would be to meet AMT and Torrance and Captain. That he was definitely going to get his picture taken with them, no matter what it cost. That maybe we could all be in cosplay and do one big photo session together with the actors. He could just take the bus from New York to Boston, it would be excellent. We could all stay at my house, right? Just like we'd all crammed into his dorm at New York Comic Con and into Todd's and Meldel's rooms at Weird World.

So my brain was flashing *danger, careful* even before Sebastian added:

"And we can meet Simon at last."

"Wait!" I said quickly. "Simon doesn't understand about fandom, remember? Also, about staying at my house? I don't know..."

"Oh. Right. I forgot." After a moment, he added comfortably, "We'll figure things out. Bloodygits always do."

I said nothing.

"Just think of it," Sebastian said dreamily. "Every single Bloodygit in the fandom will be there, if they can possibly make it!"

I nodded, feeling miserable. "Yeah."

Every single one except, maybe, me.

Scene 3

Disaster

At six o'clock inside the Con Suite, Todd raised his arms above his head in triumph and yelled, "Hallelujah! We shall not after all starve!"

Many people grinned at him. He grinned back toothily.

I had thought that Sebastian would explode into the news about AMT at Bean Con as soon as he saw the others. But in the moment, he was too busy admiring the spread of food in the Con Suite. With the part of my mind that was not fraying with anxiety, I was grateful for the reprieve.

I didn't know if I could handle Bean Con. Would having it so near home make things harder? Or easier?

"Good job, Zoe," Liv said. "We won't have to spend a penny on food." They petted a "new" scarf from the clothing swap; it was green and featured Marvin the Martian.

"It actually is pretty awesome, isn't it?" I managed.

Most cons had Con Suites in which you could find free snacks all day and into the night, provided by fans who could afford it and/or who lived locally. They would schlep in grocery bags with store-bought muffins and donuts, potato chips and cookies. There would be loaves of bread and peanut butter and jelly jars, and bowls of hard-boiled eggs. Also urns of coffee, bottles of soda, gallons of milk, flats of water.

Lilithcon took its hospitality to a new and breathtaking level.

Abundant snacks were available 24/7, yes, but the Con Suite also offered actual nutritious meals. All you needed was a reservation and an official con badge. The idea was to take care of fans who couldn't afford food on top of their badges and travel costs.

The buffet offered barbecue chicken sandwiches on rolls or gluten-free bread, vegan or vegetarian or gluten-free spinach-and-potato curry, and side dishes and salads.

Once we were seated with food, Sebastian pounded on the table. "Attention, Bloodygits!" To gasps, he told the news, and finished: "And we'll all stay at Zoe's house!"

Josie said, "If that's okay with Zoe's parents?"

The Bloodygits looked at me.

I said carefully, "I was wondering if we should cram into a room at the hotel, instead of staying at my house. So we'd be nearby to the con. Maybe I could, um, subsidize the hotel cost." Oh, God. Somehow.

"Ah. You don't want us staying with you," Todd said.

"No!" I said. "I mean, yes, I mean, no, I mean—that's not it. That's not why—I mean, it's that . . . uh, so, you all remember how I haven't exactly really told Simon about *Bleeders*? Or about you? I mean, I will tell him. I just haven't yet."

"Of course," said Liv. "But you told your parents?"

"I did," I said. "But I'm not sure how I could keep you all staying at my house from Simon. And, well, I'm not sure my parents would let me keep it from him."

"They like that Zoe is cheating on my brother," said Josie.

"I am not cheating!" I flared.

"Lying. They think it's a sign that they're going to break up." Josie started eating again.

"I am confused," said Sebastian.

I pushed my hands through my hair. "My parents just think it's a bad idea for Simon and me to go to college together. They're not pressuring me, not exactly, but . . . I feel like I'm being torn in half. I don't know what to do!"

Cam and Liv each had one elbow on the table, in mirror image of each other, with their chins propped in their hands and their eyes calm and waiting on my face. They had never looked more like twins.

"We love you," Liv said. "You'll figure this out."

"And we don't have to stay at your house for Bean Con," said Cam. "It's not a big deal."

"My parents would welcome you," I said desperately. "But Simon—I don't see how I'd keep it a secret if you were at my house. I mean, I don't *want* to keep it a secret any longer. I'm going to tell him on Monday. I've just decided! This minute, I've decided!"

"Then there's no problem!" said Sebastian.

I had to stop to pull some air into my lungs. "Only, see, Simon is a person who is totally and completely honest, and he'd never lie about anything."

Todd raised a skeptical eyebrow. "Not about anything? Ever?"

"It's true!" I said hotly.

Josie nodded gloomily. "It is true."

"I bow down." Todd waggled his eyebrows. "This Simon bro is *good*. I need to take lessons!"

I glared at him. "Believe what you like. Simon isn't going to understand that I lied." I blinked several times, hard. "*Bleeders* wasn't supposed to be a big thing. It was a *little* lie! And now I don't know what to do." I was whining. I couldn't help it.

"Do you want us to skip Bean Con altogether?" asked Liv. "We can."

"We can't!" said Sebastian.

"No!" I cried. "Of course not! You have to go! I would never, ever ask you not to go!"

"You want us to go, but you'll skip?" asked Meldel.

"*I'm* not skipping," Josie said determinedly. "I'll find a way on my own."

"I want to go, too!" I said miserably. "And it would be so, so much fun if we were all camped out at my house. We could take the T—that's the subway—into the city for the con every day. My parents . . ." I buried my face in my hands, because I could so easily imagine all my friends at my house, laughing and talking, everyone crowded together in the kitchen with my dad making pancakes. "My parents would like all of you."

"Well, I'm creative." Meldel propped her chin on her hand thoughtfully. "And you're clever. And if Simon weren't capable of being deceived, you'd never have gotten this far. Let's just make it work. I'm totally in, so how can we fail?"

"It'll be good, sneaky fun!" said Todd.

I shook my head. "Bloodygits, no. I'm done. I have to put *Bleeders* behind me. I have to become the person that Simon thinks I am. It's my only hope."

They looked at me.

"I can't change what I did," I said. "But I can stop doing it. I can do the right thing."

"I thought you were going to tell Simon," said Sebastian. "Didn't you say you were going to tell him? Just now?"

"I said that. But I don't know if I will," I said. "I know it's the right thing, but he'll hate it. I'm scared. Maybe if I just keep my mouth shut and behave from now on. Maybe that's good enough."

"I continue confused," said Sebastian.

"So is Zoe," said Liv quietly.

I closed my eyes.

"Okay," said Liv finally. "We love you. We'll go, and you won't. If that's how it has to be."

I swallowed hard.

"Zoe will change her mind," said Todd. "She'll be there with us. She always is."

"No," I said.

Josie said, in a small voice, "Maybe everybody can stay at my house instead."

I stared at her, appalled. "Josie, obviously *that* isn't going—"

I stopped. I did a double take. There was something very weird about Josie's expression. I said carefully, "Wait. Josie, your mom doesn't know about Bloodygits?" I had meant it to be a statement, but it came out as a question.

Josie cleared her throat. "I had to tell my mom. Um. Today. After we landed at O'Hare. Remember how I was gone for a long time in the ladies' room? My mom found out I wasn't at Lucy Wyatt's like I said I would be. She texted me and I had to call her back and she was, uh, pretty mad."

"She knows I'm here, too?" I already knew the answer, though.

"Yes."

I might throw up. "So she knows I lied to Simon?"

"Yes," said Josie.

My world was now balanced on the pointy end of a pin. I leaned forward. "Is she going to tell him?"

"I don't know," said Josie. "I told her your parents already knew."

"Why didn't you tell me this was happening today?" I wailed. "Why?"

"I was waiting for the right moment. Just like you've been! Maybe she won't tell Simon. She knows you don't want him to know, and she said that you weren't her business, that *I* was her business."

"Really?" I let myself hope.

"Although then again, she's really mad. Like I said."

"Did she say anything else?"

"That she needed to think and I was to check in with her like every hour while I'm here so she knows I'm okay."

"And of course you've done that," I said.

"Oh. Uh. I forgot." At the look on my face, she said, "I'll text her right now, okay? I was going to!"

I thought about choking Josie using Liv's nice long Marvin the Martian scarf.

My phone rang. Actually rang. Not a text. A call.

I looked at it, even though I knew perfectly well who it was.

I thought about not picking up.

It rang again.

I picked up.

"Zoe," he said.

"Simon," I croaked.

I knew already. I knew from the hard way that he said my name. I knew even before he said, "Tell me it's not true. Tell me that you aren't at some stupid comic con thing. And while you're at it, tell me that you haven't taken my little sister there, behind her mother's back. Do you know what that is, literally, Zoe? It's kidnapping. You kidnapped my little sister and took her to fucking Chicago!"

Simon never raises his voice. Simon never swears.

I looked at my Bloodygits, who were staring at me with their mouths open and their eyes wide. Even Todd had stopped eating, his forkful of gluten-free potato curry suspended halfway to his mouth.

Words convulsed in my throat. *I'm so sorry, please forgive me, I can explain and when I'm home, I'll tell you everything, please just listen with an open mind. And some compassion. You love me, remember? We love each other! Remember?*

I meant to say those things to Simon. I did.

Instead I said, "It's actually not true. We're not in fucking Chicago. Josie and I are in fucking Evanston."

Scene 4

Doom River

Winter Storm Natasha was in full fury outside. The wind whipped giant snowflakes beneath the yellowish light of the parking lot lamps. I hurried through the cold glassed-in hallway between the convention center and the water park. I had my thin hotel towel and my bathing suit. Maybe the storm would cause flight cancellations. Good. I could stay in Evanston late, or forever. In my head, I began a to-do list: Beg parents for help and understanding. Take the test for my GED. Get a job here doing . . . something. Attend Northwestern. Never, ever see Simon again.

It could work.

The water park was open until nine o'clock. Strings of twinkling lights above encouraged evening use, but the families had mostly disappeared. So quiet, so skanky—this water park was exactly the right place to be miserable. I gave our room number to a yawning clerk and received a purple plastic bracelet and a big black inner tube. Five minutes later, I floated alone on the Roaming River. As my inner tube drifted by a chest of plastic pirate treasure, the sound system began playing Disney music. I opened my mouth and wailed along with Elsa. She was right: it was time for both of us to let it go.

Under the fairy lights, I clutched my cell phone in front of my wet face and checked Instagram. Simon had changed his profile photo from one of him and me to a group of Senator Pratt's volunteers holding a VOTE FOR CHANGE sign.

Wow. Somehow Simon Murawski, busy, busy Simon Murawski, had found time in his schedule full of things that were bigger and more important than me and my selfish little ordinary mind and my petty obsession with imaginary people living imaginary lives in outer space. Somehow Simon Lawful Good had found the time to announce to his entire circle that he was no longer in a relationship with me. He'd done this within, what? Fifteen minutes of breaking up with me? *Impressive!* Or maybe he'd done it before even talking with me. If you want something done well and quickly, Simon's your man. I'll give you his number. He can accuse you of things without even pausing to ask if you might just possibly happen to have your own side of the story. Because he's never wrong, oh no, he's never, ever wrong.

Lawful Good is a terrible, merciless character alignment.

I wiped snot off my face and raised a trembling,

wrinkled fingertip to change my own profile picture to a photo of an orange Leuchtturm notebook, the one with creamy, dotted A5 pages, an elastic band to keep it shut, and two bookmarks. Only I hit the wrong thing and uploaded a picture of Wentworth. Wentworth! I started to try again, but my phone slipped from my hand and fell —*splash*—into the Roaming River. I attempted to heave myself out of the inner tube to grab it back, but my legs were stuck to the rubber and the tube kept moving. And really, who cared? Let people think I loved Wentworth when he didn't even like me! Fine.

It was all my fault. Everything was my fault. I was a liar and also, incidentally, Simon was correct—I was a kidnapper. Everything he said was true. He was Lawful Good, and I was not even Neutral Good. I was ... I was ...

Evil! I had to be evil. Evil people never think they're evil, which is why I'd missed my own slide into the pit of wickedness. Who'd have thought it would begin by falling in love with a TV show?

Why *should* Simon forgive me? I wasn't worthy of him and, actually, I never had been. I was shallow. Shallow as this so-called river! I'd be lucky if I wasn't arrested. Josie was underage. How come I hadn't thought *that* through? Also, Northwestern wouldn't accept me. No college would! Colleges were not interested in criminals. That Simon and I were over was only the tip of the disaster. Everything I had ever wanted was gone. And whose fault was it? Mine!

Everything came down to this one truth: I had traded in my boyfriend for a TV show.

On the bright side, at least somebody had cued up

classic sad songs here at the water park. I sang "Bad Blood."
I sang "Nine Hundred Miles." I sang "Dixie Chicken." I
sang "Killing Me Softly." I sang "Moon River." I twisted and
changed lyrics as appropriate:

> *Doom River*
> *Wider than a mile*
> *I've screwed it up in style today*
> *Dream crusher, you heartbreaker*
> *Wherever you're going*
> *I'm not going your way . . .*

I was wailing at the top of my lungs (*Doom River . . . and
meeeee . . .*) when my inner tube jerked to a stop. Someone
said my name. I forced open my salt-encrusted eyes.

I was at the landing. A long metal hook had caught my
tube and hauled it up next to the sign that said EXIT THE
RIDE VIA THE RAMP AT LEFT. Liv, who was wielding the
hook, raised an eyebrow at me. The other Bloodygits stood
there, too.

"We've been waiting for you to float by," said Liv.

"We yelled, but you didn't hear a thing," said Cam.

"We heard *you*, though," said Sebastian.

"Nice voice, nice lyrical improvisation," said Todd
approvingly. "Let me know if you want a part in my original
video project this semester."

I should have felt humiliated. But I didn't, maybe
because I had already hit bottom. Or maybe because . . .

They were here. Liv Cam Meldel Todd Sebastian Josie.
One two three four five six. They had come to find me. My

friends, my Bloodygits! They had come to pull me out of Doom River. I might be boyfriendless, but I wasn't alone.

"You've shivering," observed Meldel. "Here's a towel." She held it open for me. "It's thin, but it's clean and warm."

My friends loved me.

I was clambering out as Todd said, "I think I smell the kiddie pee."

Scene 5

From Zoe's Bullet Journal

WARDROBE FOR THE DARK SIDE

@ I showered using Meldel's French-milled shea butter soap, but I still sort of stink of chlorine. (Only chlorine. Hate Todd.)

@ Cam gave me his red tartan plaid flannel PJs to wear. Soft!

O Thought: Now that I have turned to the Dark Side, I should wear all black.

○ ~~Borrow~~ Steal (since am evil) Maggie's long swingy skirt.

◌ Pair it with black ballet flats. Or should
   a villainess wear stilettos? No, impractical for kicking butt. **Need boots.**

◌ Tight top or loose? Stupid question—
   definitely tight and slutty.

◌ Note: Cannot afford new Dark Side
   wardrobe.

   ✳ Thrift store?

   ✳ Borrow Dad's Aragorn cape?

ℰ Sebastian went out in the snowstorm
   for salted-caramel chocolate-chunk ice
   cream, which we all ate using the bells
   of the stethoscope-garrotes because S.
   only brought one plastic spoon. (For me.
   He thought I would eat it all myself! He
   was disappointed! Sorry to let you down,
   Sebastian, but I need to look my hottest
   when I sashay past Simon in my Dark Side
   slut-wear.)

ℰ I sang "Doom River" again all the way
   through, a cappella, and Josie played air
   piano and Sebastian air sax. Meldel invented
   a dance with foot stomps and hand-
   waving that became a line dance. We all

danced and sang, even Todd, then went
out into the hotel corridor and danced
down the stairs to the con meeting area.
Other people joined in and the line got long,
everybody stomping and singing and playing
air instruments.

@ Then I told everybody that I had traded in
my boyfriend for a TV show, but at least
it was a _good_ TV show, and they applauded
and asked about _Bleeders_, which Liv did a
really good job explaining, and people said
the show sounded awesome. Sebastian told
everybody to come to our _Bleeders_ panel
tomorrow to learn more. Then a Princess
Elsa cosplayer had me kneel. She gave
me her tiara and said I was now Princess
Bloody Dumpster. (I acted like a good
sport, but it was a stab to the heart,
like being told I was garbage. Meldel got
it. Once Elsa left she took the tiara
from me.)

@ We went back to our room to binge-
rewatch _Bleeders_ Season 2 and Josie sat
next to me and said it was all her fault and
she was sorry, and I said it wasn't, it was
my fault and my responsibility. We hugged.
Then Meldel said no, it was Simon's fault
also, and she talked ferociously about

why, and Liv agreed, only now I can't
remember exactly what they said. At the
time it made sense, maybe, I think, sort
of? Then Cam said even if Simon and I
weren't meant to be together forever,
I could remember the good times and be
glad about them. I said that it was too pain-
ful and he said maybe it wouldn't always
be. I can't imagine that. Then Todd asked
if sex with Simon was good for me, and
Meldel kicked him, and he said, "We're
talking about her relationship!" and she
said, "You're being nosy!" and he said, "Yes,
but also I'm her friend and I care! This is
important!" and Josie stuck her fingers in
her ears and said "La la la, I'm not listening!" and Sebastian blushed and I didn't say
anything.

℮ But the answer is yes. I write it down
here now. And if nothing else, I have to
say this is one reason why I can't ever
be sorry I was with Simon. He was a good
boyfriend! And . . . and Cam knows it's yes.
Because there was just one second after
Todd asked when my eyes met Cam's and I
could tell he read that YES in my eyes. He
looked sort of happy and sad at once for
me. Gaaah, it was like being naked! I had to
look away.

@ Simon. My first serious boyfriend. Not the last. Not the only. Not my partner, not my husband, not happily ever after. The fairy tale—gone. It's not going to be that way for me, the way it was for my parents. The easy way. The way I wanted . . . the life I wanted . . . it's over.

@ It's over. OVER.

@ MY FAULT. I ruined things. I ruined us.

@ In time, everybody else fell asleep, except me. So now I'm sitting in the dark with my bullet journal and my phone flashlight listening to them sleep-breathe while I write.

@ Question: Have I really traded in my boyfriend for a TV show? Or did I trade in my boyfriend for the friends I met because of the TV show?

@ I knew everything once, or thought I did, but now I know nothing.

@ Except this: I like listening to my friends breathe, here in the dark. And I will definitely go to Bean Con with them. That's a good thing. Bloodygits can stay at my house after all. We'll meet Captain and

Torrance and AMT. I can introduce them
to Maggie! Pancakes in the kitchen for
everyone!

☺ Deep breaths. It's not so bad. It's not so
bad. It's not so bad.

☺ Oh, God. It's bad.

TO DO.

☐ Get everybody up.

☐ Coach them on their roles for our panel.

☐ Review my PowerPoint slides.

☐ Make plans with Sebastian to get him into
his cosplay, like I promised him. Is Squirrel
Girl really coming? She's going to break his
heart and I can't save him. Love sucks!

Scene 6

An Organic Compound

Sebastian and I were in our hotel room, alone, working on his bleeder cosplay. I now completely understood why he needed help. *Completely.*

He had pieces of bubble wrap for each leg and arm and a giant one for his torso, which had a hole to go over his head. He had laid the pieces out on a bed, so that—with only a little queasiness—he could use a syringe to shoot "blood" (corn syrup and red dye) into the air pockets. Then it was my turn to brush a Very Special Glue over each bloody pocket while listening to Sebastian talk—and talk and talk—about Squirrel Girl.

Squirrel Girl knew exactly how blood was simulated in the movies. Sebastian could have bought fake blood instead of having to mix it, but Squirrel Girl thought making it was a better idea in this case because it might have been awkward for Sebastian to travel on an airplane with bags of blood. She was considerate that way. Squirrel Girl had laughed so hard when Sebastian told her about the ketchup. Squirrel Girl was majoring in chemical engineering, that was how she'd been able to invent this Very Special Glue, and wasn't I impressed? Squirrel Girl's name was Naomi. An especially pretty name, didn't I think so, too? Squirrel Girl was reading a book about the history of the Marvel-DC Comics rivalry, which she was going to loan to Sebastian. Oh, look, her flight had landed! She'd texted; she was coming by train! She would meet us at the panel.

"She thinks she'll be just in time! You'll love her, Zoe!"

"Sure," I said.

"Are you putting the glue on delicately? And thinly? Squirrel Girl says—"

"Yes. I have a totally delicate touch. And thin."

"Let me see."

"I'm doing it fine!"

He came in close, jostling me, which made me elbow over the Very Special Glue. I don't actually remember leaping up and racing for the bathroom sink to wash my gluey hands. I was just there, running the water as hot as possible—because, after a certain Squirrel Girl-ordained amount of time, the glue was scheduled to eat the bubble wrap.

I repeat: *Eat.*

"My cosplay!" Sebastian wailed after me.

Oh, for the olden, golden days when, as I understood it, one's friends made glue to sniff and get high. Maybe they still did. I wouldn't know. I had friends like Sebastian, who had friends like Squirrel Girl, who made glue as a weapon of mass destruction.

I had been scrubbing my hands for a full minute when Sebastian called, "The armpiece will be fine, so don't worry, Zoe. You didn't splash it after all."

I was still running the water hot enough to boil my contaminated flesh. I managed to say, between my teeth, "I'm not worried about your cosplay."

Sebastian finally appeared in the bathroom doorway. "Good. It's just that I understand how neurotic you can be. I figure it's probably heightened now that you've been dumped. Just remember, I'm here for you."

I reviewed my understanding of the numbers from one to ten.

"Explain to me why we weren't using gloves?" I said finally.

"Naomi didn't say we needed to. Hers is an organic compound."

I felt my lips compress. "I see. Tell me, was Luke Skywalker's prosthetic hand the left or the right?"

"Right. Why?"

"It just totally randomly occurred to me to start thinking about prosthetic hands."

"You're truly so odd. Are you finished washing? We're on a schedule here, and now we have to mix more glue since you ruined my first batch."

I looked at him.

"Or, if you prefer, you can keep on washing your hands. Until, you know, you feel done." Sebastian attempted to pat my back. I snarled. He retreated.

An organic compound! All that means is that a thing has carbon! Grimly, I continued to wash, wishing I'd brought some of Mrs. Albee's Persian Longhair soap, the formula of which included hydrogen peroxide, and wondering what everybody at home was saying about Simon's new Instagram picture. Not to mention mine. Wentworth's sudden appearance on my profile would seriously take Maggie aback, if nobody else. But without a phone to check on any of this, all hell could be breaking loose at home for all I knew. Or maybe everybody in my world was totally indifferent to my plight. Or happy!

My poor phone! Cam had somehow managed to find it in the River of Doom. It was now (theoretically) recovering from water damage in a bag of rice that Meldel bought at Target.

Who needed a phone? I was managing without so far. I had told my parents to get in touch with me via Josie. It was a relief to be out of touch. Really.

Maggie had probably left me ten thousand texts.

I turned off the tap and examined my wet, reddened, wrinkled, clean hands. Clean except for a little lying, a little kidnapping.

Maybe, just maybe, Simon had texted me? Relenting? Understanding?

I wrung my hands.

I longed for more coddling from my friends! More more more! Widened, sympathetic eyes. Patting and there, theres. Focus on me and my heartbreak! But the other Bloodygits had gone off. Liv had not even thought to loan me a scarf. Meldel wanted her picture taken with some idiot YA writer who wasn't even charging for it. And now Sebastian was doing better than me in the romance department.

Of course I wanted to support Sebastian's doomed romance.

I marched out into the room and demonstrated my selflessness by mixing the new batch of glue.

Sebastian hovered. "Are you sure you're getting the proportions right?"

"I'm taking AP Chemistry," I snapped. "I can do it. Step away!"

Sebastian stepped away.

When the glue was ready, we switched jobs. I injected blood; he painted the glue (delicately! thinly!) on the pockets. He also restarted his compulsive Squirrel Girl podcast. I listened in silence. #GoodFriend!

Until:

"Naomi has an idea for a two-person cosplay involving robot parts for the *Bleeders* Sanitation Force. She said we could do it this fall at Dragon Con. She's thinking ahead to September! Isn't that great?"

"But what about *our* group being at Dragon Con again, just us? We were going to march in the parade together."

"Naomi would be part of our group. Isn't that okay?"

"Of course," I said, after a moment.

It didn't feel okay. It felt like yet another thing in my life starting to fall apart. I reminded myself that I had had no sleep. That I was being irrational. That I would probably like Naomi. It still took everything I had to add, brightly, "Naomi's welcome!"

Luckily we were nearly done. Sebastian ducked down so I could put the torso piece over his head. I fastened the sides together with duct tape and then I taped him into the sleeves and the legs. Finally, a white long-sleeved T-shirt and yoga pants went over his bubble wrap. (What was this, his fourth set? It must have cost him a fortune.) They were tight enough to maintain contact with the bubble wrap but loose enough to permit Sebastian movement.

Sebastian bent his knees and arms and walked a few steps.

"Looking good," I said.

"Do you really think it's going to work this time?"

"I thought you trusted Squirrel Girl." I managed to keep the snark out of my voice.

"Of course I do! It's me that I—I mean, Zoe? What if I faint? Or mess up in some other way?"

Despite my mood, my heart squeezed. "You conquered the fainting. It's fake corn syrup blood. You were totally fine with it all this time while you were handling it."

"I know, only . . . only sometimes bad things happen. To me."

I knew how he felt.

"Okay, let's go," he said, only he didn't move until I took his hand and led him gently from the hotel room.

The Panel

Liv came running up in Torrance cosplay, eyes alight, waving the frying pan for emphasis. "Bloodygits, we're mobbed! They've moved our panel to the main ballroom. This is big! There's two camera guys, even." Belatedly, Liv took in Sebastian's puffy white head-to-toe outfit. "Whoa."

Sebastian bowed stiffly. His gaze skimmed ahead, searching.

"Squirrel Girl said she'd get here only just in time," I reminded him quietly. He swallowed nervously.

If she didn't show up for him today after all, or if her bleeding apparatus didn't work and he felt humiliated, I would *get* her. I'd teach her not to play with Sebastian's vulnerable heart. I'd choke her with Lorelei's stethoscope-garrote. I'd conk her on the head with Torrance's frying pan. I—I—

I was holding on by a thread. Lack of sleep. Suppressed fury. I hadn't even eaten, I realized—not since Simon called me last night. Low blood sugar? Maybe I should have someone else run the panel instead of me. Was it too late? Meldel?

No! Meldel would overdo it. And I was prepared.

"I'll wait for my cue here," said Sebastian.

"Good luck!" I said.

He managed to nod.

Liv and I wove through the crowd and into the ballroom. Sound thrummed from the hordes of prospective *Bleeders* fans. Holy cow! We were standing room only.

But . . . they would all be looking at me. Me, in my sweaty Lorelei cosplay, with red corn syrup stains down the front of my lab coat.

That was fine! That was *blood*! Anyway, for the next hour, I wasn't me. I was Lorelei. Lorelei, the most precise surgeon on the *Mae Jemison*, the mature woman who can meditate for hours, the one who speaks crisply and always to the point. Who is deadly in battle. Lorelei the loner, the enigma, the strong. Lorelei who is wrestling with the devil and maybe winning. Lorelei, not Zoe Rosenthal, would lead the panel.

Lorelei would be terrific.

At the front of the room was our table, with seven seats, three microphones, and our names printed on table tents. Our regular and our cosplay names were included: Lorelei (me), Torrance (Liv), Monica (Josie), Captain Paloma (Meldel), Tennah/Bellah (Cam), and Celie (Todd). And an unlabeled chair for Sebastian.

Meldel handed me my phone. "I got it to power on once! There's hope!"

"Really?" I tried. Nothing.

"We can put it back into the rice," said Meldel.

I nodded. I tucked it into my lab coat pocket.

Then I saw Squirrel Girl, already here, seated in the second row. She wasn't in full cosplay, but she'd worn her Squirrel headgear. She caught my eye and waved shyly, with a question on her face. I made a "back of the room" gesture and she nodded, turning, craning her neck.

I watched as she and Sebastian made eye contact.

I watched them smile shyly at each other.

I exhaled.

I was glad for Sebastian. I was.

It was time. Our presentation was cued up on the projection system. I stood before the table and took up a mic. "Hello," I said. "HELLO, BLOODYGITS!"

The room went still.

Suddenly, I felt good! Powerful. We were here in representation of *Bleeders*. It was bigger than me and my problems—and I was not going to let *Bleeders* down.

"WELCOME!" I shouted enthusiastically. "Welcome to the best science fiction show you're not watching! Welcome on board the *Mae Jemison*. Meet the crew. They're all doctors. They're dedicated to treating and finding a cure for the Bleeder virus, which . . ."

At a wave from me, one of the tech guys dimmed the lights. The video clip began, from mid-Season 1:

Two children, a boy and a girl, run through the dust of a

spaceport. They wear bright tunics and dodge around grounded ships of various shapes and sizes. "Mom!" the boy calls . . .

The audience drew in their collective breath when the mother's skin thins and her blood starts to seep out. Her arms. Her face. Her bare toes. The red stain soaks through her clothes. She stares down at herself, aghast, as every pore of skin liquifies. She tries to run from the children— her children. But her son runs, too. He throws himself on the puddle of bones and blood that her body has so swiftly become. He, too, is infected. He, too, bleeds out.

His sister, small Celie, remains. She morphs slowly into adult Celie, tossing in nightmare on her bed, on the *Mae Jemison.*

The lights came back up.

Todd stood. He should have looked ridiculous, in his dress and his hair and his fake breasts. He's way too large to play Celie. But somehow he held all eyes. Somehow he held the room riveted.

I'd been right. These were our people, here at Lilithcon.

"The Bleeder virus," Todd intoned, and the mic carried his voice to every corner of the room. "Spreading through the universe. One touch, and any humanoid is infected. How has the virus come to be? We don't know. How can the virus be cured? We don't know. Could there be a vaccine? We hope so. And what is the history of the virus? Was it actually human-engineered—and deliberately spread?"

I went on. "The renegade doctors of the *Mae Jemison* suspect that this is the case. We'll stop it if we can. But that's not all that's happening. Possibly some humanoids,"—

I leaned forward and touched my own chest delicately—
"such as Lorelei, might be wondering, secretly, if the death
of most of humanity just might be a *good* idea."

Some people were actually on the edge of their seats.

Meldel stood. "There are six of us. We are all women,
except . . ." She gestured at Torrance as Todd, working the
PowerPoint, put up a still photo of the real Torrance on the
projection system as Liv stood and waved their frying pan.
"Torrance, ship's cook and psychiatrist. If you need to play
a mind game on your enemy, he's your man. But he's no
damn good in a fight."

"By choice," said Torrance/Liv, with dignity. "I do no
physical harm. I took an oath."

Josie stood up when I pointed at her. Todd clicked to
the Monica photo. "To hell with your oath!" Monica/Josie
roared at Torrance/Liv. "You think the rest of us didn't take
one, too? These are desperate times!"

"Meet Monica," I said. "Navigator. Anesthesiolo-
gist. Monica is bipolar, and right now, she's tweaking her
medication to stay in the manic state so that she can work
harder, longer. Also, Monica is secretly in love with . . ."

Monica/Josie swiveled to stare longingly at Captain/
Meldel.

"Captain. Internal medicine. Pediatrician. Trusted
leader. And, as it happens, a gifted killer. We still don't
know why she's wearing those gloves or why she never
takes them off. Also, Captain is a mother whose children
have been stolen from her. A wife whose husband has
cruelly betrayed her."

"I don't know why," said Captain/Meldel calmly. "But

when I find him—and believe me, I will—I will discover the truth. In the meantime, I am desperate to know if my children are safe." She raised her chin. "But I allow myself to think of them only when I am alone. When there is nothing else to do." Her face hardened. "I'll be honest. That doesn't happen often. I don't *permit* it to happen often."

Oh, Meldel, I thought. You are a star after all.

"Captain doesn't know I have a heart," said Monica/Josie into the silence, as Todd showed a corroborating slide of the two of them. "I am a piece of machinery to her." She paused before adding sadly, "Maybe that's all I can ask. Maybe it's all I deserve. But I wish . . . before we all die . . . I wish for that one moment with her."

I was hardly breathing. I hadn't scripted all of this! My Bloodygits were improvising now and they were doing it brilliantly, and the room was in the palm of my—our—hands. *This matters!* I thought crazily. Fandom matters. Loving *Bleeders* matters. Never mind what Simon thinks. He's wrong! He's wrong somehow!

"Celie," I said, and Celie/Todd waved, leaned into the microphone, and said conversationally, "I'm not really a doctor yet. I'm a med tech, I'm only twenty-one, and Captain and the others are sort of homeschooling me. And yes, that was me you just saw. The little girl on the screen. That was my introduction to the Bleeder virus." Todd smiled sweetly and flipped his hair. "I'm young. And believe me, you have no idea what I'm going to become." He paused. "Unless I'm already dead."

Torrance/Liv said, "As a psychiatrist, I can tell you that Celie compensates for what happened to her in childhood with an unrelenting cheerfulness. It's annoying, especially since she's reprogrammed our ship's computer . . ."

Another clip from *Bleeders*: a compilation of scenes where the computer interrupts the crew's conversation to contribute positive, perky, and inspiring clichés. As it played, I looked at the back of the room, where Sebastian was ready for his cue to run down, to bleed. He was there, but he was frowning, patting his white arm, twisting uncomfortably—

Squirrel Girl was looking back at him, too.

"Don't forget us!" Tennah/Bellah/Cam said, with a sidelong look at me and then a longer one at Sebastian. "I take offense at Lorelei saying that there are six of us on board. There are seven, because I'm two people—I shape-shift—"

From the back of the room, Sebastian yelled, despairingly, "I'M SORRY! I'M SO SORRY, BLOODYGITS! NAOMI, IT'S NOT GOING TO WORK!"

The whole room turned to look.

Wentworth's Revenge

Squirrel Girl sidled out of her row, calling back to Sebastian. "What's going on?"

Sebastian, his expression crazed, yelled back, "Nothing, that's what!" Then he looked at me and shouted, "You messed up Squirrel Girl's glue recipe!" He appealed to the roughly two hundred onlookers. "Zoe told me she was taking AP Chem! I shouldn't have trusted her!"

Stung, I protested. "I *am* taking AP Chem!"

Squirrel Girl reached Sebastian at the back of the hall. She put one hand on his arm, pressed gently against the bubble wrap. Then she frowned toward me. "Did you tweak my formula?"

"No!" I said. "I didn't! I did it right!"

Sebastian hustled down the aisle to confront me. "You weren't careful enough!" He was visibly vibrating and emoting, ensuring that nobody in the ballroom would miss a word of our little drama. As if this wasn't enough, he added obsequiously, "Zoe's not as smart as you, Naomi." Because, of course, Squirrel Girl had followed him.

"I—I—I—" It wasn't just my mouth stuttering. My brain was doing it too.

Squirrel Girl wasn't interested in me, though. She moved to Sebastian again, and now put a hand on his chest. Again she pushed lightly. Then she withdrew her hand and looked at it before holding her hand aloft. Her smile cast beams of sunshine everywhere.

"No worries, people!" Her palm was wet and red. "It seems we just had a little issue with timing. In a moment, Sebastian is going to positively *gush* blood—"

Sebastian looked at her hand. He blinked. His mouth opened and closed. He tottered.

And then he fainted, hitting his head on a chair on his way to the floor as the fake blood seeped out from every inch of his costume.

There was shouting. Meldel raced to Sebastian, with Todd and Cam and Josie on her heels. Squirrel Girl yelled something about calling 911. Several people were immediately on their phones.

Our panel was effectively over.

The room was hot, it still stank of chlorine, and over the next few minutes people left in droves, except for the ones who were enjoying watching the chaos and the ones who were helping. I knew I should do something to help too, but all I could do was sit down very carefully in a chair.

This was twice in the last twenty-four hours that someone who was supposed to care about me jumped to the worst conclusion without even giving me a chance to explain! To defend myself!

Also, incidentally, our panel was ruined.

Eventually Sebastian stirred, moaned, and lifted his head. His lips formed words. "Na-Na-Naomi?"

"Here," said Squirrel Girl, bending down. Her face was all proper concern except for a moment when she glanced at the blood. Her upper lip curved with shy pleasure at the success of her formula.

Sebastian said things as he was hauled upright, but none of it was *Where is faithful Zoe, for I have wronged her sadly and I must beg her forgiveness.*

Liv sat down beside me. "He's going to be fine."

"Sure," I said.

"Zoe . . ."

"Liv," I said. "Don't talk to me. I'm so angry at Sebastian I could kneecap him. Also, we had this great opportunity for our panel and now it's wrecked." I dragged my hand through Lorelei's wig, pulling out the white bun and then plucking the whole wig off my head.

"I know it's not ideal," Liv said. "But it's okay. Sebastian has fainted before and he'll faint again. And we did publicize *Bleeders*—"

"Our panel failed!" I snapped. It was so unfair. I'd done just as much planning as Squirrel Girl! More! I shook my head angrily. "If *Bleeders* is canceled—"

"That won't be our fault, Zoe. Hey, want a scarf?"

I nodded miserably and tilted my head. Liv wound a warm wool scarf on me, red and gold. Gryffindor. Which was the wrong house for me; I was clearly Slytherin. Sigh.

The 911 people wanted to take Sebastian. His previously white puffy clothing was still dripping; the red corn syrup had splashed everyone and everything. This hotel certainly wouldn't be in a rush to host Lilithcon next year. Probably they would send me the carpet-cleaning bill.

I groped for my phone and tried again to turn it on. Nothing.

Liv said, "Let's plan a topic for our next panel."

"What?" I snarled. "We won't be allowed a panel. Anywhere. Ever again!"

"Oh, come on—"

"I don't want to talk about it, Liv," I said.

"We'll save it for another time, then."

That time will be never, I thought, but all I did was compress my lips.

We watched the other Bloodygits move off down the aisle and out the ballroom door with the 911 people, Sebastian, and Squirrel Girl.

"Shall we go?" said Liv. "We can get hot chocolate in the Con Suite and discuss, I don't know, menses."

I stayed put. "I appreciate it, Liv, but I'd just like to sit here for a few minutes and not talk."

"Sure. We can do that."

"Alone? I'm sorry."

"Don't be sorry. I get it. I'll check on you in a while."

"Thanks."

I stayed alone, alone, alone in the giant ballroom.

I closed my eyes and rubbed them. I tried not to think about myself but instead about AMT and Bean Con and Season 3.

Oh, God. My life sucked. Liv couldn't fully understand, especially now that they'd gotten into Smith early.

After a few minutes, I got that feeling of someone looking at me. Involuntarily, I whispered, "Simon?" and opened my eyes.

Of course it wasn't Simon. It was Cam, squatting inches in front of me. Red corn syrup had dried all over his hands and somehow also gotten smeared on his face, giving him the appearance of a psychopathic murderer.

"Are you feeling any better?"

"No," I said. "Not really."

Cam said, "You're going to be okay."

"No," I said passionately. "I'm really not. Don't you see? Simon dumped me. Also, our panel just crashed and burned, and I was the one who took the blame for it. In case you didn't notice, I was accused in front of hundreds of people. By my friend! Also, oh yeah, my boyfriend dumped me, not that I'm dwelling on it, and he was the best person in the world, *is* the best person in the world, and maybe I didn't deserve him, but all my plans for the future were wrapped up in him. And now that is completely over and I have no idea what's going to happen."

"Well, aren't you feeling sorry for yourself," said Cam.

I glared at him. "With good reason!"

"Zoe. While yes, it truly sucks and I get it, you're acting like you were done wrong by the world, and I don't think that's the right way to look at it."

I blinked. "Oh, really? What *is* the right way, may I ask?"

"I say this very gently and with love. It's time for some straight talk, girlfriend. I think you should take responsibility for your own situation."

I could not believe my ears. "I take responsibility all the time!"

"I mean for the end of your relationship. Let's take a minute and try to look at the situation from Simon's point of view—"

"Stop right there. Do you honestly think I haven't done that dozens of times? I know exactly what I did! I sneaked out to cons without telling him, which was not good. But was it really so very bad? Why couldn't he at least ask me to explain? I'm not a criminal! So I liked a TV show he wasn't interested in! So I helped his sister be part of the fandom, which, incidentally, she really, really wanted. No harm was done, Cam!"

"Luckily."

"I wouldn't have let any harm come to Josie, if that's what you're insinuating!"

"I'm not insinuating anything. I'm saying that things happen and it was lucky nothing did in this case. And when I think of it, I'm ashamed that I was a part of this, too. I should have known better, too. We all should have. We knew Josie's age."

"No," I said heavily after a minute. "It was me. You're right."

Cam was squatting in front of me. "Simon's such a social-justice warrior, upright, morally inflexible, lawful good, blah blah, whatever. You knew all that. You knew it when you started dating him. You knew it when you made up a story so you could go to Dragon Con instead of being with him. You knew it when you claimed you were campaigning in New Hampshire, or whatever it was you said the other times. Of course he'd feel that you betrayed him. You did. You abandoned the relationship first. Arguably."

I was silent.

"I thought you were my friend," I said finally.

"I am your friend. I'm just saying—"

"I am not actually evil, Cam."

"No! Of course not! I didn't say you were evil. All I was saying was that—"

"I see it!" I flared. "I've always seen it! I tell myself all the time that I must be a terrible person, and it just hurts to know you see me that way, too. Does everyone else? Liv? The others? Did Sebastian leap into accusing me because, deep down, none of you trust me? Because when you met me, I was already lying?"

"Wait, you're leaping to conclusions. I just wanted—"

My phone rang. My undead phone rang! It was the generic ringtone, but maybe it was Simon anyway. I snatched the phone from my pocket. "Hello?" Then I deflated. "Hi, Mrs. Albee."

Mrs. Albee said something.

"Wait, I can't hear you," I said. "My phone is messed up. Let me try speaker." Miraculously, the speaker icon worked.

Mrs. Albee's voice boomed with righteous fury. "Zoe Rosenthal! I could not be more disappointed in you!"

Cam's eyes met mine. Mine dropped.

I suddenly knew exactly what was coming to me.

"You went behind our backs. You made test videos with another cat. Don't bother denying it!" Over the damaged speaker, her voice went even louder.

"Please, Mrs. Albee." I hunched my shoulders. "I apologize—"

"Don't bother," said Mrs. Albee icily. "I don't care to hear it. I don't believe in your sincerity. And neither does Wentworth."

There came a furious, ear-splitting yowl.

Not without satisfaction, Mrs. Albee said, "In cat language, that means: You're fired!"

She disconnected, but not before Wentworth got in a final fart-like screech of victory. (This would, by the way, turn out to be the last noise my phone ever made.)

I buried my face in my arms.

"Well," Cam began, in his most reasonable voice.

"Go away, Cam," I said. "Go away and leave me alone to feel small."

EPISODE 6
March 2019 @Home

From Zoe's Bullet Journal

TO DO:

- ☑ Sincerely apologize to Ms. Murawski
- ☑ Write letter of apology to Mrs. Albee
- ☑ Thank Maggie for being a saintly best friend who I do not deserve
- ☑ Thank parents for their support and love
- ☑ Gracefully accept being grounded
- ☐ Look for new job, so can pay parents back for new phone ASAP
- ☐ Do not brood
- ☐ Control self-pity/anger
- ☐ Avoid Simon
- ☐ ~~DON'T WATCH THAT VIDEO!!!~~

Scene 1

Misery

Texting with Liv from home, on the weekend of Newark Con.

LIV: Hey.

ME: Hey. How's the con going?

LIV: OK. We did a Bleeders panel again. We had a really good showing, actually. It went well. We miss you, though.

ME: I miss you too. But I totally agreed with my parents about grounding me. I even sort of feel like they haven't punished me enough. They were so furious about me taking Josie to Lilithcon. I get it.

LIV: Did you say that to them?

ME: Of course I did.

LIV: We're missing Josie too. Any chance she'll be able to at least work with Meldel and Cam on fanfic again?

ME: I have no way of knowing that. Ms. Murawski really tore me a new one, which I completely understood. I abased myself. But Josie and I aren't in touch right now.

LIV: Josie told Meldel at Lilithcon that she was going to tell her mother that she blackmailed you and it wasn't your fault.

ME: Well, she did that, but you know. I have to take responsibility. As your brother would say.

LIV: Sebastian wishes you would text him back.

ME: I will. Soon.

LIV: He's very sorry he rushed to blame you about the glue.

ME: It's minor. I'm not mad at him. I'm just . . . being quiet these days. Is Squirrel Girl there with you now?

LIV: Yes. They're sweet together. But speaking of love, I suppose your heart aches and all that stuff that I totally do not understand?

ME: Well, actually . . .

LIV: It doesn't?

ME: I caught Simon sort of sneering at me, at school! And I wanted to kneecap him!

LIV: You realize I'm refraining from recommending you just take a vow to be alone for a while? No boyfriends, just figure out what you want, on your own?

ME: You and my mom and Maggie ought to get together. But you want to know what's really funny? I might miss Wentworth even more than I miss Simon.

LIV: What?

ME: Yeah. Wentworth and I had kind of an antagonistic sibling relationship or something. I've been thinking about him a lot. I have all this footage where he was just screwing around and I thought it was totally worthless, because he never did what I wanted him to do. But I've been looking it over in my spare time, which I have a lot of these days. And you know what? He's cute in his own way.

LIV: Did Mrs. Albee replace you?

ME: She took me off the contact page on her website. But there's nobody else there yet. I'm still burning with shame. I wrote to her and tried to explain that I wanted to surprise her with how good the new spokescat would be, that it would really help the business. But it sounded lame even to me. So finally I just apologized and left it at that. That's just one thing that can't ever be fixed. I have to live with it.

LIV: Personally, I thought your Ellen From Finance video was really appealing. I loved how she played foot-hockey with the kitty soaps and kicked them right into that turquoise bag.

ME: Foot-hockey was something I could never, ever get Wentworth to do. I had a fixation on it. And did you notice how that turquoise color just really suited Ellen From Finance? But still, it was all a mistake. I bet I could have worked with Wentworth if I had really tried. I just wanted to have things my own way. I like having my own way, Liv. I do.

LIV: And who doesn't? What's wrong with that?

ME: Nothing, if you go after it in an upright and honest manner.

LIV: That sounds a little, uh, Lawful Good.

ME: Sorry. I'm just trying to be a better person.

LIV: I hoped you were going to give that up and be your own person.

ME: Just because you got into college early decision, you got all this psychological knowledge suddenly?

LIV: Think about it.

ME: OK. Tell me about Smith! Isn't it great to have it settled? Are you excited? Have you heard anything else from them?

LIV: I'm going to visit next month, right after Bean Con. I'll meet the coach and the team, get a tour, you know. I was actually wondering if maybe you'd want to come see Smith again too. With me.

ME: I don't know.

LIV: You'll know soon where you got in, and maybe Smith will be one of your acceptances.

ME: Or one of the places I'm rejected. I can't make plans now. I'm not in a great place.

LIV: You're thinking about Simon and your college list?

ME: I feel sick about it. That whole list, it was all about him. I have no idea what I want. None! Except I don't want to go where he goes.

LIV: Won't you and he have to talk about it to make sure you don't?

ME: Maggie can tell me where he's going. She said she'd find out.

LIV: Look. I just need to say this once more. If you didn't feel like there was something deeper wrong between you and Simon, you wouldn't have lied about Bleeders in the first place.

ME: It doesn't matter.

LIV: It does. The people you love should respect your love for the things that you love. For your sake.

ME: Can we not talk about it?

LIV: Fine. Changing subject. Cam is touring NYU again with Sebastian.

ME: Did he get in?

LIV: He hasn't heard yet. He's anxious. He really wants to be in New York.

ME: Did Cam get Aragorn? I mailed him after I had that wee talk with my dad.

LIV: Hah. Yes, Aragorn is now in our living room. Place of honor over the fireplace.

ME: Your parents are OK with that?

LIV: Hello? You've MET my parents.

ME: You know, I have a certain black cape I might be able to send to your dad.

LIV: Please don't do that.

ME: That was a great day, when I met your parents. I loved the Dragon Con parade more than anything.

LIV: We're going again in September, right?

ME: But we'll be in college.

LIV: So? We should still go! Don't you want to?

ME: I don't know anymore.

LIV: Get over it. I'll see you at Bean Con anyway. Right?

ME: I'll see you somehow. But not at the con. I can't.

LIV: You'll still be grounded?

ME: No. That's only for a month.

LIV: Then wait a minute. You have to go. AMT. Hugh Nguyen. Jocelyn Upchurch. Remember?

ME: I can't face going.

LIV: Why not?

ME: Liv? Haven't you seen that video?

LIV: What video?

ME: Don't play games! It's tagged for Bleeders. Its views keep
climbing on YouTube. Even Maggie saw it! Don't lie to
me, Liv!

LIV: I might have seen a video.

ME: With reggae music.

LIV: Um. Yes. Cam says . . .

ME: What?

LIV: Cam says they must have still been recording after the
panel, so they caught what happened afterward on tape.
And then some troll got hold of it. I'm so sorry.

ME: Whoever made that video is my enemy until death.

LIV: It's an invasion of privacy. I was really hoping you wouldn't
see it.

ME: Well, I did. And now I can never go to a con again.

LIV: It's not that bad.

ME: It's worse.

Reggae

The anonymous person who made the video—my enemy until death—had at least done a professional job. They'd edited together footage from *Bleeders*, from our Lilithcon panel, from Cam telling me off afterward, from Mrs. Albee firing me, from Sebastian's "You told me you were taking AP Chem!" And everything else horrible. They had even included a clip of Wentworth from YouTube, overlaid with the fart noise that had come out of my phone at the end. The cuts were seamlessly spliced. Timing was expert.

What really made the video pop, however, was its original reggae soundtrack.

Fangirl lie to her boyfriend
Off to the comic con

Kidnap he little sister
Who know what they up to

Exploding blood in the spacesuit
Gal doctors know what to do
Research the wicked virus
Kill anyone in they way

Fangirl lie to her boyfriend
Off to the comic con
Destroy the evil robots
Fix up that warp drive good

Boyfriend he Goody Two-Shoes
Make Fangirl feel small
Soap for the nerdy conscience
Kitty say screw you too
(Sound effect: the fart noise)

Fangirl lie to her boyfriend
Off to the comic con
Kidnap he little sister
Who know what they up to

EPISODE 7
April 2019 @Bean Con

From Zoe's Bullet Journal

TO DO:

- ☐ Do not answer anybody re: the video. Do not react in any way. Stay off all social media!
- ☐ Sunglasses? Headscarf?
- ☐ Livestream of AMT at Bean Con, so can watch safely from home?
- ☑ Sort through college acceptances with parents, make decision
- ☐ ~~Kill Simon!!!~~ Practice yogic breathing

Scene 1

Not So Lawful Good

I didn't need Maggie to spy out Simon's college choice after all, because the news was all over school. Simon had gotten into Harvard, likely thanks to a strong letter of recommendation from Senator Alisha Johnson Pratt.

Harvard!

It was fine, I told myself. Simon had earned that letter, and in good conscience, I shouldn't resent it. Also, he'd been admitted with a strong financial aid package. Harvard can afford it. Great news for the Murawskis. Yay. No resentment.

That said.

The following are the other facts in the case:

❦ Harvard's application deadline was January 1.
❦ Simon and I were still very much together

then. And alongside sneaking off to cons,
I had spent months working hard for us
both—I thought—checking out the colleges
on our joint list.

@ Harvard was <u>not</u> on that joint list.

@ (In fairness, neither was Smith, where I'd
applied.)

@ It is therefore proven that Simon applied
to Harvard on his own, behind my back.

The day I found out, I said incredulously to Maggie, "He might have been truly angry about Josie, but he was also seizing the first opportunity to dump me! It would have happened anyway, as soon as he got into Harvard and his lies were exposed."

"You'd become his backup plan," said Maggie sagely. "For if he didn't get into Harvard and go off on his own."

"Lawful Good, my foot! He's no better than me!"

"There's something else I just found out," said Maggie. "And maybe now it won't hurt you to hear it?"

I made a "go on" motion.

"He's seeing someone else. A freshman at Harvard. She works for Senator Pratt, too. That's how they met."

"Before or after he officially broke up with me?" I asked.

"I don't know. Does it matter?"

"Oh, just wondering precisely where his character alignment lands. Maybe he's worse than me!"

When Maggie was gone, I gave up the brave front and spent the rest of the day alternately brooding, raging, and crying.

That night, my mom stroked my hair and said, "I think that somewhere deep inside, you and Simon both knew you were not ready to make a long-term commitment. That knowledge drove your actions."

"But I wanted to be like you and dad," I said miserably.

"Oh, honeybee," said my mom. "We made plenty of mistakes in our day, too, on the way to learning that it was best to communicate openly about everything."

"Yet somehow you didn't end up starring in a viral video," I said. "With all your mistakes broadcast around the world, following you everywhere forever—to a catchy reggae beat. Which is totally cultural appropriation! I'm white—I shouldn't be starring in a reggae video!"

My mom snickered. I raised my head to glare at her.

"Everyone loves you, Fangirl," she said. "Trust me."

"No, they don't."

"People love to laugh," said my mom. "Life goes on, in any case. You'll see."

"I have been globally and personally humiliated. Don't tell me it'll be fine."

"Okay, I won't. But it will be."

"You don't know that."

"Actually," said my mom, "I think I do."

I hoped she was right. Still, I said, with dignity, "I would actually like to wallow in my misery for a while."

"I recommend it."

"I'm wallowing whether you recommend it or not," I said.

"Sure."

"Because I don't need parental approval to wallow."

"You have it anyway. Enjoy."

"Wallowing is not enjoyable."

"Of course it is."

We made popcorn and settled in to watch the final episode of *Bleeders* Season 2 together. I filled her in on the backstory.

Scene 2

Handmaid at the Con

In my new cosplay, I was incognito. For insurance beyond my robe and bonnet, I'd borrowed my mother's giant sunglasses. I still felt jumpy, but as Maggie and I entered the hotel lobby, I forgot my nervousness. Because, even though just like at Lilithcon, cosplayers were outnumbered by Muggles, among those who *were* dressed up . . . well!

Never before had I seen so many Bloodygits!

Never before had I seen *any*, except us.

Eyes bright, Maggie nodded toward a group. "Oh, so sweet! The little girl Captains!"

"I know!"

They were the most adorable pair of small Captains, one aged about eleven, the other maybe eight—and oh my God, they were with a mom who was also in Captain cosplay, including the battle gear mask!

Also! There were two Tennah/Bellahs. A Torrance arm

in arm with Lorelei and Monica. A Celie. In the lobby alone!

None of these cosplayers were *my* Bloodygits. They were here somewhere, but they wouldn't recognize me at the moment, not in my all-enveloping Handmaid cosplay-slash-disguise. Also, as far as my Bloodygits knew, I was at home planning to watch the livestream of AMT's speech.

Wistfully, I checked out the Lorelei. She was tall and athletic, her exposed arms muscular. If I'd been in my own Lorelei cosplay, she'd have *seen* me. We'd have posed together for a selfie. We'd have talked about the show. In fact, in my Lorelei, I could have walked up to any of the *Bleeders* cosplayers here, shared gossip, and speculated about what AMT was going to announce.

Except no, I couldn't have. All the *Bleeders* fans here would have seen that reggae video. If I walked up to them and talked, or if I rejoined my Bloodygits, I'd be recognized. And publicly mocked!

Curses on my nemesis, the reggae videographer!

So it had to be this way, with all the other fans looking past me in my red robe and face-shading white bonnet, as if I were invisible. It was my decision—the only way I'd felt able to accept Maggie's offer.

But I was still bitter. I respected *Handmaid's Tale*, of course I did, but I was a fan of *Bleeders*, and—and that anonymous reggae video had ruined my fandom life!

I grabbed Maggie's red sleeve. "I've changed my mind. I have to go home. I'll watch the livestream."

"No." Maggie pried my fingers off one by one. "You are

staying here. I signed us up to get pictures. Every penny goes toward the show!"

"But we already paid," I whined. "No refunds! *Bleeders* gets the money whether I'm here or not!"

"*I* paid," Maggie reminded me. "So I decide. We're staying. Plus we have to go hear AMT and find out if there's going to be a Season 3."

"Livestream," I muttered.

"You're in debt to me and you do what I say."

"I'll pay you back."

"You're broke."

"I'm climbing out of the hole." I had a new job, scooping ice cream at the creamery. It would be full-time in the summer if I wanted. Tips were surprisingly good, and it was usually so busy there wasn't even time to think. I didn't feel up to anything more ambitious. (I had taken to a cowardly exit of my house by the front door, so I didn't risk seeing Wentworth—focused murderously and futilely on the house finches—at his favorite window.)

Maggie held out the photo ticket she'd bought for me. "Take this and say 'Thank you, Maggie.'"

"Thank you, Maggie. Your heart is golden, your soul incandescent, your generosity bottomless."

"Plus, I'm adorable."

"Plus, you're adorable. And you're a Bloodygit!"

"Crazy, right?"

"Crazy." We linked arms. I felt a bit better.

Maggie had (finally!) binge-watched Seasons 1 and 2 of *Bleeders.* Ironically, it was because of the reggae video, and I tried not to resent the fact that my recommendation alone hadn't done the job. The video was continuing to attract ongoing witty commentary. Do not ask me how I know.

At least Maggie was now hooked. So I had another Bloodygit friend, who was so good a friend that she'd put on the Handmaid cosplay to be here with me, instead of Celie (her first choice). Not to mention funding the con for us both.

"*Bleeders* is still your show, Zoe," Maggie said. "You have every right to be here. It's going to be all right." She paused. "Unless there's no Season 3."

I shrugged. I made sure my mother's giant sunglasses were firmly seated on my nose.

"Come on." Maggie grasped my wrist and pulled me along. "Let's go get our picture taken with the stars!"

It turned out that the Bloodygit cosplayers and fans in the hotel lobby were only the tip of the iceberg. The others—the many, many others—were in the Samuel Adams Ballroom clutching their photo tickets.

My personal problems aside, looking around at the long line was exciting. Was *Bleeders* truly catching on? I feigned nonchalance to Maggie. "This isn't so big a deal, really. You should see the lines at Dragon Con for some fandoms." Then I couldn't stand it. I dropped the act. "Maggie! There's got to be several hundred *Bleeders* fans right here! And there's more ahead—in the next area where the photos are being taken. Maybe as many as a thousand fans here? Fans who have actually left their homes! Come out in public!"

"And everyone here is willing to pay fifty dollars a picture," Maggie said.

I nodded. "Most of the time at cons the stars keep the money they make from photos and signings. A fundraiser like this is unusual. But people showed up and paid. Maybe this is what will save the show!"

"Only . . . let's say a thousand people are here, at fifty dollars a head." Maggie frowned. "Fifty thousand dollars will cover, what? A day of production? Two? Just guessing."

"Shut up," I said, deflated.

"It's still a positive sign that the fandom is building."

"But maybe not enough."

My own Bloodygits were here somewhere in these very photo lines. I suddenly really wanted—longed—to see them, even from afar, even if they wouldn't recognize me. But the room was too tightly packed. Plus, my bonnet obscured my sight lines.

"Which line?" barked a volunteer in a Bean Con T-shirt. "A for Ms. Turner, B for Mr. Nguyen, C for Ms. Upchurch."

"C for Captain!" said Maggie, holding out her ticket for scanning. She smiled winningly at the volunteer, but he didn't crack a smile back.

I would explain to her later that you shouldn't even try to charm a volunteer occupied with star-line crowd management, no matter how cute they are. They are working to move people along. They are also on the alert for rule breakers, line skippers, cheats, and of course total crazies and stalkers. This tends to make them a little tense. Not to mention the implicit con hierarchy that made volunteers, at least temporarily, our social superiors.

"A for me," I said politely. "Ms. Turner."

The heartbreaking decision between AMT, Torrance,

and Captain! I'd done some wailing and rending of garments about why the three of them weren't offering a photo op together. If I hadn't been out of money, I'd have signed up for all three. But I could hardly ask Maggie for more than the one that, out of the goodness of her heart, she'd offered.

And there was no contest, then, that I'd choose AMT.

Maggie and I parted with promises to meet outside afterward.

The photo lines snaked through grids laid out on the carpet with masking tape. I shuffled obediently along while eavesdropping. One fan was trying to control her hyperventilation and another rehearsed alternate versions of what she might say to AMT. (As for me, I planned a simple and dignified "I love *Bleeders*. Thank you.")

I kept an ear and eye out for my Bloodygits, particularly every time I turned a masking-tape corner and got a new view of the line immediately ahead of and behind me. I felt sure Meldel would want a photo with Captain, and Liv with Torrance. But the others could be here in the AMT line right now.

I froze.

I'd been wrong about Meldel. She was lined up a dozen people behind me, moving automatically along with her face half buried in a book. She was in her Captain cosplay. She was alone.

I had made it to the curtain that divided our line from the area in which the photos were actually being taken. I was being waved forward by the volunteer traffic coordinator. I almost went onward.

But I didn't.

I darted backward in line, muttering excuses. (Fans weren't upset to suddenly be one person closer to their photo op.) Then I was in front of her. Her book was called *In Other Lands*.

"Meldel?"

She was so absorbed in her book—chortling wickedly over it—that I had to say it again.

"Meldel? Shhhh. Act normal. It's me, Zoe."

I was terrified she'd draw attention to me.

She looked up. I raised my mother's sunglasses for a second.

Meldel's eyes widened in unfeigned shock.

I said quickly, "Don't say anything. Act normal. I'm so afraid people will see me!" I'd meant to speak quietly, but somehow, my voice rose with anxiety. The woman right behind Meldel turned her head to look at me.

Meldel was biting her lip worriedly, staying silent as we moved along in the line, me walking backward. (Because God forbid the line not move along.)

"It's your turn, Handmaid," said the volunteer at the curtain. With an edge in her voice, she added, "Again."

"Zoe," Meldel whispered at last. Her cheeks had reddened, and I wondered if she was embarrassed to be seen with me. "I think I'd better tell you something—"

Right then, a Tennah/Bellah fan behind Meldel yelled, "Hey! That girl! The Handmaid! It's the Lorelei from the Fangirl video!"

Scene 3

Thank You

It was my nightmare come true. Some halfwit yelled, "Fangirl! Who know what she up to?" The line burst into spontaneous applause—and then into song.

Fangirl lie to her boyfriend
Off to the comic con
Destroy the evil robots
Fix up that warp drive good

People were snapping their fingers, rotating their hips, and, inevitably, making the fart noise. (Which I had realized *had* to have been my dying phone and not actually Wentworth. Right? Do cats even fart audibly? Was Wentworth some sort of aberrant?)

The volunteer at least was not amused by the crowd. She snarled, "You two! Go, go, go! Now!" She seized Meldel and me and hustled us through the curtain as she yelled to the mob, "Sing all you want, but if anybody gets out of line, believe me, you are not getting back in! And NO PICTURE FOR YOU!"

The cacophony settled down. Slightly.

But it didn't matter anymore what was happening out there, behind us, because we were behind the curtain in the photography area.

And AMT. The real, actual Anna Maria Turner was six feet away.

Beside me, Meldel breathed, "Oh my God. It's really her."

We groped blindly to hold each other's hands.

Anna Maria Turner's dark hair was growing gray at her temples. She had combed it back severely and contained it in a bun. She wore glasses with purple rims. She was tall with a large bosom and broad hips and a small waist, which she showed off in a short, tight dress featuring a pattern of books with kittens (aarghh!) sleeping on top. She wore black capri-length leggings and classic white Converse high-tops.

It doesn't matter that you've already seen ten million pictures and videos of your hero. It doesn't matter that you fully understand that your hero isn't only a goddess of smart creativity, but also a real person in the real world. Because even if you think you know these things, it just feels different when you meet her.

No wonder that girl who was in line near me had

worried about hyperventilating. I hadn't been cooler than she was after all. She was more experienced than me. She knew.

Like Spock in the original *Star Trek*, AMT raised a single, quizzical eyebrow. Unlike Spock, a smile curved her lips, and a deep dimple appeared in one brown cheek.

She said, "Hello, you two. Photo?"

I managed not to swoon at the sound of her voice.

Meldel and I replied, unfortunately and inadvertently in chorus. "H-hello, Ms. Turner."

"I admire you so much, Ms. Turner!" burst out Meldel. "I love the show! Thank you for making it!"

I too had planned something to say. I just couldn't remember it.

"You're welcome," said AMT to Meldel. She tilted her head to one side and paused for a minute, looking at me. Then she spoke over her shoulder. "It might really be her." She was talking to a skinny man who stood behind the camera. Then to me. "Handmaid?"

I managed to nod.

"Would you please take off your bonnet?"

I figured out how to do that.

AMT laughed softly. "So it is you. Fangirl—uh, Lorelei. And Captain! Are your other friends here, too? From the Lilithcon panel?"

I froze. AMT had seen the reggae video.

I waited for Meldel to answer for me, but she didn't.

"They're here somewhere," I stuttered. "Only I'm not with them."

She raised that eyebrow again. "Did you have a fight?"

"Oh, no! No! It's just … that video." I cleared my throat. "I wasn't sure I wanted to appear in public." With one hand, I swept out my red robe as if in explanation.

"Ah," said AMT sympathetically.

I longed to pour out my whole entire sad story to her. I felt she'd understand all the complexity, the business involving Josie and Simon, the horror of being mocked online, the death of love, the disappointment in myself, the loss of Mrs. Albee and Wentworth and a job that I was good at, and the horror of having it be all my own fault. Even having Simon's voice in my head, saying—and I knew it was true—that none of these qualified as "real" problems and I should be ashamed of how I felt.

Of course I couldn't.

Also, I wouldn't cry. I wouldn't be a baby in front of her.

Meldel said, "Everybody's here, Ms. Turner. Everyone except Josie, I mean, our Monica."

"Kidnap he little sister," sang the skinny man behind the camera, sotto voce.

I gave him the hairy eyeball. "It was only a kidnapping in the strictest legal sense."

AMT bit her lip.

The photographer said, "We'd truly love to hear the full story. But if we don't move things along, there'll be hell to pay." He nodded toward the curtain, where the volunteer had just stuck her head in, one palm raised to ask a wordless, pissed-off question.

"Righto," said AMT, suddenly all business. She stretched out her arms to either side. "Come here, you two."

Meldel and I stumbled forward.

"Smile!" said the photographer.

Maggie had paid for me to get an individual picture with AMT, not a group shot. But there was no way I'd have said anything, and Meldel didn't either.

I felt the imprint of AMT's warm hug all along my side.

The picture that we got—which I will treasure until my dying day—shows a radiant AMT. Her arms are flung around the shoulders of Meldel and me. On AMT's right, Meldel smiles straight into the camera. As for me, I'm all deer-in-headlights, clutching my bonnet and sunglasses in front of my red robe, looking up at AMT as she looks down at me, with the worst hat hair of my entire life (with the notable exception of my hair in the reggae video).

What you can't see is AMT saying, "I'm glad to meet you, Fangirl. Thank you for being you."

Reunion

Meldel and I were standing together in a daze, looking in awe at our pictures.

"Um, so Zoe?" Meldel said after a couple of minutes. Her voice was uncharacteristically diffident. "I have this theory that whoever made that video possibly, just possibly, believed that, because of artistic freedom—"

I made a chopping gesture with my hand. I didn't want to talk about the video and I certainly didn't want to hear Meldel's theory of artistic freedom. Luckily, Maggie was heading our way. "Meldel, this is my pal, Bloodygit Maggie Kwan. Maggie, this is Bloodygit Meldel Delacroix."

"Maggie!" Meldel grabbed Maggie's right hand and shook it enthusiastically. "I've heard so much about you!"

"Likewise," said Maggie.

Meldel took Maggie's left hand and my right one. She

tucked them into the crooks of her arms, pulling us close to her. "You can be the first to know. I'm considering writing a novella based on my relationship with Todd. We recently had, um, a tiny little disagreement, and I won, and that means that I am currently enjoying the upper hand in our relationship."

She was talking fast. Even for Meldel.

I frowned thoughtfully.

"I thought you always had the upper hand," I observed. Meanwhile, I could feel Maggie attempting to make eye contact with me. I did not look at her, however. In the back of my mind, a suspicion was forming.

Or maybe it had been lurking there for a while.

Meldel said, still rapidly, "Yes, true, but not like now. Our relationship is evolving! Do you think it's sick? If so, it's sick in an empowering, feminist way! One that also connects to the historical power of sex." Meldel began walking, taking us with her. "I wonder if AMT might be willing to connect me with her contacts? If I include *Bleeders* and the larger context?"

I dared a glance at Maggie. She was listening to Meldel, and her brows were probably never going to return to their normal facial placement.

"You can always ask AMT yourself," Maggie murmured. She mouthed at me behind Meldel's head: *You were not kidding about her!*

I said calmly, "Oh, one tiny little favor, Meldel. Don't put me in this novella of yours."

Guilt flickered over her face. "I certainly won't. If you say not to! Of course not!"

Ah.

I did some yogic breathing.

"So anyway!" I said brightly. "Meldel, where are you taking us?"

"To the Con Suite. Everybody's there."

I stopped walking, which forced them to stop too. I fiddled with the strings of my bonnet, which I had put back on my head. "If I'm with the group, everybody will recognize me."

"Don't you think that cat's out of the bag already?" said Meldel.

I winced.

We went.

Sebastian screamed my name as we entered the room. I screamed his right back. Then Liv and Cam—and Naomi! Cam grabbed me off my feet and twirled me. I hadn't realized he was so strong. Then, as we revolved, I saw Todd.

Todd.

Ah, Todd.

He shouted, "God's blood! Zoe has returned!" But he hung back behind the others, keeping his distance. Behind Cam's back, I clenched my hands into fists.

Meldel was introducing everybody to Maggie.

"Looking like crap, Zoe." Cam put me down and tried to grab my crumpled bonnet off my head. (At this time I will admit that I had constructed the bonnet using copier paper and Scotch tape. It was holding up about as well as you'd expect. Any self-respecting cosplayer would be appalled.) "Liv was just about to text you. We knew you had to be here somewhere. And there was no way we were going to listen to AMT's speech without you there. Luckily, you were working your own side of the equation."

I beamed at him.

"Happy accident," I said. "I ran into Meldel in the AMT photo line. Events unfolded."

"There are no accidents. The Force controls all."

"I beg to differ!"

"Well, but see, I got into NYU!"

"Cam! That's fantastic!"

"I know!" Cam twirled me again. "What about you?"

"You'll know soon," I said evasively. "Now, if you'll excuse me a moment."

I turned. "Todd!"

My voice wasn't loud, but it resonated.

We faced each other, Todd and I. I looked at him and he looked at me. There was no need for me to accuse or for him to deny. We understood each other perfectly. Wordlessly.

"Oh no," muttered Meldel. "Listen, Zoe, I tried to tell him—"

Liv elbowed her. Meldel stopped talking. A little vortex of silence formed around Todd and me. I let it settle around us for a few moments. Then I spoke.

"I don't get mad," I told Todd. "I get even."

"Oh, come on, Zoe. Look at it this way. I made you a star."

I shook my head. "You are now my mortal enemy. And this I vow: you will rue the day that you crossed swords with me."

After a moment, Todd bowed deeply from the waist, sweeping aside an imaginary cape. "Bring it."

"I will, and it will," I said seriously, "be awful."

Todd's gaze faltered.

"En garde," I said, and smiled evilly.

Maggie made bug eyes at me.

Meldel—looking relieved—announced that we should now join hands in a moment of appreciative silence for our renewed group unity, and in thanks for Maggie joining us. Maggie made more bug eyes at me. Womanfully, however, she joined in.

As we stood together, I suddenly thought sadly of Josie, home alone, punished. I hoped that Ms. Murawski would at least let her watch the livestream. Although that was doubtful, if Simon had anything to say about it.

When Meldel allowed us to speak again, I looked at Liv questioningly.

Liv said, "Bloodygits! Listen up! Now it can be told! Zoe and I have decided to be college roommates! We are going to Smith!"

This started a mini riot.

In the end, it was Sebastian who said the one thing I both most wanted to hear and was most scared to hear. "Zoe, do you really have to stay in that scary, depressing cosplay?"

"Like the Bleeder viral apocalypse isn't equally scary and depressing?" I asked. But I didn't mean it. I took in a quick breath—and yelled, at the top of my lungs:

"Costume malfunction!"

Throughout the Con Suite, heads turned to me. Dramatically, I ripped off my cap and my red Handmaid's robe. I twirled them in the air and threw them away.

Underneath, I was Lorelei. With the wrong hair, of course. I reached into my satchel and shoved my Lorelei wig haphazardly onto my head.

"Fangirl!"

The room burst into cheers, meows, fart noises, and of course reggae. If some of it was mockery, I no longer cared.

I yelled, "Meet my mortal enemy, the videographer and musician!" and pointed at Todd. I mimed punching him in the face. He mimed falling over. The crowd roared. I bowed to the left. I curtsied to the right. I waved: elbow, elbow, wrist, wrist. I touched my stethoscope-garrote. I blew a kiss.

I was home.

Scene 5

Bleeders!

We waited and waited until finally our line was allowed to file into the Chowder Ballroom for AMT's speech. We got the third row: Cam, Liv, me, Maggie (alas, still in her Handmaid cosplay and a little miffed at me over it), Meldel, and Todd. Todd made a stab at saving seats for Naomi and Sebastian, but no. *They might end up standing at the back,* I thought. But that was the risk they took when they left the line.

It was sweet that Sebastian and Naomi had gone off to get some alone time. Just because love hadn't worked out for me didn't mean it was a lost cause for everybody. Not that I was going to think about love right now. Life was ahead, full of friends and possibility. The unknown might be scary, but it was also exciting.

"You don't have to be anxious about going off alone

to college," my mom had said last night. (She and my dad were happy—not to say smug—about my Smith plans.) "You'll be close to home. Plus you'll have your friend Liv!"

Indeed, I would.

I touched Liv and Maggie and pointed. "Look." It was the mom and two daughters that I had originally seen in the hotel lobby, cosplaying together as Captain. The three had seats in the second row, just ahead of us. They had their hair braided just like Captain, in a straightforward middle part with cornrows down both sides and the ends twisted into a perfect circle behind. When the mom excused herself, her two daughters stood up to let her out and turned, letting us check out how their cosplay was wittily different from each other's.

Maggie said, "The younger one has a Slytherin badge on her lab coat."

"And the older girl has Hufflepuff," said Liv. "Oh, and the younger one's got bloodstains, too! Isn't that the exact spatter pattern from Season 1, Episode 4?"

The younger girl turned around fully, a huge grin on her face. "Yes! From when Monica and Captain threw knives at the rats!" She held out her sleeve so we could admire the spatter. "I painted it myself."

"Serena loves all the gory scenes," said the older sister with all the world-weariness of her eleven-ish years.

"That one scene's great artistically, though," Liv said. "The way that all AMT actually shot was the rat shadows and then the spatters? So that we imagine rather than see anything happen?"

"And the shadow of the knives!" said the younger sister

with zest. "As Monica threw them and they stabbed the rats!"

"I hid my eyes," I said.

"She did not," said Liv.

"The first time, I did."

The older girl said, "I felt sorry for the rats. I like it better when there are human enemies for the crew to fight. Or humanoid. Or the robots."

"That's because you're a wimp," said her sister. She said to us, "My sister Gwen hates Monica, so there." The two started to glare at each other, stopped, turned, and very politely complimented our row on our cosplay. Only then did they face front and argue.

I whispered, "I'm glad those kids are right where AMT will see them when she comes in."

"And their mom," said Maggie. "Who has got to be just about the coolest mom in the world. Listen, Zoe, did you think she looks familiar? The mom?"

I shrugged. "With the mask, who can tell? You could ask her. She's coming back now."

"Yeah, no, too shy."

Liv held up both hands. Their fingers were crossed. "I'm sooo nervous. There's got to be approval for the third season."

"How about a fourth season, too?" I said. "While we're at it."

"Don't be greedy," Meldel put in.

"Shh," said Cam, craning backward. "It's her now. Be still my heart!"

AMT walked up the center aisle alongside one of the

volunteers. She was in the same book-and-kittens dress that she'd worn for the photos, and she smiled left and right and even shook a few hands. The room quieted as she reached the front where there was a simple microphone stand.

"Hello, all of you!" Her mic squealed. "Hm." A volunteer raced up to make an adjustment. "Good. We're in business. Thanks for coming, Bloodygits all!"

We cheered again.

"In a few minutes, I'm going to have Jocelyn and Hugh join me for the panel discussion. I hope there'll be chairs — okay, good, they'll bring them in. But first, I won't beat around the bush. I have a feeling that you all want to know about Season 3."

"Yes!" We roared.

"And I'm going to tell you. But first, I need to quickly explain that what I'm about to say is not what I originally had planned. Since we booked with Bean Con a couple of months ago, there's been a shift in —"

At the back of the Chowder Ballroom, someone screamed. People turned to look. Maggie gasped. Liv and Cam and Meldel laughed. I nearly bit my tongue, and Todd made the loudest and most authoritative two-handed wolf whistle I've ever heard . . .

As Sebastian and Naomi came staggering down the side aisles, arms outstretched, their bodies seeping blood through the white of their clothing.

The entire audience leapt to its feet, applauding and hooting and screaming.

Bleeders, bleeders, bleeders!

"Awesome!" yelled the two little Captains in front of us. The shoulders of their Captain mother shook with laughter.

Sebastian and Naomi reached the front and wobbled theatrically before collapsing at AMT's feet. AMT looked down, bemused, grinning. Her lips moved. You didn't need to be an advanced lip-reader to understand.

Wow.

"They did it!" Liv exclaimed in my ear. "The formula worked!"

Cam was smiling from ear to ear. We all were.

"I should have known that was what they were up to!" I yelled, my voice only just audible above the continuing din.

"You didn't guess?" said Meldel.

"No! I thought they slipped away to, you know. Canoodle."

"Oh, you sweet summer child."

"I know. I'm so embarrassed."

Things settled down as AMT made a "lower the volume" motion with her hands. "Fantastic," she said into the mic. Her eyes alight with laughter, she reached down to Naomi and Sebastian—who had not fainted!—and pulled them up. "Take a bow, *bleeders!*" They did. Then they grabbed AMT's hands and the three of them bowed low, together, with red hands. The room erupted again. People took pictures. I wiped tears from the corner of my eyes and reached out blindly for my friends. The six of us were jumping up and down together when I felt a hand on my back.

It was Josie, squirming into our row. "I'm here, I'm

here!" she shouted. I let go of Cam long enough to grab my friend, Simon's little sister, and pull her into my arms, and then into the group hug.

Josie had sneaked out! I didn't feel any guilt whatsoever about it.

Season 3

Then AMT pointed at us and shouted into the mic: "Do *you* Bloodygits out there recognize *these* Bloodygits? Especially that one—in the Lorelei cosplay?"

There was more applause, as well as stamping of feet, the inevitable fart noises, and shouting:

"Fangirl! Fangirl and the Lilithcon panel!" Someone even yelled, "Organic kitty soap! You're fired! Fired!"

"Come on, take a bow, Fangirl! All of you," AMT urged our group.

My face burned. Someone pushed me toward the end of the row. I turned with my friends to face the crowd. I flushed even hotter when someone started a reggae drumbeat, and people started to sing and dance. (White people, mostly! Who were fans of a socially conscious show! Did no one think about the cultural appropriation of mocking me with *reggae*?) And then—

I realized something. These were my people, all of them. I was having a good time with my friends, and Naomi and Sebastian had made the bleeding work, and Josie was with us too, and Maggie. And Liv and I were going to college together, not Simon and me, and—it was the right outcome for me after all.

I am Fangirl. That video is out there, and the entire world will forever be able to see me at a Very Vulnerable Yet Also Very Ridiculous Moment. So what?

I made mistakes, but oh well. I did some things right, too. I have terrific friends, and my very own mortal enemy, too, and I'm not wrong to adore them. I'm a Bloodygit and I'm proud! Also, AMT herself told me thank you! How cool was that?

"*Bleeders* forever!" I yelled, and started to dance to the reggae beat. "Season 3!"

The crowd roared back. "SEASON 3!"

"Season 3!" I grabbed my stethoscope-garrote from around my neck. I spun it in the air as if I were going to rope a steer—

And there was Simon.

He stood near the entrance to the ballroom. He was wearing his favorite blue-and-white striped button-down shirt with jeans. Across the distance, his gaze locked with mine.

He was holding hands with a girl. She was rounded, with short dark hair and deep red lipstick.

My stethoscope-garrote banged into my forearm.

Simon nodded at me coolly, his expression as grave as I'd ever seen it.

Simon is six foot one and gangly. He has shoulders to die for, and dark blond hair that is thick and long enough to tuck behind his ears. From behind his glasses, his blue eyes pierce your soul.

His glasses. I'd helped him pick out those glasses a year ago, at Warby Parker in Harvard Square. He'd tried on two dozen pairs and the store clerk kept offering opinions. He'd listened politely, but it was obvious that the only opinion he really cared about then was mine.

Then.

I could feel the chasm between us, now, wider than the ballroom.

Only, if he was here, that meant—he'd brought Josie. She hadn't sneaked out after all.

I nodded back at him. Then—maybe a little blindly—I directed a kind smile at his new girlfriend, too. Because even if that's not *entirely* who I am—kind, I mean—it's still who I want to be.

There'd been faults on both sides.

And some good, too.

My friends had noticed nothing. The crowd's shouts and singing were quieting. As everybody sat down, our group cramming together on our chairs to make room for Josie, I was relieved to face front again. I didn't want to think about Simon. I wanted to think about AMT.

She smiled at us—at everyone, but also at our group

specifically, and also at Sebastian and Naomi, who were now standing near the wall to one side, holding bloody hands.

"Your brother brought you?" I whispered to Josie, who had squeezed in and was sharing half of my chair.

Josie whispered back excitedly. "Yes! He's still incredibly annoying, but he's also been trying to be nice to me lately. Like, he even asked me to explain to him what I liked about *Bleeders* and he only rolled his eyes once. And then an hour ago, he suddenly said we should hop in the car and come. I didn't argue! He even paid for my ticket."

"I can hardly believe—"

"Shh!" Josie gripped my arm. "AMT!"

"As I was saying, before I was so delightfully interrupted." AMT waved at Naomi and Sebastian. "When I originally got in touch with Bean Con, I was planning to tell you that SlamDunk had lost faith in *Bleeders*, but we weren't giving up. That we were going to raise money to fund the next season independently. I was going to ask for your support, to spread the word and to contribute whatever you could.

"But in the last couple of weeks, our situation has changed. We're now on the map in terms of audience size and ad revenue. We're not where we want to be, not yet, but we're definitely on our way. SlamDunk is back on board. We think there are several reasons for the turnaround, including that entertaining Fangirl reggae video, along with the #bloodywomen campaign on Twitter and, of course, the wonderful podcast outreach that our actors have pursued so diligently."

She'd mentioned our video! I caught Todd's incredulous eye. He started to leap to his feet, mouth opening to yell something, but Meldel hauled him back down.

"Shh! Let AMT talk!"

He subsided.

AMT went on, "So the answer is YES! There is going to be a Season 3. We start production next month!"

The crowd leapt to their feet again. The pandemonium lasted minutes. A shiver went through my body as I looked at the widened eyes and amazed faces of my friends. We stood together, me and Liv and Cam and Sebastian and Meldel and Todd and Josie and Naomi. And Maggie!

We had made a difference.

I felt my cheeks stretch into the biggest smile of my life. I saw it reflected back in the faces of my friends.

AMT had to wave the crowd down so she could finish. She said, "I know I speak for the entire cast and crew of *Bleeders* when I say that without the passion and belief of our fans, we cannot make the show. We bring *Bleeders* to life together. You and us."

Wants and Needs

I tried to focus on the *Bleeders* panel discussion that followed—AMT and Jocelyn Upchurch and Hugh Nguyen chatted about the show and took questions from the audience—but I was hyperaware of Simon: watching, listening, thinking, *judging*. It's hard to break a longtime habit. When the Season 3 budget came up—the tremendous cost of a show like *Bleeders*—I could almost hear his whisper: *Explain to me, Zoe. Explain how you can value this over housing, food, medicine, education, childcare, and the environment?!*

Only now I was able to answer him—no, to answer *myself*. Art. Joy. Fellowship. Imagination. They too were of value and importance, and they were not secondary human needs. They were primary. And they were also, incidentally, a place where you could meet others who didn't necessarily agree with you politically.

And yet I knew: I could argue with Simon in my head all I wanted, but in real life, I had nothing left to say to him. Our paths had diverged months ago. We had both known it, and kept silent . . . and let it happen.

What if one of us had spoken up? Maybe we could have kept on being friends as we grew and changed? Because there was so much to like in Simon. And—I had to believe—in me. But instead, we'd hidden ourselves from each other . . .

I hoped to never make that mistake again.

"Zoe?" said Maggie patiently. I came back to reality to realize that Maggie, Liv, and I were the only ones left in our row. The panel discussion had ended. The ballroom was emptying.

"Oh," I said. "Sorry. I was thinking." Surreptitiously, I glanced over toward the ballroom entrance. Simon was still there, new girlfriend by his side, though they were not holding hands anymore. They also were not moving.

Maggie nudged Liv. "Simon Murawski. *The* Simon. By the door. In the pin-striped button-down."

"Really? Fascinating." Liv gave me some side-eye.

"He brought Josie," I said.

"Interesting!"

Josie reached Simon. She appeared to be introducing him and his girlfriend to Meldel and Todd and Cam and Sebastian and Naomi. They all stood in a cluster to the side, out of the way of the doors and the people who were exiting. There were nods and careful, superficial smiles—

And then Sebastian held out a bloody hand to Simon.

"Oh no," I moaned.

Simon shook his head, smiling. I saw his lips form the words "No, thanks." But Sebastian kept his hand outstretched.

I shouldn't care anymore, but I did. My stomach roiled.

I ran to get there, cutting in front of people. "Excuse me, sorry, excuse me—"

I reached them just as Sebastian was saying, "Shake. I insist. Think of it as a bloody welcome for Josie's brother!" Naomi backed him up with a merry "Don't worry, the blood's soluble in soap and water. At least, that was my intention."

Naomi would have no context for Simon. But the other Bloodygits did, and they were not intervening. Todd was grinning outright. Maybe he'd put Sebastian up to it?

Only Josie was grinning too, and fiendishly.

Simon, fastidious, carefully dressed Simon, literally had his back up against the wall. Sebastian's hand came ever closer to Simon's crisp shirt. His wet red fingers waggled in ludicrous invitation. "Come on!"

I paused, mere feet away. I put my hands on my hips and waited until Simon looked at me, as somehow I'd known he would.

"You don't have to shake my friend's hand," I told him.

"And my friend," said Josie.

There was a pause. I couldn't read Simon's expression. Then he said, with a professional smile, "Actually, I think I do." He reached out, planning to deploy—I knew—the same firm-but-not-too-tight handshake that he'd developed when working on Senator Pratt's campaign. Except his palm and Sebastian's came together with an indescribable squelch. Simultaneously, a girl's high voice exclaimed: "Simon and Shelley! Mom, it's Simon and Shelley from your office!"

A deeper, amused, feminine adult voice answered, "So it is. What a surprise. Hello, Shelley. Hello, Simon. I had no idea you two were *Bleeders* fans!"

Simon's gaze went behind me. His mouth opened. Closed. Opened.

He said, *"Senator?"*

I turned. The Captain-mom and her two Captain-daughters were a few feet away. The Captain-mom pushed her battle gear mask up on her forehead.

"Well met!" said Massachusetts State Senator Alisha Johnson Pratt. Her smile glanced off Simon's bloody hand. "Look at you. In cosplay!"

"Uh. You too, Senator." Red seeped slowly up Simon's face as he blushed. Chin. Cheeks. Nose. Forehead.

"Oh, I'm all in," said Senator Pratt easily. "It's good for the soul. So, *are* you a *Bleeders* fan, Simon? Shelley?"

"I just might get into it," said Shelley, Simon's new girlfriend.

Simon looked appalled. "No. I'm not."

"Too bad," said the senator. "It's such a good show. I'd love to be able to gossip about it at the office."

"Uh." Simon fixed his gaze desperately on the senator's two daughters. "Hi, Serena. Hi, Gwen."

"You were infected, like, two seconds ago," the little one informed Simon expertly. "In a few minutes, you'll be gushing blood! Then you'll be dead!"

Simon looked blank. He started to wipe his hand on his pants but stopped just in time. His eyes met mine again.

Need is different from want. I had *wanted* a boyfriend. But what I *needed* was my fandom and my friends, with all their chaos and enthusiasm and hope and confusion. I needed the self I had discovered and was still discovering when I was with them. I had wanted certainty about my future. But what I needed was possibility.

"Listen, Simon," I said. "How about if Maggie and I get Josie home later? So you two don't have to hang around here waiting for her." I nodded pleasantly at Shelley.

He hesitated. "I thought I'd take her home right after the speech."

"Please, Simon," said Josie. "I want to stay with my friends."

Another moment before Simon nodded. "Okay. Since it's important to you, Josie. Thanks, Zoe. Maggie. If it's not too much trouble to take her home."

"No trouble," I said.

"A pleasure," said Maggie.

Simon left with his new girlfriend, who may—or may not—have cast a curious glance backward.

I turned to my friends, my Bloodygits, so that we could enjoy the rest of the con together.

EPISODE 8

August 2019 @Dragon Con

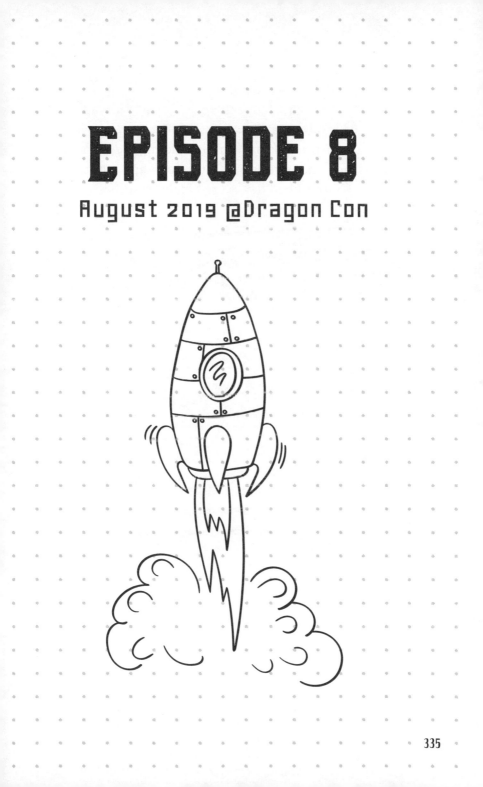

Epilogue

It was Labor Day weekend in Atlanta. It could not have been hotter. In a few days, college would start for most of us, and Maggie would return to her apprenticeship. But today, we were in the Dragon Con parade staging area, in full cosplay. I linked arms with Cam and Liv and Josie and Meldel and Todd and Sebastian and Naomi and Maggie. We weren't the only Bloodygits here today, however. We were part of a group that was fifty-something strong.

Fifty!

Later—I smiled evilly to myself—I had a tiny little surprise planned for Todd.

But now, we hoisted our fabulous *Bleeders* banner.

We marched.

Acknowledgments

Writing about Zoe and the Bloodygits filled me with joy in a time that wasn't always joyful. In no small part, my happiness in making this book was also because of the following people who supported me.

Warm thanks to Daniel Berry, Julie Berry, Rob Costello, Erin Dionne, Deborah Kovacs, Ammi-Joan Paquette, Diana Peterfreund, and Kathleen Sweeney, my early readers and critiquers, for their thoughtful comments and for their laughter. Rob, your insights were especially important and I couldn't be more grateful. My appreciation also to William Alexander, who listened to a (very) early description of what I wanted to write and asked, "Do you know about character alignment charts?" Love to Sarah Aronson, Toni Buzzeo, Jacqueline Davies, Jennifer Jacobson, Jane Kurtz, Jacqueline Briggs Martin, Dian Curtis Regan, Joanne

Stanbridge, Nicole Valentine, Deborah Wiles, and Melissa Wyatt, for writerly emotional support.

Hooray and gratitude to my insightful editor, Miriam Newman, at Candlewick Press. Miriam understood Zoe and the Bloodygits, was a pure delight to brainstorm with, and is—simply and in every sense of the word—just exactly right. She's also a titling genius. Thanks also to Liz Bicknell at Candlewick, who knew instantly that Miriam was the right editor for Zoe and me. Appreciation and gratitude to crack Candlewick designers Matt Roeser for the super-cool cover and Lisa Rudden for the fun interior, and also to copyeditors Julia Gaviria and Jackie Houton and proofreaders Emily Stone and Emily Quill for making sure every detail was in order—just as Zoe would like it to be. I'd also like to thank super-publicist Jamie Tan, Lara Armstrong in foreign rights, Lydia Abel for her meticulous reading, and Amanda Bellamy for production coordination.

Finally, and as ever, thank you to my love and husband, Jim McCoy.